"THIS IS WHO I AM.

"Mary's the flamboyant, exciting one; she can go around disrupting the world and reinventing herself whenever things get dull. But that isn't me, Patrick. I'm the staid, sane one."

"Bull." He held her, his gaze journeying over her upturned face. "If you were all that sane, Amelia, you'd know better than to stick with a job that's boring you to tears."

"I'm not bored to tears," she protested halfheartedly.

"You think everything you do has to fit this arbitrary role of yours. You've got to hold down a tedious job because it's your role. You've got to run away from me because it's your role."

"Nonsense," she scoffed although she didn't sound terribly convincing.

"No, Amelia, it's not nonsense," he said, his voice low and husky. "Quit the damned role, sweetheart. Walk out on it. Be yourself." His hands slid slowly up her arms to her shoulders. "Kiss me."

ABOUT THE AUTHOR

Freedom is a right Judith Arnold cares deeply about—and in this latest book she examines the noble sacrifices it entails. Never at a loss for interesting heroes, she has created one of her most unique in lawyer Patrick Levine—half-Irish, half-Jewish, all-charmer. Recently Judith and her husband and two sons relocated to the Boston area.

Books by Judith Arnold

HARLEQUIN AMERICAN ROMANCE

139—JACKPOT
149—SPECIAL DELIVERY
163—MAN AND WIFE
189—BEST FRIENDS
201—PROMISES*
205—COMMITMENTS*
209—DREAMS*
225—COMFORT AND JOY
240—TWILIGHT
255—GOING BACK
259—HARVEST THE SUN
281—ONE WHIFF OF SCANDAL

*KEEPING THE FAITH SUBSERIES

HARLEQUIN TEMPTATION

122—ON LOVE'S TRAIL

TURNING TABLES

JUDITH ARNOLD

Harlequin Books

TORONTO • NEW YORK • LONDON
AMSTERDAM • PARIS • SYDNEY • HAMBURG
STOCKHOLM • ATHENS • TOKYO • MILAN

Published July 1989

First printing May 1989

ISBN 0-373-16304-5

Chapter One

If it hadn't been for the rumor floating around the campus all day that *Live at Five* was going to air a public-relations piece about the Hibbing School, Amelia wouldn't have bothered to turn on the television when she got home from work. Five o'clock usually found her puttering around the kitchen, preparing dinner to the accompaniment of classical music on her stereo. However, her loyalty to Hibbing—as both an alumna and assistant to the Dean of Students—compelled her to switch on the television in her living room and listen to the chatty light-news show while she fixed herself a chef's salad across the hall in the kitchen.

So it was quite by chance that she happened to overhear one of the show's hosts announce, "A controversial art exhibit in the sleepy Catskill village of Wisherville led to a street disturbance this afternoon, as angry protestors..."

Amelia dropped her knife and raced into the living room. A combination of controversy, art, disturbance and Wisherville could mean only one thing: Mary had cut loose. Again.

Staring at the television screen with a mixture of alarm and so-what-else-is-new impatience, Amelia

watched the on-location report. "I'm standing in front
of the Potts Gallery on Main Street, here in the sleepy
Sullivan County town of Wisherville," announced a
fresh-scrubbed young correspondent holding a microphone. She stood in front of Mary's gallery, which
was partially blocked from view by a small crowd of
people mugging for the camera. "At around noon today, Mary Potts, the owner of this gallery, placed a
terra-cotta sculpture of her own creation on display in
the front window—a sculpture that apparently nu-
merous residents of Wisherville found obscene." The
camera panned from the reporter to the gallery's display window, which was constructed of rectangular
panes of glass held together by a grid of polished
birch. Two of the panes were broken, and the spot-
lighted pedestal centered in the window was empty.
"Witnesses confirm that, responding to complaints,
Wisherville Mayor James Dunphy personally visited
the gallery to request that Ms. Potts remove the
sculpture, and that she refused. Within an hour, a
group of town residents calling themselves the Wisherville Citizens Brigade organized a protest outside the
store. *Live at Five* was on the scene to capture the
dramatic end of the melee."

The segment cut to a tape of the demonstration. The
grandly named Wisherville Citizens Brigade com-
prised no more than twenty people, but they were vo-
cal and angry. So was Mary, who stood in the open
doorway of the gallery brandishing a weighty abstract marble statue at the tiny mob and shouting,
"Freedom of expression is guaranteed by the Constitution!"

There were shouts of "She's trying to intimidate
us!" and "Look out—she's armed!" and then a rock

soared through the air and shattered one of the panes. The cameraman zoomed in to a close-up of the broken window, while a police siren and another crash of breaking glass drowned out the continuing shouts of the mob. Within a minute, Mary was shown being led out of the gallery in handcuffs by a police officer.

Nearing the camera, she grinned defiantly, held up her hands to flaunt the handcuffs and hollered, "Power to the people!"

The report continued with a brief interview with Mayor Dunphy, who described the statue as "vulgar in the extreme" and "a potential affront to tourists—Wisherville's primary source of income," followed by an interview with one of the demonstrators claiming that Wisherville, New York, was a nice, clean town, and there was no place in it for "smut masquerading as art." Mary Potts, the reporter concluded, had been booked on charges of disturbing the peace, disorderly conduct and a breach of public decency.

The instant *Live at Five* paused for a commercial, Amelia's telephone began to ring. Grimacing, she returned to the kitchen to answer it.

"Do something," her mother said without preamble. "Your sister is running amok."

Amelia let out a long weary breath. Mary was constantly running amok, and Amelia was constantly being ordered to do something about it. "Mom—"

"She was on TV. In handcuffs."

"I saw."

"Not that I can blame them for handcuffing her. Did you see the way she was waving that marble monstrosity around—you know, the one she made for that artist friend of hers that he forgot to take with him when he moved to Patagonia last year? She still hasn't been able to sell it. You'd think she would have planted it in someone's rock garden by now."

"Maybe she wanted to keep it on hand in case she needed it to protect herself," Amelia returned dryly.

"Protect herself? Amelia, you heard the report. The sculpture was obscene!"

"Just because the reporter said it was obscene doesn't mean—"

"I can imagine," her mother said, cutting her off. "When Mary called us from the police station, she described it as a depiction of the ultimate expression of human love."

The ultimate expression. Like her mother, Amelia could imagine. "Obscenity is in the eye of the beholder," she said in her sister's defense.

"In this case, obviously, it was in the eyes of too many beholders. Please go and get her out of police custody, Amelia. I'll call Bartholomew and have him meet you up in Wisherville tomorrow. I'm sure he'll be able to fix everything."

"Mom, I—"

"If there's a problem with bail, have them contact your father and me. You know we'll cover it. Just get Mary out of jail—or wherever she is—and sit on her until Bartholomew gets there."

Amelia scowled. If her parents wanted to rescue Mary, that was their business. But she was tired of being recruited to serve in the front lines. With Bartholomew's help, Amelia had rescued Mary last Labor Day when she'd been arrested for skinny-dipping in a public lake on the outskirts of town, and six months earlier when she'd been expelled by a professional gallery owners' association for denouncing its board of directors in pungent language, and a few years ago when she'd been cited for painting a mural on a wall at a construction site in Manhattan, and more than a few times when the gallery's accounts payable exceeded the accounts receivable, and on and on.

Amelia loved her sister. They were fraternal twins, and even though they were as different as they were alike, they adored each other. But enough was enough.

"Mom, I really don't want to go to Wisherville."

"But you must! You've got to help Mary straighten out this mess!"

"I always help Mary straighten out her messes, Mom," Amelia protested. "I'm sick of it."

"Now, now, we're counting on you," her mother cooed. "You're the responsible one, Amelia. You're the sane one. Mary's expecting you to go, and your father and I are depending on you, too. You're her sister and she needs you. So be a good girl, Amelia, and—"

"No," Amelia said, summoning all her reserves of strength. Who had ordained that she always had to be a good girl, sane and responsible? Why was she perpetually being called upon to do damage control for Mary until Bartholomew arrived on the scene for the final mop-up? "I'm sorry, Mom," she said resolutely, "but this time I absolutely refuse to go."

Two AND A HALF HOURS later, Amelia steered her Saab into the parking lot adjacent to Wisherville's police station, which occupied the basement and ground floors of the town-hall building, overlooking a charming village park. Amelia was familiar with the police station from Mary's last brush with the law. She had sworn then that she'd never again set foot inside this building to bail Mary out. Yet here she was in New York's Catskill Region, resigned and compliant, doing exactly what was expected of her.

Her resentment had simmered down during the drive from New Milford. If she was irritated now, her irritation was directed not toward Mary but toward herself for having once more caved in to her parents' demands.

The police station's front room was surprisingly lively, considering the village's small size and the relatively late hour. Three uniformed officers sat at desks behind the counter, pecking away at manual typewriters. A woman sat at the switchboard, and a clerk was talking to a cluster of civilians armed with notepads and cameras—reporters, no doubt, here to write stories about the maniac with the lewd statue. After all, this was the most exciting thing to happen in Wisherville in a long time.

Drawing in a deep breath, Amelia straightened her crisp cotton camp shirt, which had developed a few wrinkles during the drive from Connecticut, and smoothed the gathered waistband of her skirt. Then she tossed back her long black hair and approached the counter. "Excuse me," she called to one of the police officers. "Can you tell me if Mary Potts is here? I'm her sister."

All three officers looked up from their typewriters. Abandoning the clerk, the reporters swarmed around Amelia and peppered her with questions. "What's your opinion of the sculpture?" "Do you have a statement?" "Does your sister deal in pornography?"

Lacking a better idea, Amelia covered her ears with her hands. Through her fingers she heard her sister's clarion voice echoing in a back hall. "Melie? Is that you?" Turning, she saw Mary emerge through a door and hurry down the corridor, her arms outstretched and her smile glowing with unfettered joy.

Amelia wasn't naive enough to believe her arrival was the source of Mary's elation. Mary was happy because she was causing a ruckus. Here, in the police station, the focus of half a dozen avid newspaper reporters, she was in her element.

Mary engulfed her sister in a crushing hug. She was taller by two inches, larger-boned, more curvacious and rounder-faced. From the moment they were born, Mary had been the bigger twin. Family folklore had it that Mary had overwhelmed Amelia from conception on, squashing her into a cramped corner of the available space and hogging most of their mother's womb for herself. As explanations went, it made perfect sense; no matter where she was, Mary had the tendency to overwhelm everyone around her.

She was prettier than Amelia, too—or so Amelia believed. Mary's eyes were wide, her hair lush with untamable dark curls, her fingers long and thick, her breasts and hips pleasingly full. Amelia, on the other hand, was small and skinny—or petite and delicate, as her mother euphemistically described her. Amelia's eyes were darker and narrower, her nose pointy, her cheeks almost gaunt and her hair a limp, listless spill of black, which she managed to dress up with strategically placed barrettes. Amelia had the uncanny ability to fade into just about any background, while Mary attracted the spotlight wherever she went.

Amelia briefly returned Mary's hug, then drew back and gave her a comprehensive appraisal. "What have you gotten yourself into this time?" she asked, annoyed by her sister's apparent glee. She wished she'd been more adamant about refusing to come to Wisherville. She wished that for once Mary had avoided making a scene and getting into trouble.

But that would have been out of character for Mary—as out of character as it would have been for Amelia to refuse to come.

Mary turned to the assembled press people and police officers, beaming as if they were guests at a gala being held in her honor. "I'd like you all to meet my sister, Amelia Potts," she said, presenting Amelia to the group. "She's the sane one in our family. I'm the fruitcake." With that succinct identification, Mary swung around and hugged Amelia again.

Amelia disengaged herself from her sister's clutches. "Come on, Mary, tell me what's going on. Are they holding you here on bail, or can you leave?"

"No to both," Mary replied. "I've been released on my own recognizance, but I refuse to leave unless they let me take my sculpture with me. They claim it's been impounded, and they won't give it back."

Amelia did her best to ignore the reporters, who leaned forward en masse to eavesdrop on her conversation with Mary. "If the thing's impounded," she pointed out, "they can hold it here for days, or weeks. You can't stay here all that time."

"First of all," Mary argued, "it's not a *thing*. It's a beautiful sculpture entitled *Liberty*, and I plan to exhibit it at the gallery until July the Fourth—even if it gets purchased before then. The police have no right to hold my property—"

"Mary, can't we go someplace and talk about this quietly?" Amelia pleaded, knowing as soon as she spoke that she'd just asked for the impossible. Mary was inherently unable to do anything quietly.

"I'm staying right here," Mary declared. "On the advice of my lawyer—"

"What lawyer? Has Bartholomew gotten here already?"

"I have another lawyer," Mary announced, her eyes twinkling with a blend of mischief and delight. "He's taken my case for free."

"Bartholomew doesn't charge you for his legal services," Amelia reminded her.

"Bartholomew doesn't promise to fight my cases to the Supreme Court, either," Mary pointed out in a lofty tone. "Bartholomew compromises and makes settlements. Patrick is a fighter. He's planning to take my case as far as he can."

"What case?" Amelia rolled her eyes. "You've been charged with disturbing the peace. Bartholomew will get you off with a small fine and you'll write a check, and that will be the end of it. Now come on, Mary, let's go."

"Hell, no, I won't go," Mary intoned echoing the words of an earlier decade—one to which she would have been much better suited, Amelia thought grimly. While she tried to think of a way to persuade her twin to leave the police station, the reporters clustered around Mary, interrogating her about her plans. Amelia glanced away. She'd seen her sister in action too many times to be impressed by her spirited performance.

Peering down the hall, she noticed a scruffy-looking young man swinging through a door at the far end and striding in a loose easy gait toward the front room. His apparel—baggy gray T-shirt, faded blue jeans and leather sneakers—marked him as a plainclothes detective, but when she ran her gaze up his tall lanky body to his face she discarded that possibility. He had long, sandy-blond hair, riveting blue eyes, a sharp nose and a day's growth of beard darkening his upper lip and his harsh square jaw. His lack of grooming notwithstanding, he was, quite simply, too handsome to be a policeman.

Now that was a stupid thought, Amelia reproached herself. Who said policemen couldn't be handsome?

Besides, he wasn't really all that handsome, she decided as he neared the reporters congregating around her sister. He was much too grungy-looking for Amelia's tastes. His T-shirt did little to flatter his broad shoulders and streamlined chest, and the slogan printed across it—I Brake for Whales—struck her as bizarre. She had always preferred clean-cut, clean-shaven types. This man looked like a bum.

Maybe he *was* a bum, someone who'd been picked up for vagrancy. Or a narc, duded up in a sloppy costume in order to fit in with drugged-out teenagers. Or a janitor, or—

"Patrick!" Mary bellowed, extending her arm above the heads of the milling reporters and waving at the blue-eyed man. "These reporters have some questions for you."

Patrick? Amelia mouthed silently. Her sister's newly acquired lawyer, the one Mary had described as a fighter? His taking clients for free might explain his seedy attire, but he certainly didn't look like someone who could argue cases before the Supreme Court.

Frowning, she took a protective step backward as he approached the group. He didn't seem to notice her—

typical, given that nobody ever did when Mary was in the vicinity doing one of her star turns. From her unobtrusive vantage, Amelia spied on him, trying to figure out exactly who, or rather what, he was, why Mary felt free to call him by his first name, why he had shown up dressed as if he'd just returned home from a three-day camping trip. She wondered if he was, in fact, a genuine lawyer, and if he was more than just a lawyer to Mary.

"Ladies and gentlemen of the press," Mary intoned with her customary flair, "I'd like you to meet my attorney, Patrick Levine."

The man smiled tolerantly, then slipped his hand around Mary's elbow and said, with a slight beguiling whiff of a southern drawl, "Nice meeting you all, but we have no comment at the present time. We'll be willing to talk further in the morning. Mary, I think we're going to have to take our leave.

"I've received adequate assurances that the sculpture will come to no harm as long as it's here. In fact it's safer here than it would be at your home or the gallery. We'll try to get it released tomorrow."

Giving her elbow a gentle but emphatic yank, he successfully guided her through the tight knot of reporters. His eyes met Amelia's and he hesitated, his lips curving into a smile that had a distinctly unsettling effect on her. Amelia didn't believe that anyone with eyes as beautiful as his ought to look at her that way, so incisively, so inexplicably seductively. It violated her nervous system, which sent a flutter of mysterious and totally unwelcome signals through her flesh.

"You look familiar," he said, sweeping his gaze over her, taking in her slim, almost boyish figure and then studying her hollow cheeks, her pursed lips, her high forehead and her almond-shaped brown eyes. "Have we ever met before?"

"No, but you seem to be on intimate terms with my twin sister," Amelia said, then clamped her mouth shut and fought the blush she felt creeping up her neck to her face. She and Mary loved to shock strangers by proclaiming they were twins, but Amelia hadn't meant to imply that this man was actually intimate with Mary.

"Patrick, this is my sister, Amelia. I warned you she'd be dispatched to Wisherville to put a tether on me. Our family is so predictable." Mary shook free of Patrick's relaxed grip and arched her arm around Amelia's shoulders. "Melie, this is my lawyer, Patrick Levine. Isn't he cute?"

Amelia hastened to unscramble her thoughts. She couldn't argue with Mary; Patrick Levine was definitely cute, in a derelict sort of way. But if he was truly a lawyer, why didn't he look like one? Why wasn't he wearing a suit and tie, for heaven's sake?

His smile widening, he gathered Amelia's right hand in his and gave it a firm warm shake. "It's a pleasure."

"How do you do?" she said frostily. In spite of his reassuring handshake, she didn't trust him. She would humor him and Mary until Bartholomew arrived in town tomorrow, and then...then she'd make sure Patrick was dismissed.

If he detected her unvoiced disapproval, he didn't comment on it. His smile unwavering, he released Amelia's hand and touched his palm to the small of Mary's back. "Let's go someplace and talk strategy," he suggested, steering her to the exit and then glancing over his shoulder at Amelia. "You'll join us, won't you?"

You bet I will, she answered under her breath. With a cool smile and a nod, she followed them out of the police station, taking note of the fact that her sister's height complemented Patrick's, and that her bright blue jumpsuit, which displayed her hourglass figure quite nicely, just happened to match his eyes.

To her dismay, Amelia felt a twinge of jealousy toward her flamboyant, gregarious sister, who could command the attention of reporters and Wisherville's entire police force—and an unkempt but undeniably sexy-looking small-town lawyer.

Mary had crowded Amelia in the womb—and Amelia couldn't shake the annoying feeling that her sister was still crowding her.

AMELIA FOLLOWED Patrick's open-roofed Jeep through town. Mary had opted to travel with her sister, but the drive was too short to afford Amelia an opportunity to talk Mary into dropping him from her case. Mary dominated their conversation with a description of how generous the police had been in allowing her two calls, one to their parents and one to Patrick. Amelia wondered whom Mary would have phoned if she'd been limited to a single call. And while she was at it, she questioned whether Mary had phoned Patrick for his expertise as an attorney, or for some other reason.

Before Amelia could think of a tactful way to ask, Mary was nudging her arm and pointing out the window. Patrick had turned into a parking lot alongside a café. A striped awning extended over the broad sidewalk from the front wall of the building; below it stood a dozen circular tables, each adorned with a winking citronella candle and a cluster of daisies in a bud vase.

It was a pretty place, Amelia thought with relief—and a bit of peevishness. She had almost hoped Patrick would take them to a dive, some dingy, dimly lit bar decorated with stuffed moose heads. If he had, Amelia might have found it easier to convince Mary that he was unsuited to represent her.

Moose-head bar or no, he didn't seem at all suitable to Amelia. As he hopped out of his Jeep, she noticed that the hems of his jeans were frayed and his hair fell below the neckline of his shirt. A small gust of wind lifted the thick dirty-blond hair at the side of his head, and she glimpsed a tiny gleam of gold at the bottom of his earlobe.

"Oh, my God," she gasped. "He's wearing an earring."

"Just a little one," Mary whispered, as if that was supposed to reassure Amelia. "I think it's cute."

Amelia stifled the urge to shudder.

"Ladies," he greeted them, crossing the lot to where Amelia had parked. "If it's all right with you, I'd like to sit outside. It's such a pleasant evening."

"Yes, let's," Mary seconded, curling her fingers around the bend in Patrick's elbow. He eyed Amelia for a moment, as if considering whether he ought to offer her his other elbow. Evidently he discerned her wariness, because he merely angled his head toward the outdoor tables and ushered Mary to one of them.

They took their seats, Mary positioning herself between Patrick and Amelia so that they faced one another across the flickering candle. Sizing him up, Amelia found herself wishing his eyes weren't quite so striking, wishing the blond waves framing his face didn't appear quite so silky, wishing the candle didn't throw his rugged features into such striking relief. Wishing the wind would pull at his hair once more so that she could see his earring and remember that he was much too weird to be considered attractive.

A waitress came outdoors to take their drink orders. As soon as she left, Patrick directed his attention to Amelia. "It was nice of you to drive all the way here from— Where was it?"

"New Milford, Connecticut," Mary answered for her.

He nodded, but his eyes remained on Amelia, their piercing radiance making her shift uneasily in her chair. "That's a long way to travel on such short notice."

"Mary's my sister," Amelia said, as if that explained everything.

"Your twin." Patrick directed his gaze to Mary, then back to Amelia, comparing the two. He chuckled and shook his head. "I never would have guessed."

"We aren't identical," Amelia said. "We're really just sisters who happened to be born at the same time."

"I was born twelve minutes before you," Mary boasted.

"That must be why you're so much more mature than I am," Amelia said sardonically. Then both women burst into laughter. They'd had similar conversations many times, pretending to bicker, pretending to be competitive. Their laughter told Patrick that he shouldn't take the exchange seriously.

In case there was any doubt in his mind, Mary elaborated, "We're nothing alike, you know. She's the sensible one, and I'm the troublemaker. She's the good one, and I'm the naughty one. She's the little one, and I'm the big one. We were named after our grandmothers, but in personality, I'm more of an Amelia and she's more of a Mary."

"That's your opinion, not mine," Amelia interjected. She had grown to appreciate the fact that she'd been endowed with the baroque name and her sister with the plain one. Being named Amelia was the only dramatic, unusual aspect of her existence, and she treasured it.

"She's our parents' favorite, of course," Mary went on, undeterred.

"No, I'm not," Amelia protested. "I'm the one they rely on. You're the one who keeps them entertained."

"I scare them."

"Fear is more entertaining than reliability."

The waitress arrived with their drinks, drawing Amelia's attention from her sister to Patrick. She had almost forgotten he was present, witnessing their sisterly repartee—which was, in fact, a fairly standard routine for them; when they got into one of these dialogues Amelia tended to recite her lines by rote. For so many years she'd been labeled reliable and sane and sensible by the family. For so many years she had seen her parents wring their hands over Mary's escapades and fret about what was to become of her. For so many years she'd understood that her function in the family was to be the daughter her parents didn't have to wring their hands over, a fact that didn't make her the favorite but merely the one they didn't have to invest much time and energy on. It made her the one they could take for granted.

But she didn't want to go into all that in front of Patrick. As far as she was concerned, he was a complete stranger—and completely strange. Recalling his glinting gold earring, she decided not to waste any more time before setting things straight for both her sister and Patrick.

"Look, Mr. Levine," she said with brisk formality, "Appearances to the contrary, you may be a fine lawyer. But we've got a family lawyer who takes care of Mary when she's in legal hot water. I appreciate what you've done for her, but he'll be in Wisherville tomorrow—"

"Bartholomew's coming?" Mary asked, her eyes growing round. "Tomorrow?"

"Of course he's coming. Didn't Mom tell you?"

"She didn't mention it."

"He always comes," Amelia reminded her. "Whenever you get into trouble."

"Which is rather often," Mary said with a self-congratulatory smirk.

Patrick took a long swig of beer from the bottle. When he lowered it, a residue of foam remained on his upper lip. He licked it off with a small agile movement of his tongue that Amelia noticed—and responded to, in some deep secret part of herself.

"Bartholomew?" he asked. "What kind of name is Bartholomew?"

"Bartholomew Driscoll," Mary told him. "It's a very Waspy name."

"What kind of name is Patrick Levine?" Amelia asked, suspecting that the best way to defend Bartholomew was to attack Patrick.

He smiled, and his stubble of beard seemed to thicken in the curves on either side of his mouth, indicating dimples lurking beneath. "It's the kind of name you wind up with when your mother is Irish and your father is Jewish."

"Irish and Jewish," Amelia echoed, fascinated in spite of herself. "That's quite a combination."

"What it boils down to," he explained, his eyes sparkling, "is that I lose my temper a lot, and then I feel very guilty about it afterward."

"I see." She resented his sense of humor. She resented everything that drew her attention to him—which was just about everything about him.

"So," he said, expanding his gaze to include Mary, "this Bartholomew Driscoll fellow is planning to come here tomorrow and take over your case?"

"He may try," Mary answered, "but I won't let him."

"Because I'm willing to take you on for free?"

"Because you're affiliated with the American Civil Liberties Union. This is a constitutional issue, Amelia." Mary directed her words to her sister. "It's a matter of freedom of expression and respect for private property. I have the right to display my sculpture in my gallery."

"In the front window? If the thing is so obscene, couldn't you at least have displayed it in the back?"

"It's not obscene! And even if it were, there's no law saying I can't use it to attract customers. Our highways are lined with billboards of half-naked women inviting drivers to smoke cigarettes and drink Scotch. Who says I can't have a tastefully erotic sculpture luring customers into my gallery?"

Amelia eyed Patrick dubiously. "Have you seen the sculpture?"

"Yes."

"Would you call it tastefully erotic, or obscene?"

He shot a quick look at Mary, then turned back to Amelia. "Do you want my personal opinion?" he asked soberly. "I'd say it's borderline obscene."

"Patrick!" Mary shrieked, balling up a napkin and throwing it at him.

Laughing, he deflected the paper missile, then took another swallow of beer and cleaned the foam from his lip with a deft, curiously sensual swipe of his tongue. "That doesn't mean I don't think it's art. I think some of Salvador Dali's paintings are obscene, and Picasso's *Guernica*, and all those fat, luscious nude ladies painted by Rubens and Titian in the Renaissance. And a lot of other things are obscene, too—certain songs, dances, movies . . . and a few of my favorite poster pinups," he concluded with a sly smile that Amelia sensed was intended solely for her, although she couldn't guess why.

"The thing is," he went on, a faint Dixie drawl once again filtering through his voice, "what *I* think is obscene is irrelevant, just as it's irrelevant what Mayor Dunphy thinks is obscene, or the Wisherville Citizens Brigade. All that matters is that the town had no right to force Mary into removing her sculpture from the window. In so doing they abrogated her constitutional rights."

Fair enough, Amelia conceded. His unorthodox jewelry notwithstanding, he talked like a lawyer. His speech contained just the right dose of passion, a soupçon of legalistic jargon, a hefty portion of conviction—and that husky Southern flavor that against her better judgment Amelia found intriguing.

"And what do you plan to do about this heinous abrogation of Mary's constitutional rights?" she asked wryly.

His eyes hardened slightly as he allowed her sarcastic tone to register. "First, we're going to have the charges against Mary dropped." He continued to address Amelia alone, aware that she was the one who needed convincing. "Then we're going to demand an apology from the town and a written assurance that her gallery displays will never again be interfered with. We may also push for sanctions against the Wisherville Citizens Brigade—they could be charged with harassment, vandalism, inciting to riot and so forth. I doubt we'll accomplish such sanctions, or even the apology, which means we'll have to take our complaints to a higher jurisdiction."

"Watch out, Supreme Court," Amelia muttered. As spellbinding as his speech had been, there was a limit to how much of his plan she could accept with a straight face.

"Why not the Supreme Court?" he asked. "It's the ultimate forum for constitutional interpretation."

"And you're going to argue Mary's two-bit case there?" she asked skeptically.

"I'm qualified to, if that's what you're asking. I've passed the bar exam and I'm licensed to practice pretty much anywhere, Ms. Potts—may I call you Amelia?"

"Sure," she said with some misgivings. She would have felt safer maintaining a certain formal distance from him, but since he and Mary were on a first-name basis, she couldn't bring herself to demand that he use her last name. "It's not that I question your qualifications," she explained, unable to look directly at him, "but Bartholomew always takes care of Mary's legal affairs."

"Bartholomew is Amelia's fiancé," Mary interjected.

"That's not true!" Amelia objected, more vehemently than she should have. It *was* true that Bartholomew was the son of her father's best friend, that he was as sane and responsible as she was, and that just about everyone in the Potts and Driscoll families assumed that she and Bartholomew would get married someday. It was also true that they were good friends, and that they'd gone out on dates a number of times, and that they'd once shared a bed, although they'd kept their pajamas on and, after a couple of kisses, gone to sleep. But while they were both well aware of the others' expectations, they never discussed marriage themselves. Amelia assumed that if a wedding were to come about, it would be a result of their mutual respect and their prodigious sensibility, not passion.

She tossed Patrick a nervous smile, unwilling to consider why it was so important to clarify her relationship with Bartholomew for him. "He's an old friend of the family," she explained. "His father and our father roomed together at Yale, and we kids all grew up together. He's quite fond of Mary, too."

"He thinks I'm a fruitcake," Mary claimed.

"Which only proves how observant he is." Amelia shaped a more confident smile and swiveled in her chair to confront Patrick. "I appreciate everything you've done for Mary—" which wasn't exactly true, since one of the things he'd done for Mary was fire her up for a needless court battle "—but I really think it would be best if you let Bartholomew take over her defense from here."

Patrick glanced at Mary, then leaned forward, bearing down on Amelia with his gaze. "And *I* really think it's up to Mary to decide what's best for her. She's under no obligation to me. If she wants to fire me the minute your old family friend arrives, she's free to do so. On the other hand..." He gave Mary another quick glance, and then turned his smile back to Amelia. "On the other hand, if she wants me to represent her, I will. It's not for you to say, sweetheart."

Amelia bristled indignantly. Patrick couldn't be faulted for failing to understand the dynamics of the Potts family. He didn't know that when Mary got herself into a fix, it definitely *was* for Amelia to say. It was her duty to map out the best course of action, to save Mary from her own recklessness.

But he didn't have to call her "sweetheart" in such a facetious tone.

"We don't have to decide anything tonight," Mary was saying. Amelia smothered her anger and gave Mary her full attention. "Bartholomew will be here tomorrow, and we'll get his input. He's a very intelligent man," she assured Patrick, "even if he is a stuffed shirt. Anyway, the most important thing right now is for me to get my statue back."

"Don't worry about it," Patrick reassured her. "We'll get it back."

"It really upsets me to think of *Liberty* sitting on a shelf in the town-hall basement overnight. It's a very valuable piece, you know."

"It's probably doubled in value since people started rioting over it." He grinned. "After all, now that the world knows that the statue is obscene—"

"It's not obscene," Mary grumbled.

Patrick ignored her. His eyes locked with Amelia's and he murmured, "If you ask me, obscenity has a lot going for it. Don't you agree, Amelia?"

"No," she snapped, vexed by his mocking grin. "I most certainly do not."

And then she looked away, acknowledging that what bothered her most about Patrick Levine was not his teasing but that, for an immeasurable instant, when she'd stared into the bewitching blue depths of his eyes, she had almost believed he could get her to agree to anything.

Chapter Two

Patrick spotted the white late-model Saab parked at the curb in front of Mary's gallery and smiled. Mary had mentioned once that her sister was the assistant to the Dean of Students at some snooty all-girls boarding school, and he didn't think assistant deans at prep schools earned enough money to be able to afford Saabs. Then again, Mary didn't earn much money from the Potts Gallery or her own artistic creations, yet she owned a winterized cottage in what was considered a pricey vacation area within weekending distance of Manhattan.

The Potts family was rich. From the bits and pieces Mary had told Patrick about her past, he deduced that she and her sister had been raised to pursue the careers of their choice, secure in the knowledge that beneath whatever tightropes they chose to traverse lay a thick safe cushion of Potts money. Mary had also told him, late one night after several daiquiris, that she had continually rebelled against the privilege of her youth, while Amelia had been the family's official goody-two-shoes.

Mary hadn't told the whole truth, he realized now. She hadn't told him that she and her sister were fraternal twins. And she hadn't told him about the sparks of energy animating Amelia's dark eyes, the intelligence illuminating her face. Mary hadn't done anything to prepare him for the possibility that he would find the official goody-two-shoes of the Potts family altogether enchanting.

He understood Mary. He understood artists and rebels and carefree young women who imbibed banana daiquiris. But Amelia, with her deceptively dainty build and her ballerina posture, her porcelain complexion and her determined chin and her stubborn, surprisingly sensuous mouth...

Amelia challenged him. And Patrick Levine loved a challenge.

He parked a few cars ahead of her and strolled back down the block to the gallery. He suspected that Amelia would view him with less distrust today than she had yesterday, given that he was clean-shaven and dressed in a summer-weight khaki suit, a white shirt, and a brown necktie knotted but not drawn against his throat. Later that morning, at eleven-thirty when he was due back at his office, he would tighten the tie in honor of the press conference he'd scheduled to answer questions and explain Mary's position regarding Wisherville's trashing of her civil rights. He'd leave the tie snug and straight, as well, for his afternoon appointment at Keppler's, one of the resort hotels where he performed nuts-and-bolts legal duties.

His work at a few of the region's resort hotels and summer camps paid him well, which freed him to tilt at windmills whenever the opportunity arose. That was the way he liked it, the way he'd envisioned his future years ago when he'd chosen to attend law school. He had never wanted to become a paper pusher at some Wall Street firm or a hired gun for some *Fortune 500* company. He wanted to fight the good fight, save the universe, remain true to his ideals. He also wanted to eat. Therefore, he exerted himself to maintain a balance between principles and money.

Today, the equilibrium was perfect: a morning of chest thumping over Mary Potts's constitutional rights, followed by an afternoon of billable hours at Keppler's. Grinning, he raked his hair back from his face and swung open the front door of the Potts Gallery, glimpsing the two broken and boarded windowpanes on his way in.

Mary was engrossed in a conversation with a man Patrick had never seen before. They were standing near a polished wooden sculpture displayed on a pedestal in the rear of the showroom. At first glance, the wooden sculpture appeared to be a tame abstract shape, but the longer Patrick stared at it the more phallic it seemed. His grin widened and he shook his head. When Mary made that remark yesterday about her family's predictability, she must have been referring to herself as much as to her sister.

At the sound of the door closing, Mary and the man flinched and fell silent. Mary, Patrick noted, seemed in a surprisingly cheerful mood, considering the fact that less than fourteen hours ago she'd been arraigned on an assortment of petty criminal offenses, fingerprinted, photographed and offered temporary accommodations in the police-station holding cell. This morning she was dressed in a bright orange sweat suit with padded shoulders. It looked good on her, but Patrick wasn't sure it was suitable for the press conference. He would have to ask her to change into something a little more demure—and she'd probably accuse him of trying to censor her. She'd be correct, too. But if she wanted to play the game, she was going to have to wear the proper uniform.

The man with her was certainly in proper uniform, Patrick observed. He stood a head taller than Mary, and his lightweight tweed jacket and pleated cotton-flannel slacks covered a body that was considerably better contoured than Patrick's lanky physique. The man's strawberry-blond hair and clean-cut features gave him a youthful appearance that didn't seem to match the expensive styling of his outfit.

"Patrick!" Mary shouted with a big smile that, for reasons that eluded him, looked almost guilty. "Good morning! Come meet Bartholomew Driscoll. Bartholomew, this is Patrick Levine."

That explained the guilty smile. Patrick had just barged in on her while she was conferring with another lawyer. He'd have to let her know he had no objection to her discussing the case with her old family friend. Competition didn't threaten Patrick; it invigorated him.

"How do you do?" he said, shaking Bartholomew's hand. He skimmed the gallery with his gaze, wondering where Amelia was. Her absence disappointed him, but he didn't have time to dwell on it right now. Turning back to Mary, he asked, "Do you have an estimate on the cost of replacing those windowpanes?"

"I think my insurance will cover it," she answered, flashing Bartholomew a quick grateful grin. "It's thanks to Bartholomew that I even have insurance," she added. "He told me I had to have it or I'd be in big trouble. He was right."

"Don't let your insurance company pay for it," Patrick cautioned her. "It's a tangible loss. We'll get the town to pick up the tab."

"Um, excuse me," Bartholomew broke in, favoring Patrick with a supercilious glare. "Miss Potts and I have been reviewing her situation. In my estimation, she ought to have her insurance company reimburse her for the window repair, plead nolo contendere to the disturbing-the-peace charge, pay her fine and return to life as normal. We could have the entire incident cleared up in a matter of days."

"In *my* estimation," Patrick said calmly, "your estimation is the pits—no offense intended. This is a case of an artist being denied her freedom of speech—"

"This is a case of a broken window," Bartholomew interrupted. "I appreciate your input, Mr. Levine, but I'll take it from here."

"Now, Bartholomew—" Mary silenced her friend with a reproving look "—I haven't yet decided which way I want to handle this. Please don't make up my mind for me."

Patrick offered Mary an unvoiced cheer. Bartholomew, he concluded, was a pompous fool. He simply couldn't imagine the guy, no matter how well-toned his musculature, being engaged to Amelia.

Then again, Mary was the one who'd identified him as Amelia's fiancé, and Amelia had promptly refuted it. There was still hope.

Hope? What, precisely, was he hoping for? He'd thought his only aim at the moment was to parlay Mary's case into something exciting, something as significant as the principles that lay at its foundation. Ever since he'd met Amelia Potts last night, though, and those dark, doubting eyes of hers had dug in and taken hold of him, he'd been hoping for something else, something that had absolutely no connection to principles or freedoms. He wasn't sure what it was, but another brief glance at the phallic wooden statue filled him with all sorts of marvelous ideas.

The sound of the gallery's front door opening broke into his thoughts, and Patrick spun around to discover that one hope of his had just been fulfilled. Amelia had arrived.

She was dressed in a prim lavender shirtwaist dress—the sort of dress Mary ought to wear to the press conference, Patrick thought. The pale pastel set off Amelia's creamy complexion and black hair in a becoming way. Her hair was parted in the middle and held back from her cheeks with a simple silver barrette, and despite the warm morning, her slender legs were sheathed in hose. She was carrying a white paper bag. Her gaze circled the room, halting when it reached Patrick. An odd, slightly anxious expression crept across her face.

"Here's the coffee," she said, walking across the room until she reached the glass-topped desk at the rear where Mary generally sat when she wasn't dealing with customers. Amelia set down the bag and removed three styrofoam cups, then pried off the lid of one. "I'm sorry, Patrick," she said, briefly meeting his gaze again. "If I'd known you'd be here, I would have bought four."

"That's all right," he said. "I had some at home."

"I didn't." Amelia scowled at her sister. "Mary's coffee maker is broken, and I can't stand instant." She took a bracing sip of the coffee she'd just purchased, then emitted a contented sigh.

"Instant tastes fine to me," Mary declared blithely, rummaging in the bag for sugar. "But then, nobody ever said I had any taste." She emptied three packets into her cup, then handed the remaining cup to Bartholomew.

Surveying the sculpture exhibited around him, Patrick found himself agreeing that Mary's taste was questionable at best. A peculiar chrome statue stood on a shelf against one wall, an equally peculiar blob of tinted blown glass stood on another, and a few ceramic shapes were displayed on tables placed strategically throughout the room. Not all of the pieces looked phallic, he acknowledged; a few of them were rounded, with enigmatic hollows and folds. It was a wonder the police hadn't confiscated the entire collection.

None of which was relevant to her legal case, he reminded himself. She had the right to sell any artwork she wanted, no matter how tasteless. The community-standards yardstick couldn't be used against her; whether or not one cared for it, this stuff was being marketed for its esthetic value, not its prurient value. It was art, not pornography.

"Well," Amelia said, her alluring eyes once again finding Patrick's, "I'm glad you've had a chance to meet Bartholomew. I take it he's explained to you how he's going to handle Mary's situation."

"He's offered an opinion," Patrick said blandly.

"I believe I did more than that," Bartholomew argued in a meticulous tone. "I'm not questioning your professionalism, Mr. Levine. However—"

"Bartholomew." Mary cut him off with a bright smile. "Patrick is willing to take my case to the highest court in the land if necessary. Are you?"

"The highest court?" he sputtered, nearly spilling his coffee over his fancy tweed jacket. "This is just a minor contretemps with the local authorities, Mary," he lectured. "You don't need to blow it out of proportion."

"You may be right, Bartholomew," Mary said steadily, "but I haven't yet made up my mind which way I want to take this." She directed her smile at Patrick.

"Why don't you see if you can convince her that your way is better than mine?" he suggested to Bartholomew, optimistic that Mary would ultimately decide in his own favor. "Meanwhile, I'll see if I can get the statue out of police lockup. Amelia, why don't you join me? Mary probably needs a little more time to go over her case with Bartholomew." This last recommendation popped out unexpectedly, and Patrick congratulated himself on its excellence. Not only could he attempt to retrieve Mary's sculpture, not only could he give Bartholomew a fair chance to persuade Mary that a timid, boring defense was preferable to fame and glory and her name immortalized in a Supreme Court decision, but he could spend a few minutes alone with Amelia, trying to erode her overt distrust of him.

He watched her, holding his breath as he waited for her to accept his invitation. After lengthy deliberation, she yielded with a slight nod. "I'd like to see this masterpiece of yours, Mary," she said, leaving Patrick to understand that that was the only reason she agreed to accompany him.

Whatever her reason, at least she'd said yes. Patrick smiled and motioned toward the door. "We'll be

back shortly," he promised. "Don't forget, Mary—
the press conference begins at eleven-thirty."

"What press conference?" he heard Bartholomew
roar just before the door closed behind him and
Amelia.

Without looking at him, Amelia started toward her
car. He gently touched her arm, then steered her down
the sidewalk to his Jeep. "We'll take mine," he said,
letting his hand drop from her elbow before she had a
chance to pull away. "If you drove, I'd have to hold
the sculpture—assuming we're allowed to take it. I'd
rather you hold it on the trip back to the gallery. It's
kind of fragile, and I'm all thumbs."

She peeked at his hands and snorted. "I doubt
that," she muttered, then averted her eyes as her
cheeks darkened with a pretty pink flush.

Patrick checked the impulse to grin. Her comment—and her blush—implied that she was aware of
him in a way that transcended their superficial ac-
quaintance. Daring to press his luck, he curved his
fingers around her arm again as they reached the Jeep,
and assisted her onto the seat. She acknowledged the
gesture with a stiff smile.

He strode around the vehicle to the driver's side and
climbed in behind the wheel. Then he revved the engine and eased out of his parking space. A refreshing
gust of air descended into the open Jeep as he pro-
ceeded down the street. The wind swirled around
them, tangling their hair and causing the skirt of
Amelia's dress to billow. Opting for safety, Patrick
reluctantly kept his eyes on the road instead of her
legs.

"If you ask me, the old family friend seems a mite
conservative," he remarked.

Amelia tossed him an unreadable look, then smiled. "He is. Preserving the status quo is his forte."

"I'm not a big fan of the status quo, myself. Few worthwhile things have been accomplished without overturning a few tables. I believe in fighting the good fight wherever it arises."

"I'm sure Mohammed Ali would support your view," Amelia said dryly. "On the other hand, the Potts family tends to be as conservative as Bartholomew."

"Speak for yourself, Amelia. Mary is all psyched for a brawl."

"Thanks to you," Amelia shot back, twisting in her seat to face him. "You've got her thinking her case is going to change the future of America."

"And why not?" He pulled into a parking space in the lot at the town hall and switched off the engine. "If we publicize her situation effectively, all of America may hear about it. She's already made the local television news broadcasts."

"Much to my parents' chagrin."

"I'm not working for your parents," he pointed out, struggling against his reflexive impatience. "I'm working for Mary."

"For free," Amelia grumbled. "What's in it for you, Patrick? Why have you taken her case?"

"Because she asked me to," he said, conscious that that wasn't the complete answer. Amelia's dubious expression implied that she knew there was more to it, too. "I believe in certain values, Amelia," he elaborated with forced patience. "I'm a civil libertarian, and I believe that artists—and business owners, too—should be left in peace to do whatever it is they want to do, as long as it isn't hurting anybody."

"How noble."

"It's the truth." He felt an imperative urge to win her trust. "I didn't just stumble over these ideals yesterday, you know. I've paid my dues. My first job out of law school was with Common Cause—that's a citizens' rights lobby in Washington. After that, I worked for a while on the staff of the American Civil Liberties Union. I've got impeccable credentials."

"And now, according to what Mary told me last night, you represent Borscht Belt hotels for a living."

He would be the first to agree that negotiating union contracts and liability coverage for resort hotels wasn't the most heroic work in the world. But he had a mortgage to pay, for crying out loud. "I got tired of city living," he explained in a contained voice, refusing to let her see how much her disapproval grated on him. "I wanted to settle down someplace where the air was clean and the trees weren't in little wrought-iron cages. Two years ago, I turned thirty and discovered I had zilch in the bank. I want a healthy life for myself. I want to get married and have a couple of kids someday, and that costs real money. So, yes, I do some profitable work these days—a hell of a lot less profitable than what your buddy Bartholomew must be doing, but I'm not ashamed to admit I earn a comfortable living working for the hotels. That doesn't mean I've sold out, Amelia. I still like to take a case that matters, and what's in it for me is a sense of pride."

"Excuse me," she said melodramatically. "Where's my handkerchief? I'm moved to tears."

His exasperation began to build. He admired her pluck, he appreciated her combativeness, but dammit, he wouldn't have her ridiculing him. "Why is it so necessary for you to think the worst of me?"

"Do you want to know?" she retorted, her eyes blazing and her chin thrust forward pugnaciously. "Do you really want to know why?"

"I asked, didn't I?"

"You showed up at the police station yesterday to represent Mary looking like a street bum, wearing a T-shirt and jeans. Not just a T-shirt, but one with a silly slogan on it! Mary is my sister, and I want her represented by a lawyer who has enough dignity to dress properly when he's working on her behalf."

Patrick's impulse was to lambaste Amelia for making unfounded assumptions about him. The truth was that Mary had phoned him at home while he'd been doing some yard work, and she'd asked him to come right away, so he'd dropped everything and raced over without taking time to change his clothes first. How dare Amelia accuse him of failing to represent Mary adequately?

But he held his tongue until his anger faded. He was touched by Amelia's protectiveness toward her sister. Mary might be the senior twin by twelve minutes, but Amelia was clearly the caretaker of the two, the guardian, the one who looked after her sister and worried about her.

Besides, he knew as well as Amelia did the importance of dressing appropriately. If he didn't, he'd be willing to let Mary show up at the press conference in her Day-Glo orange sweat suit.

"You're right, Amelia, I wasn't dressed for the occasion last night," he admitted, willing to stifle his self-righteousness in the hope of winning her favor. He shifted in his seat to display the suit he had on now. "Does this meet with your approval, at least?"

"Your collar is undone."

"Easy to remedy," he pointed out, fastening the top button.

"And your tie—"

"Slides right into place, once the collar is buttoned." He demonstrated. "Is it even?"

She automatically reached to adjust the tie, then let her hands fall to her lap. "It's fine," she mumbled, glancing away.

He appraised her for a minute, trying to interpret the tension emanating from her, trying to figure out the reason for it. "Somehow I sense that even when I'm willing to strangle myself on a necktie, you still don't approve of the way I look."

"I don't," she confirmed, keeping her gaze on her lap. "You're wearing an earring." She spoke the work "earring" as if she'd uttered a blasphemy, and another rosy blush flooded her cheeks.

The earring? Was that what was bothering her? A few polished molecules of gold attached to his ear? He threw back his head and laughed.

Amelia wasn't laughing, though. She crossed her legs and folded her arms, contorting her body in a classic pose of rejection. When she risked turning her head and lifting her eyes to him again, they were filled with apprehension, and maybe a bit of fear.

He immediately grew solemn. "What's wrong with my earring?" he asked. "It's pretty discreet, I think."

"But...but it isn't the sort of thing I associate with men," she said, her voice faltering in a way that tugged at him. He comprehended that it wasn't his earring that disturbed her but something deeper, something about his attitude as much as his appearance.

He gave her a tentative smile. "Of course you don't associate this with men. And piloting jets isn't the sort of thing I associate with women. Or fighting fires, or running businesses, or driving trucks."

"That's sexist!"

His smiled expanded. "So it is," he agreed, allowing her to make the connection herself.

Chastened, she unwound her limbs and sank against the upholstery of her seat. "I'm sorry, Patrick. It just...makes me nervous."

Was it his earring that made her nervous, or Patrick himself? Hoping to put her at ease, he tucked his hair behind his ear so she could see the tiny gold stud for herself. "That's all it is, Amelia," he murmured. "Something I did a long time ago because it gave me a kick. Check it out."

She did. Unbuckling her seat belt, she leaned toward him, closer than he'd expected, close enough for him to feel her warm breath brushing lightly against the side of his neck. Impulsively she extended her index finger and fondled the small gold bead. Her touch jolted them both, and she jerked her hand away in embarrassment.

"I forgot to warn you about the wiring," he joked, surprised that her innocent caress could have had such a strong impact on him. "Lesser mortals have electrocuted themselves doing what you just did."

She laughed, too, a shy breathless laugh that shot along his nerve endings, making his quip about electrocution seem distinctly unfunny. He was almost relieved when she shifted her gaze to the dashboard. He wasn't sure he wanted her to realize the effect she had on him.

"You make me uncomfortable, Patrick," she whispered, so softly he had to strain to hear her.

He absorbed her confession with mixed emotions. He wanted her to feel comfortable with him, comfortable enough to accept him and what he stood for, to give her blessings to his taking on Mary's case—and comfortable enough to welcome a sexual overture from him, if it ever reached that point. Because she turned him on in an astounding way, and that made him damned uncomfortable, too.

He considered matching her in honesty and confessing his own feelings. Then he thought better of it. "Let's go liberate Mary's statue." He pocketed his key and climbed out of the Jeep before he did anything more to shock her.

THE PROPERTY LOCKUP was located in the cellar. Amelia followed Patrick and the police clerk along a hallway, down a narrow flight of stairs and along another hallway, this one walled in clammy cinder block. "It's kind of damp down here," Patrick observed as they strolled through the underground corridor. "Too much humidity might ruin Mary Potts's sculpture."

"If my hair isn't frizzing, it can't be too humid," the clerk assured him, selecting a key from the ring strapped to her belt and using it to unlock a door. Inside was a small anteroom furnished with a long wooden table and a few folding chairs. The anteroom was separated by a chain-link barricade from dozens of metal storage shelves cluttered with impounded items. "You can look at it if you want," the clerk informed them, unlocking a gate in the chain-link barricade, "but I can't release it. It's being held as evidence."

"Evidence of what?" Patrick inquired.

"Hey, don't ask me." The clerk closed the gate behind her and wandered along the shelves, searching. "Talk to the arresting officer."

"Is he here this morning?"

"Huh-uh."

Patrick swore under his breath. "Isn't it fun dealing with the bureaucracy?" he whispered to Amelia.

She was having too much trouble dealing with Patrick to worry about dealing with the bureaucracy. Why had she touched his earring? Why had touching it felt so good? Why was she letting this man rattle her?

She envied his poise as he addressed the clerk. "Do you know why they impounded Ms. Potts's terra-cotta sculpture and not the marble statue?"

"The weapon, you mean?" The clerk's voice floated out to them from behind a freestanding shelf.

"The *alleged* weapon."

The clerk guffawed. "There was nothing alleged about it, Mr. Levine. Mary Potts confessed to waving it at the demonstrators in a threatening manner."

"She confessed to that before she'd been properly Mirandized," Patrick argued. "It's inadmissible in court. And nobody's contending that she waved the terra-cotta sculpture at anyone. It remained on the pedestal throughout the entire episode. Why was it impounded?"

"You want to know why?" The clerk reappeared, cradling a hefty ceramic sculpture in her arms. "Don't say I'm your source on this, Mr. Levine, but we're talking curiosity factor here. The guys on the force were curious—to say nothing of the politicos upstairs. More people have asked to get a look at this thing than any property we've taken since back in the seventies, when a bunch of rowdy Hell's Angels came through town and Joe Calhoun confiscated thirty-one knives from them." She carefully set the sculpture down on the wooden table, read the identifying tag and closed the gate with a shove of her hips. "There it is," she said. "Feast your eyes."

Amelia neared the table cautiously. The earth-toned sculpture depicted, without the slightest ambiguity, two human figures posed in an erotic confrontation. She took note of the delectable plumpness of the female figure's derriere, the unnaturally high thrust of her breasts, the arched arms extended toward the male figure. When she reached the opposite side of the table to view the male figure, she gasped. Protruding from his lower abdomen was an absurdly long, thick appendage. "Good Lord!" she muttered, feeling her cheeks grow hot. "That's...that's..." Unable to come up with an adequate term, she pressed her lips together and glanced away.

Unfortunately, turning from the table brought her gaze directly in line with Patrick's. He was measuring her reaction to the sculpture, his hands shoved into the pockets of his trousers and his hair tumbling rakishly over his brow. His mouth reflected a mere hint of a smile, but his cheeks were scored with dimples, and his vivid blue eyes were bright with laughter. "Are you outraged beyond words?"

"No, n-not really," she stammered, her embarrassment doubled because Patrick was there to witness it. "It's just . . . I can't help but wonder what Mary must have been thinking when she made this."

"It's pretty obvious what she was thinking."

"I mean..." Amelia felt her face grow even warmer, and she took a deep breath to calm herself. "I mean, this seems rather...exaggerated."

"Oh?" Patrick stepped toward the statue, scrutinizing it with a scholarly intensity. "In what way?"

He was baiting her, and she tried to maintain her composure. "As far as I know," she said, her tone admirably even, "Mary has always appreciated the human...form." She gulped in another deep breath. "This—" she gestured vaguely toward the male figure "—is hardly human."

"That's exactly what it is. Human and hard."

"It isn't an appreciation—it's a parody."

"Not necessarily."

Amelia glared at him. "Do you mean to tell me you think she's got the proportions right?"

He gave her a slow, insinuating smile. "I reckon it depends on the man, sweetheart."

Amelia had the choice of laughing or slapping him. She laughed. "Next thing I know, you're going to be bragging that you posed for this."

"If you're interested, I can think of one easy way to find out," he said, resting his hips against the table and eyeing her above the sculpture.

"Haven't you got a job to do, Patrick? You're supposed to be getting this thing out of police custody." Deliberately turning from him, she gave the piece a final inspection and then stalked to the door leading out of the storeroom. She would have preferred to keep going, to hurry through the basement corridor, upstairs and outside, to escape from Patrick until she'd collected herself. She didn't like the way he could make her blush and stutter, the way he could fluster

her when all she was doing was examining one of
Mary's creations.

She'd been critiquing Mary's artwork for years, ever
since their freshman year at the Hibbing School, when
Mary had renounced her ambition to become a movie
star and took up art—mainly because she'd had a
crush on one of the art teachers. All through prep
school and then through college, and on through the
next several years, when Mary had moved back into
their parents' Sutton Place apartment and devoted
herself to defacing the temporary walls at construction sites in Manhattan, declaring that such acts were
an artistic statement, and on until three years ago,
when Mary had taken a vacation in the Catskills with
some fellow she'd been dating, discovered a store for
rent in Wisherville and decided, on a whim, to open a
gallery, Amelia had been Mary's staunchest sup-
porter—and in private her harshest critic.

Some of Mary's work was magnificent, and some
of it was rotten. This so-called *Liberty* thing, this tex-
tured arrangement of copulating clay figures with their
distorted anatomies . . . well, it certainly wasn't magnificent.

She heard the clank of the gate as the clerk shut and
locked it. Turning, Amelia found Patrick close behind her. "I'm going to have a chat with the chief of
police," he said, "and see if I can get anywhere with
him. If you can wait, I won't be more than a few minutes, and then we can head back to the gallery. Personally, I think we're better off if the police refuse to
hand over the sculpture."

"I agree," Amelia muttered, thinking that the piece
would cause a lot less trouble if it remained locked
away in the town-hall basement.

Patrick smiled patiently. "If the police don't release the sculpture, we can accuse them of confiscation of property without due process," he explained. "It's one more charge, one more bit of ammunition for our side."

When they reached the top of the stairs, Amelia told Patrick she'd wait for him outdoors. She sorely needed some fresh air. As soon as she stepped outside, her gaze fell on his Jeep, and she recalled her impetuous decision to touch his ear. Drawing in a sharp breath, she pivoted and crossed the street, entering the park and following one of the meandering paths through the painstakingly landscaped grounds until she found an empty bench. She sat on it and sighed. The air was rich with the scent of pine, and a cool sweet mountain breeze washed over her, relaxing her.

There was no need to become overwrought about Patrick. He was just a man; his ear was just an ear. Touching it hadn't been any more intimate an act than shaking hands with him—although, as she reflected on it, she'd been unusually conscious of the size and warmth of his hand when he'd closed it around hers last night.

All right, so he was an attractive man. So he stirred some unexpected feelings inside Amelia. Whatever she felt toward him was basically irrelevant; what mattered was what sort of impact his inspiring principles were going to have on her sister's legal problems.

Closing her eyes, she considered his strategy. Granted, it differed greatly from Bartholomew's low-profile approach, but she couldn't deny that Patrick's reason for wanting the police to keep the statue was shrewd, and that when he'd talked about civil liberties he'd stirred her sense of justice and fairness. If only her sister weren't at the heart of the matter, Amelia would support Patrick's position. But Mary *was* at the heart of it, and Amelia didn't want to see her subjected to years of legal maneuvering and public scrutiny just because a rabble-rouser from the Catskills felt like making a test case.

"That duck is a pig." Patrick's husky drawl reached her from over her shoulder.

Jumping, she spun around to find Patrick resting his forearms on the back of the bench with his hands clasped together, his tie once again loose and his hair windblown as he gazed past Amelia toward a small flock of ducks waddling among the willow trees that grew along the edge of a pond at the center of the park. She took a moment to recover from the start he'd given her. "How can a duck be a pig?" she asked.

"Whenever I come down here with bread crumbs, he bullies the other ducks away and gobbles all the bread crumbs up himself. One of these days, he's going to explode. I hope I'll be here to see it—armed with my camera and a roll of film."

"I bet you'll get some lovely photos," Amelia commented wryly. "Perhaps you'll be able to enlarge and frame them, and Mary will exhibit them in her gallery."

"Not a bad idea," he pondered aloud, his eyes glittering with humor. "*Exploding Duck—Works by Patrick Levine.* I like the sound of it."

"She wouldn't call it *Exploding Duck*," Amelia argued. "She'd probably call it something strange, like *Liberty*." Standing, she dusted off her skirt and ambled out of the park with Patrick. "I take it you were unable to gain custody of her statue."

"I didn't try my hardest," he admitted with a grin. He glanced down at her and his smile became quizzical. "Did it really shock you all that much?"

His question had been asked honestly, and she weighed her answer before speaking. "I suppose I shouldn't be shocked by anything Mary does," she granted. "I mean, she is the family fruitcake and all."

"I don't care if she's the family pizza with anchovies," he said. "I want to know what your true opinion of the sculpture is, Amelia. You seemed so mortified in there."

"I guess I was."

"Not that I'm a great art critic or anything, but I think that's the point. Mary created it for its shock value."

Amelia smiled faintly. "You're right, Patrick. Much of what Mary does is for shock value."

Patrick nodded and opened the Jeep's passenger door for her. "And what about you?" he asked, his casual tone contradicted by the intensity of his gaze.

She bought a minute by settling herself in the seat, smoothing her skirt and hooking the seat belt. "Much of what I do, I do for the sake of peace," she finally admitted.

He closed the door and rested his elbows against the ledge; his unwavering eyes were level with hers. "In other words, you've got noble principles, too," he said, smiling gently.

"I don't mean peace in the antiwar sense," she corrected him. "Of course, I'm against war, too, but I mean a calm, temperate existence, where a person knows what's expected of her and does her best, where she doesn't go looking for trouble. That probably makes me very staid and dull, but—"

"Oh, no," he murmured. Casting her a dimpled grin, he sauntered around to the driver's side, his hands in his pockets and his earring winking provocatively in the morning sunlight. "It makes the temptation to shock you that much greater."

Chapter Three

"Why did I let you talk me into this?" Amelia muttered. She was seated beside Patrick in the Jeep, her palms flattened against her knees to keep her dress from being blown off her lap as he accelerated out of yet another S-shaped wiggle in the road. The back routes connecting the towns and villages of the Catskill region tended to be gloriously picturesque, their bucolic beauty magnified by their dramatic twists, turns, ascents and descents as they conformed to the hilly terrain.

He risked a quick glance in her direction and then turned back to the snaking road ahead. "I don't know why," he answered, "but I'm glad you did."

Amelia wasn't glad. She was irked, not so much by Patrick as by herself for having agreed to accompany him to Keppler's Hotel for the afternoon. She hadn't taken a day off from her job at the Hibbing School and driven all the way to Wisherville to gallivant through the mountains with a stranger. She'd come to help her sister.

Maybe that was why she was with Patrick now—to help Mary. After the press conference at Patrick's office, Mary had dragged Amelia into the rest room, locked the door and announced, "I'm still pretty mixed up," which Amelia considered the understatement of the century. "Meeting with the reporters and talking about my position was a lot of fun," she continued, "and I really think Patrick knows what he's doing, but...Bartholomew wants to spend some more time reviewing the situation with me. I sort of feel I owe it to him, seeing that he's practically family."

Amelia bristled at her sister's insinuation. Then she realized Mary might simply have been referring to the fact that Bartholomew was a close friend, not that he was her sister's future husband. Too many of her relatives implied that he was, and even if she ultimately did marry him, she considered such hints awfully presumptuous.

"I think you owe it to him, too," she concurred, hiding her uneasiness by examining herself in the mirror above the sink and fidgeting with her hair. "He's got your best interests at heart, Mary. You've got to give him a fair hearing before you do anything rash with Patrick."

"Then you understand." Mary smiled. "I want you to give me a few hours alone with Bartholomew to chew things over. We'll converge for a strategy session at dinnertime, okay?"

Amelia accepted Mary's plan with some reluctance. She did want Mary to chew things over with Bartholomew, but she hadn't expected to be excluded from the chewing. What was she supposed to do all afternoon while her sister and Bartholomew were in closed session? Window-shop? Hang out on the front porch of Mary's bungalow? Take a dip at Halley's Pond?

Or drive to Keppler's with Patrick? "It'll be fun," he insisted, once the Potts sisters emerged from their bathroom powwow, joined Patrick and Bartholomew in the eclectically furnished reception area, and announced Mary's plan. "We'll have lunch there—the chef is excellent. And you can bring a swimsuit and relax by the pool while I work. Or you can get one of the horses at the stable next door to Keppler's and take a nice long ride through the woods. Or take a rowboat out on the lake, or shoot some billiards or play shuffleboard. Or all of the above. I should be done by four o'clock or so, and then we'll come back for dinner."

"Doesn't it bother you that my sister's going to be in consultation with your rival all afternoon?" Amelia asked, casting her gaze toward Mary and Bartholomew as they departed from the office, which was housed, along with a barbershop and a real-estate agency, in a modest brick building a block off Main Street.

"Is Blond Bart my rival?" Patrick countered with a nonchalant shrug. "Hey, I want what's best for Mary just as much as you do. If the Potts family counselor can convince her that she's better off eating crow and turning her back on her principles, then so be it. I happen to think Mary is made of sterner stuff."

"You also happen to have an enormous ego."

"A healthy one," he corrected her. "So. How about coming to Keppler's with me?"

And here she was, going to Keppler's with him. She hadn't packed a swimsuit when she'd left New Milford the previous evening, but she kept a spare one, along with a couple of changes of clothing, in the guest bedroom of her sister's bungalow to accommodate her spur-of-the-moment visits. Lolling by the pool at a resort hotel for a couple of hours would be a pleasant diversion, so she'd accepted Patrick's invitation and asked him to swing by her sister's house in order for her to get her suit and a towel.

"What did you think of the press conference?" he asked, apparently choosing not to comment further on her misgivings about spending the afternoon in his company.

"It was a media circus."

"All press conferences are by definition media circuses," he pointed out. "I thought it went well, myself. Mary looked great, didn't she?"

What Mary had looked was uncharacteristically demure. At Patrick's request, she'd worn an unpretentious beige linen dress for the conference. "Bartholomew was impressed," Amelia told him. "He said he thought she could pass for a senator's wife."

"I imagine that's his idea of sexy," Patrick said with a snort.

"Well, she dressed for you, not for him," Amelia reminded him. "She must have assumed that you wanted her to look like a senator's wife, too." She heard a twinge of bitterness in her voice and hoped he hadn't picked up on it. It wasn't exactly fun to stand quietly aside while two notably attractive bachelors wrestled for the right to represent Mary, who was so pretty she could fix herself up to impress one of them and, without any extra effort, manage to impress the other.

"I didn't want her to look too flamboyant," Patrick explained. "We don't want to come across as if she's simply grandstanding. We don't want her clothing to attract more attention than her fight for civil rights.''

''Fine,'' Amelia said, cutting off the lecture he seemed to be on the verge of. ''The bottom line is, you arranged the press conference to attract attention, and you succeeded.''

''We had reporters there from New York City, from Albany, from Ithaca and Binghamton—and someone from the Associated Press.'' Patrick smiled triumphantly. ''My secretary is an absolute whiz. She made a few calls this morning, and presto!''

''Is her ego as huge as yours?'' Amelia asked sardonically.

Patrick laughed. ''I think Mary handled herself well. You were standing in the back with Bartholomew. How did the event seem to you?''

''Bartholomew thought the whole thing was absurd. He tends to share my family's aversion to notoriety.''

''I didn't ask what *he* thought of it, Amelia. I asked what *you* thought of it.''

She gazed at the trees blurring past and sighed. She had wanted to dislike Patrick's strategy as much as Bartholomew did. But the truth was, as she'd stood at the back of the crowded conference room in Patrick's suite of offices, listening while Patrick and Mary fielded questions from the score of reporters in attendance, she'd thought not about Patrick's questionable methods of getting Mary's case before the public but about his presence, his savoir faire, his sharp mind and his charisma. She'd thought about how well prepared he was, and how subtly he came to Mary's aid whenever she began to founder, and how adroitly he kept the press conference on course. She'd thought about his hypnotic blue eyes. She'd thought about how he, like Mary, attracted attention without any apparent effort, and about how utterly lacking Amelia herself was in the art of getting people to notice her.

She'd thought about whether Patrick and Mary were lovers, and if not, why not.

It occurred to her that Patrick was waiting for her to say something. Sighing again, she turned to him. "That stuff you said about how Mary had the support of creative artists around the country—was that true?"

"Do you think I'd lie to the press?"

"I wouldn't put it past you."

He shot her a swift, inscrutable look, and then his face relaxed into a smile. "All right, I've been known to gussy up the truth on occasion. All good lawyers do. I'm sure even Bartholomew does."

"I'm sure he doesn't."

Patrick muttered something under his breath about how Bartholomew probably wasn't such a good lawyer. Aloud, he said, "As far as the press conference goes, what I said was the absolute truth. My office has gotten at least a dozen telephone calls in support of Mary, as well as telegrams from three artists' organizations, two writers' groups, the faculty of an art school in Chicago and the publisher of a skin magazine."

"Wonderful." Amelia grimaced.

"The more publicity Mary's case gets, the more support she'll receive."

"I understand the need for publicity," she allowed. "But this is my sister we're talking about. If your strategy backfires, she'll be the butt of ridicule."

"For trying to assert her constitutional rights?" Patrick shook his head. "No matter what the outcome, her position is sound. No one could ridicule her for it. Besides—" the corners of his lips turned upward in a sly grin "—she seems to love publicity. Whatever the circumstances, your sister thrives on being in the spotlight. Even if she were the butt of ridicule, I have the feeling she'd enjoy the attention."

He slowed the Jeep, turning off the road and onto a paved driveway flanked by white rail fences, with a freshly painted sign reading Keppler's marking the entry. The tires bumped along the ruts in the driveway, passing rolling emerald-green meadows dotted with purple clover blossoms and yellow buttercups. The early-June splendor of the scenery distracted Amelia from her debate over Patrick's methods.

He coasted into the parking lot abutting the rambling main building of the hotel. It was a white clapboard structure, three stories high, with symmetrical wings of rooms extending on either side of the sprawling front porch, which was furnished with heavy redwood lawn chairs and planters of scarlet geraniums. A few guests sat on the porch, reading magazines and paperbacks, chatting among themselves, sipping cold drinks and enjoying the unseasonably warm late-spring weather. All in all, the atmosphere was one of cleanliness and congeniality.

"I like this place," Amelia blurted out, startling herself. She still hadn't figured out what she was doing at Keppler's with Patrick, but for some unfathomable reason, she was delighted to be there.

"I only work for clients as high quality as your sister," he joked, lifting his briefcase and Amelia's tote bag from the narrow space below the back seat of the

Jeep and then helping her out. He escorted her up the three steps to the front porch, then through the double screen doors to the lobby, which was actually an airy breezeway extending the width of the building.

The attractive young woman posted behind the registration desk noticed Patrick, and her face lit up. "Patrick! Hi! I didn't know you were coming today."

This might explain why Mary and Patrick weren't lovers, Amelia thought, giving the woman a quick perusal. She appeared to be barely out of her teens—too young for a man who'd seen his thirtieth birthday come and go a couple of years back. But then, Patrick was the sort to flout respectability. Maybe, having reached the ripe old age of twenty-eight, Mary was too old for his taste.

"Hi, Sue," Patrick greeted the desk clerk, his smile a bit more restrained than hers. "Is Rae Keppler around? She should be expecting me."

"Hang on, I'll find her." The clerk dialed Rae's office.

"She certainly seems happy to see you," Amelia murmured, pretending to be fascinated by the ornate brass fan hanging from the vaulted ceiling, the light wicker chairs and tables, the carefully placed arrangements of fresh flowers and the intricate mosaic of tiles decorating the floor.

"I think she has a crush on me," Patrick said, sounding less than thrilled. He almost cringed when the young woman hung up and sang out his name, her eyes bright with infatuation. Amelia stifled a chuckle.

"Mrs. Keppler's in her office. She said to send you on in," said the woman.

"Thanks, Sue."

"Will you be here long?" she called to Patrick as he ushered Amelia to one of the hallways leading out of the lobby.

"As long as it takes," he answered, allowing his hand to settle against the small of Amelia's back.

She didn't object to the gesture. In part, she understood that it was his polite way of informing the smitten desk clerk that he wasn't interested in her, and in part it nullified the sense the clerk had conveyed that Amelia was invisible. She was used to going unnoticed, but she didn't like it. Patrick's gentlemanly touch let her know that even if Sue had overlooked her, he hadn't.

And his hand felt nice where it was, molding gently to the hollow of her waist, his long fingers fanning out against the smooth fabric of her dress. It felt very nice.

Patrick stopped at a door halfway down the hall, rapped on it and then pushed it open. The office he and Amelia entered was sunny, the walls lined with birch bookshelves, the furniture upholstered in flowery chintz, the curving leather-top desk adorned with a bud vase holding a spray of daffodils. Broad windows opened onto the property at the rear of the main building; through the screens wafted the sounds of guests talking and laughing, and birds chirping as they flitted through the trees surrounding the property.

An inner door opened and a matronly woman emerged. She was a few inches taller than Amelia, solidly built, and she strode toward her guests with the energy of a varsity athlete, her steps sure and purposeful, her arms swinging. She wore a stylish pantsuit of gauzy cotton, and her bleached-platinum hair was coiffed to perfection. Amelia estimated the woman's age to be somewhere around sixty, although her youthful face and natural vivaciousness seemed to belie that.

"Patrick! Darling!" she bellowed before giving him an affectionate hug, which he willingly returned. For a brief moment Amelia wondered whether this older woman, and not the young clerk at the reception desk, was Patrick's current inamorata.

Her beaming smile as she turned to Amelia implied otherwise, as did her words. "And who is this lovely young lady you've brought with you? Don't tell me you've hired a new secretary."

"No, Marilyn is holding down the fort in Wisherville," Patrick told her. "Things are pretty hectic there at the moment. This—" he pressed his hand into Amelia's back, urging her forward "—is Amelia Potts, a friend of mine who came along for the ride. I told her she could use the facilities here while I worked."

"Of course she can," the woman said, gathering Amelia's hands in her own. "I'm Rae Keppler. I own this place, headache that it is. Patrick, I'm so glad you're here. I've got troubles you wouldn't believe. That condo developer? He sent me a package of papers that could be in another language for all I understand them. I think the guy's trying to chisel me. You'll check it all for me, won't you, darling?"

"That's what you're paying me for, Rae," Patrick said with a grin.

"I love this boy," Rae confided to Amelia, pinching Patrick's chin between her thumb and index finger. "Look at him. Is this gorgeous, or what?"

Amelia smiled weakly. She hadn't yet recovered from Patrick's having introduced her as his friend. She wasn't about to cast her vote on his looks.

"All right." Rae released Patrick's face and pointed him toward the inner door. "I've got everything in there for you. Tons of documents, Patrick, I'm warning you. It's enough to make an old lady weep. Go find out what that thief is trying to pull over on me."

Patrick eyed the door. "Any chance I could grab a bite to eat first?" he asked. "I promised Amelia some lunch."

"You want lunch? I'll send something in for you," Rae promised. "There's too much stuff in there for you to go through. You shouldn't be dawdling over a meal. I'll have Roger send in some salmon, okay, sweetie? It's so fresh, it's to die from. And a nice iced tea, the way you like it." She turned to Amelia. "You, I'll feed myself. He's got to get to work or he'll be here all night."

Before Amelia could protest, Patrick handed her her tote bag and vanished through the inner door. Linking her arm through Amelia's, Rae led her out into the hall. "I'll tell you, that boy—you grab a hold of him and don't let go," she whispered conspiratorially. Evidently she'd come to the conclusion that Amelia was more than friend to Patrick, even though Amelia believed she was considerably less than a friend. "He's quite a catch, darling. Now. You like salmon? This is so fresh, and the way Roger fixes it, broiled with just a little fresh parsley and lemon butter, it melts in your mouth."

"It sounds marvelous." Amelia wasn't sure what to make of Rae Keppler, but for the time being she felt the wisest course was to remain agreeable.

They entered an enormous dining room, atmospherically lit and filled with attractively set linen-covered tables, some of them occupied by diners. "I tell you what," Rae suggested, steering Amelia through the room to a row of French doors. "Why don't we eat on the porch? The breeze is so much nicer there." She opened one of the doors and they entered a screened dining porch that offered a spectacular panorama of the sloping lawn, the Olympic-size pool surrounded by lounge chairs and striped umbrellas, the volleyball net, the shuffleboard courts, the children's swing set and jungle gym, and in the distance, through a stand of evergreens, a small tranquil lake.

"You like it?" Rae asked about the vista.

"It's beautiful," Amelia replied, enthralled. Once again she thought about how unexpectedly pleased she was to be in this warm friendly place.

"Sit." Rae pointed to a table for two and left the seat with the better view for Amelia. A college-age waiter in a crisp white shirt, black trousers and a black bow tie hustled over and filled their glasses with ice water. "Good afternoon, Mrs. Keppler. What can I get for you ladies today?"

"She'll have the salmon," Rae spoke for Amelia, who didn't dare to contradict her. "As for me," she went on, "I ate earlier, so just some fruit—some berries and cream—would be nice. And a cup of tea. What would you like to drink, Amelia?"

"Water is fine," she said, taking a sip and determining not to let the woman cow her. For all Rae's bossiness, Amelia was growing to like her.

"So," Rae said, once they were alone again, "how long have you known Patrick?"

"Less than a day," Amelia admitted, figuring she ought to set Rae straight. She had enough of people hooking her up with Bartholomew. She certainly didn't want to be hooked up with Patrick. "Actually, my sister is . . . I guess you could say a potential client of his."

"Your sister," Rae repeated. "Potts is the name?" She frowned, searching her memory, and then wagged her finger at Amelia. "I thought there was something familiar about the name. Your sister's the meshuga with the sexual statue, right? I saw her on TV last night."

"That's right," Amelia said with a long-suffering sigh.

"Matter of fact, there was some talk around here that some of the guests were going to drive down to Wisherville just to see the statue."

"If they do, they'll be disappointed," Amelia warned. "It was impounded by the police. Patrick tried to get them to release it this morning, but he wasn't able to."

"And here I thought that boy could do anything," Rae said, smiling. She leaned back when the waiter arrived with their food. "Try that, darling," Rae urged Amelia, gesturing toward the juicy pink slab of fish on her plate. "You're such a skinny little thing, you could use a few pounds. Not that salmon's going to help—it's very dietetic, you know—but you'll have some cake for dessert. Roger makes an almond cheesecake that you ought to have to pass a cholesterol test before you're allowed to have any, it's so rich. But eat, Amelia. Tell me what you think of that salmon."

Amelia tasted it. "It's delicious."

Rae nodded smugly. She sipped her tea and gazed out at the hotel guests frolicking on the lawn. "So, maybe Patrick can't do everything. He's still a fine lawyer, a very fine lawyer.''

"I don't doubt it," Amelia murmured. She might have doubted it as much as a half hour ago, but there was something contagious about Rae Keppler's enthusiastic endorsement of him.

"See those trees down there?" Rae said, pointing to the copse of pointed firs by the edge of the lake. "There's a developer who wants to buy some of my land and put up condos there. Not to deprive the hotel of lakeside property, but more to complement what we've got here—or so he says. Lots of the resorts are building condos these days."

"Isn't that self-defeating?" Amelia asked, amazed that she found the topic interesting. "If people buy condos, they aren't going to take rooms in your hotel."

"But they'd still make use of the facilities and they'd pay for that. The theory is, we'd have more people coming in and spending money." Rae scooped a spoonful of blueberries from the cut-glass bowl the waiter had placed before her. "I don't know. Maybe it means less work for me. Sooner or later, this whole place is probably going to go."

"Go? Where?"

"To developers," Rae said with a pensive smile. "My father-in-law, may he rest, founded this hotel, and my beloved husband, may he also rest, ran it until the day he passed away. Now I'm running it, and I love it. But look at me. I'm an old lady. I've got three wonderful children and five grandchildren I love so much I could eat them up, and not a single one of them wants to take over Keppler's. My son, my wonderful son, thinks I should sell the whole place right now and spend the rest of my life taking cruises. My daughters want me to move near them, which could cause some problems since one of them lives in Ann Arbor and the other one lives in Austin, so what are they going to do, cut me in half? This is my life. I love this place. But once I'm too tired to run it—and that's going to happen soon, Amelia—who's to say? It's a lot of work, running a hotel like this. Maybe my son is right. Maybe I should sell the whole thing to the developers, and take the money and go on a cruise."

Amelia listened sympathetically. Keppler's was such a lovely hotel, and the guests seemed to be enjoying it greatly. She'd hate to see it turned into condominiums. "Have you thought about selling it to someone as it is?" she asked. "I mean, someone who would continue to run it as a hotel?"

"Find me that person and I'll close the deal tomorrow," Rae swore with a sad smile. "Nowadays, anyone with enough business smarts to run a place like this would rather be an investment banker, making millions of dollars. To run a place like Keppler's takes more than brains—it takes dedication. It isn't going to make anyone rich."

Amelia was saddened by Rae's claim. Keppler's wasn't her concern, of course. In the three years since she'd been visiting Mary in Wisherville, she'd never even heard of the place, let alone visited it. Why should she care about the hotel's fate?

Yet she did. She felt comfortable here, and she admired Rae Keppler, and she thought it would be a crime if the resort was turned into condos.

"Eat," Rae commanded, her expression brightening. "Finish your fish. In the meantime, I'm going to make sure Roger saves you a piece of his cheese-cake.''

PATRICK STOOD, stretched, and crossed to the window. He'd been reading documents for two and a half hours, taking notes, marking up clauses with his blue felt-tip pen. Papers were scattered almost the entire length of the mahogany conference table. His open briefcase occupied one end, and the tray of empty dishes from his lunch occupied the other. Even while eating, he hadn't permitted his concentration to stray. He hadn't given any thought to Mary Potts, her sculpture, the publicity that might result from the press conference. Nor had he given any thought to Amelia. Patrick had long ago mastered the necessary skill of tuning out everything but the task at hand.

Single-mindedness was one of the most useful attributes a lawyer could possess, but after a while it took its toll. When the muscles in his neck began to stiffen up and he discovered himself rereading the same paragraph three times, he knew he needed a break.

Loosening his tie, he gazed through the window at the hotel grounds, taking in the lake with its reflection of the tufted clouds scattered across the wide blue sky, and then the trees, and then a raucous game of volleyball in progress on the lawn, and finally the swimming pool. It wasn't too crowded; the afternoon really wasn't warm enough for swimming, although he noticed one brave figure doing laps at a slow steady crawl. He couldn't see her face, but her one-piece swimsuit was a bright fuchsia that stood out against her aqua-blue surroundings. Her legs were long and sleek, her arms graceful as they cut through the surface of the water, and her long locks of hair floated around her head like black ribbons.

Reaching the far end of the pool, she hoisted herself out onto the tiled patio and Patrick's suspicions were confirmed. Amelia Potts might come across as fragile and somewhat timid, but she had the guts to take a leisurely swim even though the afternoon temperature hadn't broken the eighty-degree mark. She had the guts to tackle the water, the strength to give herself a vigorous workout and the verve to wear a garishly colored bathing suit.

From his vantage, half a story above the pool and some sixty feet away, he could scarcely make out the particulars of her slight figure. He could tell only that her skin was pale and her body slender, and that her legs were much longer in proportion to her torso than he'd realized.

He wished he could abandon his work and race outside for a closer look. He wished he could check out the fit of the swimsuit—its snug elasticity would undoubtedly hint at the feminine assets lurking underneath. He wished he could see her chest pumping as she caught her breath, and the droplets of water rolling down into the hollow between her breasts, and the smooth skin of her thighs....

A low laugh escaped him as he considered the direction his thoughts had taken. What anyone else might interpret as an exhausted swimmer he interpreted as a mermaid, a sea nymph, a vision of sensual delight. Even if she disapproved of him, even if the act of touching his ear for all of one second that morning had scared her out of her wits, even if she was promised to that big blond oaf in his expensive tweed jacket... Those were the concerns of a cautious mind, and one thing Patrick's mind wasn't was overly cautious.

He watched Amelia as she wrapped her body in a fleecy towel, then unwillingly tore his gaze from the window and returned to the conference table. It was time, once again, to tune out everything but the chore of figuring out how many different ways the condominium developer was trying to bamboozle Rae Keppler.

An hour later, he packed up his briefcase and left the conference room in search of Rae. At the reception desk, he approached Sue, who had been flirting with a busboy who'd wandered out of the dining room for a breather between his lunchtime and dinnertime shifts. As soon as she saw Patrick, however, she turned her back on the busboy. "Hi, Patrick," she said with a coquettish smile.

"Can you track down Rae for me?" he asked coolly.

Sue batted her eyes. "Last time I saw her, she and Jeff Wurtzel were cruising around on a golf cart, inspecting the outbuildings."

"I'll try to head her off," Patrick said, departing from the lobby. He exited onto the back porch and surveyed the grounds, spotting the cart rattling up the grassy slope toward the main building. He signaled Rae with a wave, and she waved back, said something to the man driving the cart and hopped off as soon as he slowed the vehicle.

"That terrible thunderstorm we had last week!" she lamented, jogging over to Patrick with the vitality of a woman half her age. "The recreation building down near the stables, where we have dances, is a mess. A rain gutter knocked off, some roof tiles loose, I tell you..." She shook her head and clicked her tongue. Then her eyes met Patrick's and she grinned. "All right, so what's the word? Should I sell to that chiseler and let him tear down the barn and put up a high rise?"

"What you should do, Rae, is let me rewrite the entire contract. He's inserted lot of mumbo jumbo in there that I don't like, and I think we've got to clarify a number of points. If you're absolutely certain you want to sell, that is."

"I don't want to sell, Patrick. You know that as well as I do. It's just..." She threw up her hands. "What am I going to do? One of these days I'll have to retire, and then what?"

"We've already discussed your options, Rae. You could sell the entire complex as a working resort."

"And who's going to buy? At least with the condos, I'm guaranteeing myself some money now, am I right? This is my pension we're talking about. I shouldn't die penniless, you know."

He slung his arm around her shoulders and gave her a reassuring hug. Although he worked for Rae—and charged her a substantial fee for his labors—he felt more like her devoted nephew than her attorney. "Let me rewrite the preliminary sales contract," he advised. "He's fudging on the price per acre, and I have some questions about the surveyor's report, and we need to be a lot more specific about how much disruption the construction is going to cause. The way he's got things written, he could drive his construction equipment right over your lawn here, and you wouldn't be able to do anything about it."

Her eyes widened in horror. "We can't have that, Patrick!"

"I intend to fix the contract so he can't do it. Don't worry."

Rae returned his hug, then strolled arm in arm with him toward the back porch. "So how was the salmon? Was it to die from or what?"

"It was to die from, Rae."

"Amelia's a doll," she went on. "A very sweet girl. You going to date her, or what?"

"I don't know yet, Rae." He flashed a broad grin. "I've got hopes, though."

"I like her. You can bring her along with you any time you come here. She's a very nice girl. Smart, too. A little skinny, but you send her to me and I'll fatten her up."

"Thanks, Rae." Patrick scanned the lawn. "I guess she's still over by the pool. I'd better go and get her. You take care now. I'll be in touch."

He ambled across the lawn, feeling absurdly over-dressed in his suit and tie while everyone around him was clad in resort wear. Reaching the pool, he saw Amelia lying face down on a lounger in the protective shade of an umbrella. Her arms were folded beneath her head and her body was motionless. He wondered if she was asleep.

He walked around the pool and lowered himself onto the empty lounger next to hers. When she didn't turn to acknowledge him, he took a moment to study her. Rae was wrong. Amelia wasn't really skinny. She was slim, small-boned, slight. The ridge of her spine stretched delicately between her shoulder blades, and the high cut of the swimsuit legs revealed not a hint of flab on her hips. Her calves and upper arms were pleasantly curved, and her rear end was smooth and economically shaped. Her hair was wet but brushed, and when he leaned toward her he could smell its delicious scent, a blend of chlorine and shampoo.

"Hey, sweetheart," he murmured, patting her shoulder. "Time to wake up."

She lifted her head, then rolled onto her side, groping for the towel that had dropped to the patio next to her lounger. "I wasn't asleep," she said.

Patrick focused for a moment on the soft shifting of her breasts as she leaned over and picked up the towel. Her breasts, like her bottom, were compact, but they had an enticing roundness he wouldn't mind exploring further. Even the hard cynical look she gave him as she sat back up and draped the towel discreetly around her upper body couldn't extinguish the fantasies he was enjoying simply by looking at her.

"I'll get dressed," she said.

"Don't do me any favors," he countered with a roguish grin. "Did I mention how good that bathing suit looks on you? The color's mighty becoming."

"The color," she argued, "is brassy. Mary talked me into buying it. It's really more her style."

"I can't imagine it on her. I think it's your style."

She scrutinized him for a minute. "Why does that drawl of yours come and go, Patrick?"

He hadn't anticipated the question, but he didn't mind it, any more than he'd minded her inquiring about his earring. He appreciated any evidence that she took a personal interest in him.

"That drawl of mine is a result of my childhood in North Carolina. I haven't lived in Dixie since I left for college fifteen years ago, so the accent has gotten pretty diluted. However, it sometimes sneaks up on me—usually when I'm in the presence of a beautiful lady."

She glanced dubiously at him, then lifted her tote bag from the patio and pretended to be engrossed in its contents.

"Don't you like being complimented?" He leaned close enough to get another enticing whiff of her hair.

"I don't mind if I think the person complimenting me is sincere," she mumbled into her bag.

"You don't think I'm sincere?"

"I don't know." She raised her eyes to his, searching his face. If he hadn't already recognized how beautiful she was, the haunting darkness of her eyes would have convinced him. "You're ogling me, Patrick. That's not the sort of behavior I tend to associate with trustworthy men."

"Just normal men," he conceded with a chuckle. "Go ahead and get dressed, if you must. Deprive me of my innocent thrills."

"Innocent? Ha." She picked up her tote and stalked off toward the shower room to change.

Granted, innocent wasn't a term he would apply to himself at the moment. Not when he replayed in his mind the image of her breasts moving beneath the taut, damp surface of her swimsuit, not when he envisioned her long creamy legs and that tantalizingly narrow strip of fabric connecting the front and back of the suit between her thighs. Not when he recalled the dark resonance of her eyes as she courageously met his stare.

The thoughts he was entertaining about Amelia Potts were far from innocent. And he wasn't the least bit ashamed.

Chapter Four

"I really think this is the best way to proceed for now," Mary was saying, her pretty eyes darting around the table. She, Amelia, Patrick and Bartholomew were seated at a sidewalk café, this one just off Main Street in Wisherville. Mary had traded her demure senator's-wife dress for a flamboyant slacks outfit featuring a loosely woven fabric with a loud pattern of magenta and turquoise poppies. The blossom-shaped purple earrings dangling from her earlobes made Patrick's tiny gold post seem downright conservative. "I think that the more mileage we can get out of the case, the better," she said. "Plea bargaining would be easier, but nobody ever said fighting for justice was easy. Look at the American Revolution. Look at Martin Luther King and the civilrights marches of the sixties...."

Amelia nibbled at her pasta salad, swatted the occasional fly who deigned to alight on her shoulder, and focused her attention on Mary. Likening her measly legal plight to the War of Independence or the civilrights movement was laughable, but Amelia preferred to concentrate on her sister rather than on Patrick. He sat across from her, and every time her gaze met his he gave her a disconcertingly seductive smile.

"Now, now," Bartholomew eventually interrupted. His stern gaze seemed to be intended for Mary alone, leaving Amelia with the same impression the clerk had given her in the lobby at Keppler's—that she was invisible. Being overlooked by a flirtatious young woman was one thing; being overlooked by her presumed fiancé was quite another. "You've got to keep things in the proper perspective," he admonished Mary. "I'm willing to admit that magazines like *Playboy* and *Penthouse* have a legitimate right to be published, but I'm not convinced you want to place yourself in their company."

Mary bridled self-righteously. "I want to place myself in the company of every individual voice struggling to be heard in this society of ours."

"The issue isn't your voice," Amelia noted dryly. "It's your sculpture." She was growing impatient with the apparent love-fest blooming among the other three people at the table. Mary had announced over predinner drinks that she had decided to let Patrick continue to press her case against the town, and to allow Bartholomew to serve as her personal adviser. "You had four hours alone with her," she complained to Bartholomew. "I thought you were going to talk some sense into her."

One corner of his mouth quirked upward in a lopsided smile. "Mary can be very headstrong when she wants to be. As far as I'm concerned," he added sanctimoniously, "since I haven't been entirely shut out, I still have a chance to influence the outcome of her situation."

"Was that how she presented it to you? Either do it her way or she'll shut you out entirely?"

"It was . . . a bit more complicated than that," Bartholomew mumbled. He shifted in his chair and dug into his food.

Amelia scowled. It wasn't like Bartholomew to let Mary manipulate him or to evade Amelia's questions. When she turned to her sister for an explanation, Mary smiled sheepishly and took a long drink from her second banana daiquiri. "I know I'm a fruitcake, Melie, but Bartholomew doesn't think there's anything wrong with letting me try it Patrick's way first."

"I'll tell you what's wrong with it," Amelia flared. "What's wrong with it is—" *Patrick*, she nearly said. There was something seriously wrong in allowing that long-haired, earringed man to turn a trivial legal hassle into a major brawl because of some ludicrous dream about storming the Supreme Court and making history.

But she couldn't say that. She especially couldn't say it when Patrick had his enchanting eyes zeroed in on her, glowing with interest and curiosity and a vaguely taunting gleam. "What's wrong with it," she said in as steady a voice as she could muster, "is that it's going to bring a lot of embarrassing publicity down on the family, and on you, Mary. Particularly on you."

"I, who don't know the meaning of embarrassment," Mary countered with a carefree sniff.

Amelia again turned to Bartholomew in search of an ally. To her dismay, he laughed. Disgruntled, she glanced toward Patrick. He was smiling, too, a quiet, self-assured smile.

What on earth was going on? Mary's behavior was totally in character, and so, she assumed, was Patrick's. But Bartholomew was supposed to be on Amelia's side. He was supposed to be reasonable and rational. His purpose in Wisherville was to douse the little brushfire Mary had set, not stoke it into a huge conflagration.

Frowning, Amelia nibbled on a limp green noodle and tried to revive the feeling of contentment she'd experienced that afternoon at Keppler's. She still wasn't sure why she'd felt so serene there, why Rae Keppler, a woman unlike the people with whom she usually associated, had made her feel so much at home. Keppler's was an alien environment, but Amelia had loved the place. Until Patrick had started flirting with her by the pool, she'd been utterly at peace.

Now, on relatively familiar turf, flanked by two people she'd known since birth if not before, she felt out of place. Oddly enough, it wasn't Patrick who provoked that feeling, but rather her sister and Bartholomew. There was something awfully peculiar about the way Mary avoided looking directly at her, and the way Bartholomew wasn't fulfilling his usual role as the voice of reason.

"Tomorrow's Saturday," Patrick remarked, "which is usually a slow news day. If we're lucky, newspapers will be likely to run a human-interest item they've picked up from the wires, like the piece on the press conference. Once we get a handle on how good the coverage was, we'll be able to position ourselves for a counterstrike against Wisherville."

"If you're so concerned about Mary's civil rights," Amelia argued, "what difference does it make how good the coverage is? Fight for her civil rights regardless, if you really believe she's been wronged."

"I intend to do just that," Patrick said patiently. "The amount of coverage we get will help to determine our method of attack. Lots of press coverage will make the town more eager to accommodate Mary."

"Of course. *They've* got the good sense to be embarrassed by publicity."

"Their publicity would be negative publicity," Mary piously pointed out. "Mine is positive publicity."

"Right. You stick a statue of two people fornicating in the window of your store, where children can see it, and you think you're going to get positive publicity?"

Just as Mary was about to respond, a fly dive-bombed her head. Recoiling, she fanned the air with her hands. Bartholomew gallantly leaned across the table and swatted the fly away, knocking over Amelia's water glass in the process. Some of the water spilled onto the tiled patio, but most of it splattered across Amelia's lavender dress. With a small yelp, she shoved back her chair.

"Oh, Amelia, I'm sorry!" Bartholomew leaned over and used his napkin to dab at the damp circle spreading across her lap.

Glowering at him, she shoved his hand away. "Never mind. It's only water."

"But look, you're soaked." Bartholomew redoubled his efforts with the napkin.

"I'm okay," she snapped. Her irritation seemed grossly out of proportion to the minor spill. She knew she was reacting not so much to the mess as to Bartholomew's unnecessary fussing.

Trying to contain her annoyance, Amelia blotted her dress with her own napkin. She wished she could laugh off the entire incident. Although she occasionally envied the attention Mary attracted, she wasn't used to being the center of attention herself. Knowing that her dinner companions were all gawking at her increased her discomfort. "It'll dry," she mumbled, hoping to deflect their concern.

"Don't feel bad about it, Amelia," Patrick drawled, his eyes sparkling with a meaningful glow. "You happen to look terrific when you're wet."

Amelia felt her cheeks grow warm. She knew he was referring to that afternoon when he'd found her lounging by the pool, drying off from her swim. The bathing suit she'd had on at Keppler's hadn't been indecent, but the way Patrick had looked at her *had* been. The way his gaze had followed the curves of her body, focusing on the shadow of her cleavage and the rise of her hips and then skimming down her legs, had made her feel uncomfortably exposed, even though many of the women sunbathing near the pool had been wearing much skimpier swimsuits. During the drive back to Wisherville, neither she nor Patrick had mentioned their exchange by the pool. But even as Patrick had answered her questions about Keppler's and described the condominium developer's preliminary plans, Amelia hadn't been able to shake her memory of him gazing at her and calling her beautiful.

It wasn't as if nobody had ever called her beautiful before. Her parents had, of course, and Bartholomew occasionally told her she looked nice.

But Patrick... Patrick was different.

"Excuse me," she said, standing and peeling the wet dress away from her thighs. "I'm going to the lady's room." Without giving the men a chance to rise to their feet, she hurried among the patio tables to the inside of the café.

Once in the rest room, Amelia let go of her skirt and eyed her reflection in the wide mirror above the row of sinks. Her face was still flushed and her eyes glistened with panic. Maybe Bartholomew and Mary hadn't been acting strangely over dinner, after all. Maybe Patrick had gotten Amelia so keyed up that she was the one acting strange, relating to the world around her from a skewed perspective.

The strangest thing of all, she realized, was that Patrick could key her up so much. Who was he, after all, other than a small-town lawyer with sun-streaked hair and a penchant for delivering extravagant compliments? He had probably chosen Amelia as the target for his sweet talk because she looked like an easy mark. She was merely a visitor in town; he didn't have to worry about the long-term ramifications of his flirting. Since she'd established herself as his opponent when it came to Mary's legal situation, he probably figured he deserved to have a little fun at her expense.

In the mirror she saw the door behind her swing open, admitting Mary. "Are you okay?" she asked, looking genuinely worried.

"Of course I'm okay," Amelia said a bit too brightly, not bothering to add that two rest-room conferences in one day were too many. She tugged a few paper towels from the dispenser on the wall and busied herself with her dress.

Mary watched her for a minute. "You went so pale when Patrick made that remark," she said.

"Well, I'm not pale anymore."

"Right. You look feverish now. Are you sure you're all right?"

Amelia considered the excuse Mary had inadvertently provided for her. "I don't know," she hedged, tossing the soggy paper towels into the garbage pail and straightening up. "It's been a long day, and I'm not feeling my best."

"Maybe I should take you home."

"No, that isn't necessary," Amelia assured her. "Really. You're having such a nice time with Bartholomew—"

Mary looked momentarily abashed, and then let out a weak laugh. "I've been with him all afternoon, Melie. I can take you home."

"No. Please." Once again, Amelia felt awkward about being in the spotlight. She wondered how Mary could stand so much attention, let alone enjoy it, for Amelia found it rather unpleasant. "It's only a few blocks' walk," she noted, longing for the solitude of a quiet stroll to Mary's place. "The fresh air will do me good. And my dress will dry off on the way."

Mary scrutinized her. "Did something weird happen with Patrick this afternoon?"

Amelia almost replied that something weird had happened the moment Patrick had first accosted her with his mesmerizing gaze, and had continued to happen with regularity ever since. All she said, though, was, "Patrick isn't my favorite person, and I'm disappointed by your decision to let him continue to represent you. I'm kind of surprised that Bartholomew consented to that, too."

She expected to hear Mary retort that Bartholomew didn't have the right to consent or not consent to anything—and she'd be correct if she said so. But

Mary only gave Amelia a nervous smile and shrugged. "I guess Bartholomew has faith in me," she said. "He knows I know what's best for myself. It doesn't bother you, does it?"

"That he knows you know what's best for yourself? Sure, it bothers me," Amelia shot back, giving a few more swipes to her dress with a fresh paper towel. "It bothers me that you're pursuing this harebrained scheme. I for one *don't* think you know what's best for yourself."

Her words clearly rankled her twin. "Maybe I'm not as much of a flake as everybody thinks I am," Mary asserted. "Maybe I'm willing to take responsibility for my own decisions and suffer the consequences, whatever they may be. If I want to do things my own way, that's my choice. I'm an adult."

"You don't act like one. Skinny-dipping in a public pond—"

"That was last year," Mary quibbled.

"So you're nine months older. You don't seem particularly wiser."

"Give me a break!" Mary railed. "Bartholomew trusts me. Why the hell can't you?"

"Mary—"

"You're always treating me this way," she raged. "Like I was an idiot! Well, I'm not, and the sooner you get off my back—"

"Get off your back? I'm trying to help you, Mary, and if you don't realize that, you *are* an idiot."

"Thanks for the vote of confidence," Mary retorted with a sneer. "I don't want your help. I don't need it. I don't want you managing my life anymore, Amelia. Go be a good girl for Mom and Dad, and leave me alone!"

Amelia sank against the counter and let out a slow steadying breath. Mary had never spoken to her so vehemently before, so angrily. She'd always laughed when Amelia came to her rescue in the past, accepting the inevitability of it and apologizing for her silliness. She had never rejected Amelia with such bluntness.

Amelia wanted to reciprocate with a few equally wounding barbs. She wanted to tell Mary that in all honesty she was sick and tired of helping her, that she wanted nothing better than to leave her alone and get off her back and that Mary could make as much of a fool of herself as she damned well pleased. It was Mary's life and Mary's reputation, not her own. The only reason Amelia had felt compelled to intervene was that that was what she always did.

Somehow, it didn't seem like a good enough reason anymore.

"All right," she said, simmering. "Do what you want."

"Do you trust me?" Mary pressed her.

"Of course not," Amelia shot back impatiently. "But you don't care, so what does it matter? You've got your two devoted lawyers to advise you, Mary. You don't need advice from me, too." She took another deep breath, and when she spoke again her voice was low and weary. "I think it would be better if I skipped the rest of this dinner party. I'm really not feeling like myself tonight." She was suddenly overwhelmed by a desperate urge to get away, to be by herself for a while, so she wouldn't have to see Patrick and Bartholomew tripping over each other to offer their services to Mary. She didn't want her sister to detect her envy. "Would you please make my excuses at the table? I don't feel like going back."

"You can't just sneak off without saying good-bye."

Amelia smiled sourly. Mary could sneak off, but Mary had never given a hoot about the proper courtesies. Amelia, however, didn't have it in her to be rude. Sighing, she tried futilely to fluff out her sodden skirt, then gave up and reached for the doorknob. "Okay. I'll go and say goodbye."

The men both stood as Amelia and Mary neared the table. Amelia couldn't help noticing that Bartholomew had a couple of inches on Patrick, and at least twenty pounds. Bartholomew wasn't fat, but for the first time, she thought he looked, well, a bit heavy. There was just too much of him.

Unfortunately he chose to put his bulk to decisive use. As soon as she announced she was tired and wanted to leave, he grabbed her arm and said, "I'll drive you back to Mary's."

"I'd rather walk."

"I'll drive you back," he repeated, as if she hadn't spoken.

She didn't have the strength to argue. Glancing at Patrick, she noticed his gaze shuttling between her and Bartholomew. "I'll see you later, Amelia," he murmured, his lips hinting at a smile.

Bartholomew led her to his car, a silver Porsche of which he was colossally proud. He had spent a fortune buying it, and he spent an additional fortune garaging it in Manhattan. It was an ostentatious car, Amelia thought—high-powered, but not as much fun to ride in as a Jeep. Air-conditioning couldn't compare to fresh breezes on a scenic mountain road.

"Is it something I did?" Bartholomew asked once he'd pulled away from the curb.

Amelia gave him an amused look. "Sure, it's something you did," she mumbled, even though that wasn't true. Her malaise was probably more Patrick's fault than Bartholomew's, but if he wanted to take the credit, she would let him. "You were supposed to convince Mary not to turn this situation into a federal case."

"I tried," he insisted, then became very absorbed in the flow of traffic on Main Street.

"Not hard enough, it would seem," Amelia commented. "Her personal advisor, Bartholomew—what kind of nonsense is that? You're letting Patrick Levine run the show."

"I'm giving him enough rope to hang himself."

"And what if he hangs Mary in the process? She's my sister."

"I know exactly who Mary is," Bartholomew said curtly. He downshifted and turned the corner. "Trust me, Amelia. She'll come around in time."

They had reached Mary's bungalow, and Bartholomew braked to a stop. Amelia unclipped her seat belt and eyed him dubiously. It made a certain sense not to trust Mary in circumstances like this. But Amelia had always trusted Bartholomew in the past. For some reason, she wasn't sure she trusted him this time. Not that he didn't know what he was doing, not that he didn't have a firm grasp on his professional obligations, not that he didn't have a healthy respect for the Potts family, but . . . she just didn't trust him.

"Thanks for the lift, Bartholomew," she said, blocking his hand before he unfastened his own seat belt. "Please go back to the restaurant and finish your dinner."

"Will you be all right? You really look rather piqued, Amelia."

"That's all it is," she reassured him. "I've had a long day and I'm worn out."

"Let me walk you to the door and see you safely inside—"

Amelia cut him off. "Mary gave me her spare key. I'll be fine." At his hesitation, she added, "I'm not sure it's such a good idea to leave Mary alone with Patrick."

"You've got a point." Bartholomew leaned across the gear stick and gave Amelia a perfunctory peck on the cheek. "We'll come back here straight after dinner," he promised, reaching across Amelia's lap to open her door. "I'm really sorry about your dress, Amelia."

"Forget it. I'll see you later." She climbed out, shut the door and waved him off. When he drove around the corner and out of sight, she let out a sigh of relief.

She shouldn't have experienced relief at the disappearance of the man purported to be her future husband. But she really did want to be alone, and she couldn't dismiss the suspicion that Bartholomew hadn't wanted to spend any more time than necessary with her. He'd seemed to be in a big hurry to get back to Mary. But then, Amelia was behaving too wretchedly for anyone to want to remain in her company for long.

With another sigh, she trudged up the front walk and let herself into the house. In the guest room, she removed her dress and hung it from the curtain rod in front of the open window to air out. Then she donned a pair of shorts and a shirt and wandered into Mary's kitchen, thinking that a glass of wine might relax her. Mary's liquor cabinet contained only esoteric beverages: Cointreau, Midori, an unopened bottle of sake, a nearly empty bottle of ouzo. Wrinkling her nose at the selection, Amelia returned to the front porch empty-handed.

The sky was rapidly fading to a deep blue, and the mild evening air vibrated with the song of crickets. Sitting on the porch step and resting her back against a support pillar, Amelia gazed up at the first faint stars to pierce the night. She inhaled deeply, holding the crisp, menthol mountain air inside her lungs for almost a full minute. Exhaling, she forced herself to empty her head of all thoughts about Patrick and his come-hither eyes, Bartholomew and his uncharacteristic clumsiness, and Mary and her meshuga art.

She hadn't expected the Yiddish word to spring into her mind, but as soon as it did she felt a sense of well-being descend over her. She wished she could be at Keppler's right now, instead of here in the midst of Mary's latest debacle. She wished she could simply turn her back on everything and return to the beautiful hotel nestled cozily into the forested hills, with its grand old buildings and verdant lawns and crystalline lake. She felt that she could fit in there very easily, that she could become a part of Keppler's and even contribute to it in a way she couldn't contribute to solving Mary's mess in Wisherville. She didn't belong here, and while she could think of no rational explanation for it, she felt as if she did belong at Keppler's.

The purr of a sports car approaching the house jolted her from her ruminations. She gazed toward the street to see Bartholomew's Porsche edging to the curb and stopping. He and Mary climbed out.

"How are you?" Mary asked, hurrying up the front walk. The gaudy flowers printed across her top and trousers seemed to glow in the waning evening light.

Managing a smile, Amelia answered, "Drier, thank you."

Bartholomew joined the sisters on the porch, although he remained standing while Mary squatted beside Amelia. "Your color's better. You were looking pretty ghastly earlier, all waxy and grayish—except when you were blushing."

"I'm okay. Really."

Mary studied her for a minute longer, then looked away bashfully. "Melie, listen, I'm sorry if I lost my temper a little bit," she said under her breath.

Amelia snorted. "A little bit?"

"Well, you lost your temper, too, Melie."

"Not as much as you." Arguing over who had lost her temper more was ridiculous, especially since it was totally in character for Mary to rant and rave in anger, and Amelia to withdraw. "If you really want me to get off your back, Mary, I'll be happy to."

"No, I don't want that at all. I don't know what got into me in the bathroom, but—"

"But maybe you spoke the truth?" Amelia concluded, her voice rising in a question.

Mary considered. "The truth is—" She smiled hopefully "—I'm afraid to think of what I might do if I didn't have you on my back."

"So am I."

"I just..." Mary considered her words. "I just wish you'd take me seriously sometimes, Melie."

"I do take you seriously. If I didn't, do you think I'd have taken a day off from work during the hectic final weeks of school and come to Wisherville?"

"You came because Mom asked you to," said Mary. There was nothing accusatory in her tone, yet Amelia couldn't deny that her words held more than a grain of truth.

She gave a small wistful nod. "One of these days, Mary, let's take Mom and Dad by surprise. Let's do something totally unexpected."

Mary mirrored Amelia's modest grin, the delicate curve so similar to Amelia's that an onlooker might actually take them for the twins they were. "I keep trying to surprise them by doing totally unexpected things," she said. "The trouble is, that's exactly what they expect."

"One of these days," Amelia swore, "We'll get the better of them."

"Count me in." Her smile brightening, Mary squeezed Amelia's hand. "Friends?"

"Friends."

Satisfied, Mary straightened up. "It's getting late, Melie. I'm about ready to hit the hay."

"I'll be in in a while," Amelia promised.

"Bartholomew's going to be on the living-room couch."

Amelia glanced curiously at her sister, wondering why she'd felt the need to mention the sleeping arrangements. She certainly had no intention of sharing the guest room with Bartholomew—and she doubted he had any designs in that direction, either.

Then she realized that Mary's remark could have been an innocent reminder that the living-room couch wasn't far from the front door. "I'll be quiet when I come in," she promised, nodding at Bartholomew. "I won't wake you up."

He returned her nod, wished her a good night, and escorted Mary into the house.

Amelia settled back against the pillar, not minding its rigid surface along her spine. She was glad to be alone again, glad to know that she wouldn't have to deal with her sister and Bartholomew for the rest of the night. Closing her eyes, she let the chorus of crickets serenade her and imagined what her life would be like if she could swim laps in a pool every day and then stretch out to rest on a comfortable lounger beneath a protective umbrella. She tried to imagine what her life would be like if she could cast aside her responsibilities, even if only for a few days.

She tried to imagine what her life would be like with someone like Patrick in it, telling her that she happened to look terrific when she was wet. She didn't have to imagine that, though. Patrick was already in her life, telling her.

To her amazement, the notion didn't make her go pale, and it didn't make her blush. It made her smile.

THE HOUSE WAS DARK, but in the hazy glow of the half-moon overhead, Amelia was visible on the front porch. She sat motionless, her posture-perfect back propped against one of the support beams that flanked the porch steps. Her hair fell sleekly behind her shoulders, and her face shimmered like alabaster in the silver light.

He almost kept driving, continuing past the house and heading for home. It would be a sin to disturb her when she looked so tranquil. But he couldn't just drive by. He had to talk to her.

Her abrupt departure from the restaurant a couple of hours ago had disturbed him. He hadn't been ready to say goodbye to her yet. Perhaps she'd been ready to say goodbye to him, but Patrick wasn't easily defeated by an unspoken rejection. Or even a spoken one.

Evidently she heard the Jeep coasting toward her. Her eyes came into sharp focus on Patrick, and she stiffened. The corners of her lips turned down. Cripes. He hadn't even gotten out of the car, and he was already making her uncomfortable.

He might enjoy a good challenge, but Amelia had already come to mean more than merely a challenge to him. He wanted her friendship, her respect, her company, and—no point in denying it—he wanted those long, graceful legs of hers wrapped around him in passionate abandon. Even now, in a nondescript pair of cotton shorts and a short-sleeved white blouse with an open collar, her mouth pressed into a grim scowl and her gaze cold enough to cause frostbite, he found her sexy.

Praying for luck, he yanked on the parking brake and got out of the Jeep, leaving his jacket and tie on the passenger seat. He'd removed them shortly after dinner, and he'd rolled up his shirtsleeves during a long aimless walk through the park by the town hall, during which he'd tried without much success to figure out how to break down Amelia's resistance. Why was it so simple to come up with a strategy for Mary's defense, and so difficult to come up with a strategy for dealing with Mary's sister?

"Hi," he said, ambling slowly up the front walk.

Amelia eyed him with foreboding, but she didn't order him to leave. She didn't say anything at all. Her eyes remained on him, vivid and dark, as he covered the length of the walk to the steps and lowered himself beside her. He was careful to leave plenty of room between them, but she seemed to shrink from him.

"I'm glad you haven't already retired for the night," he said in what he hoped was a casual tone of voice.

She wrapped her arms protectively around her raised knees, each hand gripping the opposite elbow. "It's awfully late," she said. "As a matter of fact, I was just getting ready to go inside."

He didn't believe her, but he wasn't going to make her more defensive by calling her a liar. "Then I reckon I got here in the nick of time."

"Patrick—"

"Look, Amelia, let's get a few things straight between us," he plunged in, refusing her the opportunity to stop him. "When I compliment you, I mean it. When I tell you you look terrific, it's because you do look terrific—and if you don't understand that, then somebody's done a nasty job on your self-esteem. You're a very attractive woman, Amelia. So stop acting like a virginal twit every time I say something nice about you."

She gaped at him. He himself was startled by what he'd said. He attempted to soften his words with an ameliorating smile.

To his surprise, Amelia responded with a smile of her own. "A virginal twit?"

"That's a figure of speech."

"I know what it is."

"I didn't say that you were one," he hastened to clarify. "I said you were acting like one."

"Oh. Thanks. I feel so much better now."

He took heart in her lingering smile. Her lips looked soft, her teeth small and white. "I admit I've been coming on to you," he said, "but I'm not going to apologize for it."

"Fine. Don't apologize."

This wasn't going as he'd expected, or as he'd hoped. He had hoped that she would fling herself at him and moan, "Take me, I'm yours," or something to that effect. He had expected that she would tell him to get lost. But he wasn't prepared for her to treat him with such detached poise.

"I think we could be good together," he plowed ahead. "Call me a cockeyed optimist, but—"

"I'll call you cockeyed."

He laughed in spite of himself. If she ever guessed how much her fighting spirit turned him on, she might stop fighting.

Deciding to try a different tack, he asked, "What were you thinking about when I drove up? You had such a dreamy look on your face."

She appraised him thoughtfully. "Do you really want to know?" she asked, sounding dubious.

"I really do," he said earnestly. Coming on to her was fun, but getting to know her—taking a peek at her most private thoughts—would be infinitely more rewarding.

"I was thinking about Keppler's."

He took a moment to absorb this revelation. While he'd been strolling through the park, sidestepping the ducks and plotting his game plan for winning Amelia's affection, he'd figured that if she didn't outright tell him to drop dead, they'd probably wind up talking about Mary's legal plight or possibly Bartholomew's matrimonial intentions. Never had Patrick predicted that Amelia would mention Keppler's.

Maybe the past afternoon hadn't been an unmitigated horror for her. Maybe she had enjoyed herself. Maybe she'd even enjoyed being complimented by him at the pool. "What about Keppler's?" he asked.

"It would be a shame if Rae sold the place to condo developers."

"I'm going to do everything in my power to make sure that doesn't happen," Patrick said, adding silently, *See? I'm really a good guy.*

"I like Rae. She's so warm, even if she is kind of overwhelming."

"She's a great lady."

"I don't know why I keep thinking about the place, Patrick, but I just..." Amelia got that hazy faraway look in her eyes again. Her clear pale skin shimmered in the moonlight. "It's so unlike any resort I've ever been to."

"What resorts do you usually go to?"

She directed her gaze to him again. He was thrilled to see that her expression was devoid of hostility. "There's a yacht club in the Hamptons," she told him. "My parents are members, and so are the Driscolls— Bartholomew's family. My father and Edgar Driscoll own identical sailboats. They like to race each other."

"How upper crust," Patrick muttered.

"I know," Amelia let slip, her tone mimicking Patrick's. "When they aren't sailing, they play golf."

"Where do you take your vacations?" he asked. "I don't mean your family. I mean you, on your own."

She smiled. "I come here. I visit Mary. At least twice over the winter I'll take a long weekend and we'll go skiing. And in the summer, well, I spend a lot of time here looking after her and getting her out of tight spots. It would be kind of fun to come up here just to relax, instead of having to take care of a catastrophe.''

"Feel free to relax," Patrick suggested. "Bartholomew and I can take care of this catastrophe for you."

Something darkened in her eyes, and she shook her head. "No, Patrick, it's my job."

"Oh? Since when are you a lawyer?"

"Mary doesn't need me to be a lawyer. She's obviously got more than enough of those. She needs me to be..." Amelia drifted off, gazing past Patrick at the moon.

"What does she need you to be?"

"Her sister."

"You're very good at that." He meant it, too. He had a sister, but Terry was seven years his senior, practically a different generation. They'd never been particularly close, and they didn't look after each other, bicker playfully or communicate nonverbally the way Amelia and Mary did.

"Patrick, all this stuff about Mary's civil rights and all..." She faltered, staring at him, completing the question with her eyes.

Unfortunately, he couldn't translate her gaze into words. "What about it?"

"Mary isn't a principle," Amelia said slowly. "She isn't a concept or a law. She's a human being, and as fired up as you've got her..." Amelia gave her head a slight shake. "I don't want you exploiting her just to make a point."

"Mary wouldn't let anybody exploit her," he insisted, moved by Amelia's abundant concern for her sister.

"You're not really in a position to be objective about it," she noted.

"Neither are you. In light of which, I think we ought to let Mary make her own decision."

"Yes, but..." Again her voice faded as she wrestled with her thoughts. "You yourself said that Mary likes to shock people. Well, her sculpture shocked people. She accomplished what she set out to do. Why can't we simply leave it at that?"

"If she asked me to stop representing her, I would. But she wants me to stick with it, so that's what I'm going to do."

"Why did you come here tonight?" Amelia asked abruptly.

She was looking directly at him. The moonlight spilled across the dainty features of her face, emphasizing the edge of her nose, the sharp tilt of her chin, the delicate indentation in her upper lip. "I wish I could say it was to talk about Mary, but it wasn't." He inched closer to her on the step. "I think you know why I came, Amelia."

"If you've got any ideas about making another pass at me, please don't," she implored him, bravely meeting his gaze. "It has nothing to do with my self-esteem or anything like that. I'm flattered, I really am. I admit I'm also surprised."

He stifled the impulse to brush away the gossamer lock of hair that a breeze blew across her cheek. "Why are you surprised?"

"It's obvious, Patrick. You're not my type."

"Is that a fact?" He smiled, undaunted. What was obvious to him was that Amelia was as attracted to him as he was to her. If she wasn't, his presence wouldn't make her so uncomfortable. He wouldn't be able to affect her at all. "What's your type, Amelia? Beefy blond hunks who dress like models for Brooks Brothers and knock glasses of water onto your lap?"

"That was an accident," she said. "Bartholomew isn't usually like that."

"Do you honestly think you can convince me he's your type?"

"I don't know whether or not I can convince you, but he is."

"I bet he'd hate Keppler's. I bet he thinks racing sailboats and playing golf are the ultimate thrills."

"Well..." She kept her gaze locked with his, a show of courage that impressed him. He noticed the light dancing in her eyes as she wrestled with her thoughts. "That's irrelevant," she finally said. "He's a fine upstanding man. I've known him all my life and I know exactly what to expect from him..." She hesitated, then shook her head again, her expression adorably bewildered. "I take that back," she said, half to herself. "I didn't expect him to let you represent Mary."

"So he's decided to try doing the unexpected. Why don't you?"

"By the unexpected, I assume you're referring to yourself?"

"Sure. Try me," he dared her with a grin.

She looked uncertain. Her tongue nervously circled her lips and she leaned back against the pillar, measuring him with her eyes. He noticed the subtle motion of her Adam's apple as she swallowed. She said nothing.

"All right, maybe I'm not your type," he granted, sliding closer to her. His knee brushed hers, but she didn't flinch. "My hair's long and I've got an earring, and I'm not a rich Anglo-Saxon Protestant snob who hangs out at yacht clubs. I'm the son of a couple of labor organizers who've spent most of their professional lives trying to unionize the North Carolina fabric mills and getting chased off the grounds by management thugs. And I grew up to believe in certain things and to act on my beliefs. One thing I believe is that you and I could be good together. I think we could be spectacular.''

"Mary's more your type,'' Amelia argued. There was a strange, almost desperate edge to her voice.

"If Mary were my type, I'd be saying all this to her. I'm not. I'm saying it to you.''

"But I'm—'' she sighed "—too sensible, Patrick. And this doesn't make any sense.''

"It makes perfect sense to me,'' he asserted. "You and I want each other. That's all the sense it has to make.''

"Speak for yourself,'' she mumbled, breaking from his gaze and lowering her eyes to her knees.

He slid his hand under her chin and lifted her face back to his. "One kiss,'' he whispered. "Just give me one little kiss. If you can honestly say I'm not your type after that, I swear I'll leave you alone.''

It was a big risk for both of them. If he had in fact misread her, one kiss could totally destroy his chances with her. If, on the other hand, she was feeling what he was feeling, allowing him to kiss her would rob her of the ability to pretend she didn't care for him.

He was willing to take that risk.

To his great relief so was she. Taking a deep breath, her eyes open and wary, she angled her body slightly toward him. Her lips brushed his, but before the brief contact could register on either of them, she retreated. "There," she said in a shaky voice. "I haven't exactly been swept away."

"You haven't exactly been kissed," he pointed out, sliding even closer to her and moving his hand from the soft underside of her jaw to the nape of her neck, beneath the black fall of her hair. Twining his fingers through the silky locks, he steered her mouth back to his.

"You said only one—"

He smothered her protest with a kiss, a real kiss, one she couldn't escape from so effortlessly. His lips covered hers, coaxed them, nibbled and teased and tasted until her mouth began to move on its own. He saw her eyelids sinking until her long lashes cast shadows on her cheeks, and then she let herself go with a small sigh.

He deepened the kiss. He was acting, as he so often did, on instinct rather than logic, tightening his hand against the curve of her head, cupping his other hand over her cheek, stroking downward with his thumb to tilt her face and ease her lips apart. As soon as they opened to him he stole inside, savoring the moist sweetness of her inner lips and the slick surface of her teeth, then probing deeper, seeking her tongue with his.

Her quiet moan incited him. His tongue surged against hers, and his hand caressed the velvety skin of her cheek. He felt his body tensing, veering out of control, but he didn't care. He wouldn't stop, not when everything about this moment felt so good, so incredibly good.

"I want to touch you," he whispered, forgetting his earlier promise to limit himself to one kiss.

"Patrick..." His name emerged on a ragged breath. Her voice held a distinct warning but he chose to ignore it. He skimmed his hand down the slender column of her throat to her shoulder, then farther, to the curve of her breast. Her nipple was already hard when he molded his palm to the small, womanly mound.

She gasped, then tore her lips from his and rested her head on his shoulder. She seemed to be struggling for air. So, he realized, was he. Every time she drew in another rasping breath her breast pressed deeper into his hand, and his control slipped another notch. As if by reflex, his fingers kneaded the sensitive swell of flesh, provoking another helpless moan from her.

"You said only a kiss," she mumbled, the words emerging brokenly.

"I know." But he couldn't bring himself to let go of her.

She covered his hand with her own, held it there for a fraction of an instant, and then gently pulled his fingers away. Simultaneously he and Amelia straightened and gazed at each other. She looked as stunned as he felt. He really hadn't meant to push beyond a single kiss.

"Let's make love," he said. It seemed like a reasonable suggestion under the circumstances.

"Patrick!" She let out a faint, anxious laugh, then shook her head. "How in the world do you get from 'just one little kiss' to 'let's make love'?"

"It's easy," he answered. "I'll show you."

"No," she said, a steely resolution replacing the humor in her tone. "You won't show me. Good night, Patrick." She rose to her feet.

He stood with her and reached behind her to grab the support beam, temporarily blocking her path to the front door. "At least admit I'm your type." His smile softened the blunt demand.

She ducked under his arm and crossed the porch, making a beeline for the door. "I won't admit to anything," she swore as she yanked it open and hastened inside.

He had made her uncomfortable again—and himself, too, he thought wryly, leaning against the railing until his pulse slowed to normal and his body unwound from its aching state of arousal. He'd made them both damned uncomfortable, but that was all right. As any good lawyer knew, half the battle in winning a case lay in proving to your opponent that the truth was on your side.

He'd proven the truth to Amelia tonight. He may not have won the case yet, but he was well on his way.

Chapter Five

About eight miles out of Wisherville, Amelia pulled to the side of the road and turned off the engine. Through the car's open windows she heard the rustle of leaves caught in a breeze, the creaks of ancient trees swaying deep in the forest surrounding the road, and the buzz of a cicada. The stars seemed uncommonly bright in the midnight sky.

Sneaking away from Wisherville in the dead of night was cowardly. It was also ill-mannered. But Amelia didn't care. Right now her primary goal was to regain her bearings and return to the safe predictable world she was accustomed to.

Patrick had scared her. It was as simple as that. The power of his kiss had shaken her to her soul. Whether or not he was her type didn't matter. The way his mouth had taken hers, the way his hand had moved on her body, magically awakening responses even in places he hadn't touched, the way he'd smelled and felt and tasted had thrown her entire world off its axis. Even if he *was* her type she would have panicked at her overwhelming reaction to him. But with his hair—admittedly beautiful but much too long—and his eyes—also beautiful, but much too perceptive—and his personality—too strong, too forceful, too damned appealing...

He wasn't her type. He wasn't.

Maybe if she said it enough times, she'd start to believe it.

Her heart had continued to race long after she'd shut herself safely inside Mary's house. For a while she'd leaned against the closed door, as if afraid Patrick might try to follow her indoors and continue kissing her. When her body temperature returned to normal, she'd peered out the window and seen that his Jeep was gone. Her pulse had been drumming so loudly in her ears, she hadn't even heard him drive away.

Tiptoeing into the living room, she'd found Bartholomew fast asleep, his knees bent in order to squeeze his tall body onto the couch, the blanket drawn up to his chin. Listening to his muted snoring, Amelia had contemplated him with a heavy heart. Never, in the many years they'd known each other, in the years they'd been viewed as an inevitable twosome, had Bartholomew made her feel anything as shattering as the sensations Patrick had awakened within her. She loved Bartholomew—as a friend, a companion, practically a brother. But his kisses had never burned through her, never made her feel so vulnerable, never aroused such an inconsolable desire in her.

She'd realized then that, no matter what else happened, she couldn't marry Bartholomew. She would have to explain this to him. It was only fair.

But not now.

She'd crept down the hall, thinking at first that she would simply crawl into bed and go to sleep. By the time she'd reached the guest room, however, she knew she would never be able to rest, not while she could still feel Patrick's tongue mating with hers, not while her breast still throbbed with the heated imprint of his hand.

If she spent the night in Wisherville, she would have to see him in the morning. She would see him, and he'd look at her and know he'd gotten to her, and she would be mortified.

So she'd packed her things, left Mary a note explaining that she was sorry to have to leave, but that she had no doubt Mary's legal problem was being adequately attended to, and she'd taken off.

The road was empty. A few minutes ago a car had traveled past her in the opposite direction, but other than that she was alone. Propping her arms on the steering wheel and resting her head on her arms, she remained parked on the shoulder, wondering why even with eight miles between her and Patrick Levine she was still suffering the aftershocks of his kiss.

Somewhere not far away an owl hooted. She tilted her head so she could see out the windshield. The forest's shadows seemed alive, eerie and mystifying, and the air was redolent with the clean fragrance of pine. She wondered what it would be like to camp out in the woods—the Catskills was a popular region with backpackers and outdoor types.

Amelia herself had never camped out before; it had always seemed like a dirty, vaguely uncivilized enterprise. She wouldn't be surprised if Patrick camped out. He seemed the sort. She could imagine him stretched out inside a sleeping bag beneath the stars, relaxed and smiling and bare-chested....

These were obviously the thoughts of a cloudy mind at a late hour. With a sigh, she straightened up and started the engine. As soon as she got back to New Milford and her familiar routines, she'd feel like herself again.

Resolved, she pulled back onto the winding road, heading for the highway.

"MELIE, ARE YOU all right?" Mary's voice blared through the telephone receiver.

Amelia had known the caller would be Mary before she even lifted the receiver from the wall phone. Nobody else would dare to call her at seven o'clock on a Saturday morning, even under normal circumstances. The circumstances today were far from normal.

Despite her exhausting moonlit drive the previous night, Amelia had had difficulty falling asleep once she'd arrived back at her apartment. She had unpacked her bag, washed, collapsed into bed and stared at the ceiling, wondering how it was possible for a kiss and a caress to have such an enduring effect on her.

By the time Mary called, she'd given up on the possibility of getting any sleep and was in her kitchen, preparing a pot of coffee. "Hi," she said into the telephone, then yawned and pulled a mug from one of the cabinets. She filled it with coffee and took a greedy gulp.

"I knew it. I knew you looked under the weather yesterday," Mary babbled. "You must have been delirious, running off in the middle of the night like that. You should have said something, Melie. You should have awakened me. I would have taken care of you."

"That'll be the day," Amelia muttered under her breath.

"I mean it. Driving all that distance when you're not feeling well, Amelia, that was really stupid. You're usually so sensible."

Amelia sank against the counter, the telephone wedged between her ear and her shoulder and her hands cradling the steaming mug of coffee. She had thought that leaving Wisherville was the most sensible thing to do. Maybe she'd thought wrong.

"All right, so it was stupid," she granted, less than thrilled by the possibility she could be mutating into a fruitcake like her sister. "Deprived of a reliable source of real coffee, I became demented." She sipped from her mug and smiled at the rich fresh-brewed flavor.

"Amelia, this isn't a joke." Mary sounded stern. In fact, she sounded a lot like Amelia. "You've left me here with Bartholomew," she continued when Amelia remained silent. "What am I supposed to take that to mean?"

"You're supposed to take it to mean that I know you're in good hands."

"But . . . but he's your . . . well, you know."

Amelia wasn't ready to discuss the decision she'd reached last night concerning her relationship with Bartholomew. "You're the one in trouble, Mary, not me," she commented, sidestepping the issue altogether. "Bartholomew will get you out of it. He'll make sure Patrick doesn't lead you on a wild-goose chase."

"Patrick wouldn't do that," Mary argued.

Amelia gritted her teeth. She didn't want anyone defending Patrick to her. "Bartholomew could settle your case and be back at his desk in midtown Manhattan by nine o'clock Monday morning,'' she said. ''Why don't you let him take care of everything?''

''I called you to talk about you, not me,'' Mary chided. ''Anyway, you've got a hell of a nerve giving me advice when you've been acting so weird.''

''Me? Acting weird? Just because I left Wisherville a little earlier than planned?''

''Earlier than planned? You snuck out of here like a cat burglar, for crying out loud! What time did you take off? The stroke of midnight?''

''I don't remember exactly.''

''Why did you leave like that?'' Mary's tone grew plaintive. ''It wasn't anything I did, was it? Melie, I apologized—''

''No, of course not.''

''Was it Bartholomew? Are you angry with him? He really didn't mean to spill water all over your dress.''

''I'm not angry with him.''

''Then...I know it's asking a lot, Melie, but would you come back? I don't like your being home all alone when you're not feeling well, and I can't come to New Milford when there's so much going on here.''

''I'm feeling fine, Mary. Honestly.''

''Would you like me to send Bartholomew?''

''No. Really. You need him more than I do.''

Mary didn't say anything for a minute. Then, ''I guess I'll check in with you later, Amelia. There doesn't seem to be much else I can do.''

''There's nothing you need to do.''

''Okay. I'll be in touch.''

Amelia hung up the phone and finished the coffee in her mug. After rinsing it, she trudged to the bathroom for a shower. She moved slowly; the previous night's insomnia had rendered her utterly exhausted.

Still, she couldn't spend the day shut up inside her apartment. There was too little to do there, and too much to think about. As soon as she was dressed, she left for the Hibbing campus to finish up the paperwork she'd left undone when she'd hurried off to Wisherville Thursday night.

Her apartment was located on the second floor of a quaint Victorian house a few blocks from the campus, and Amelia decided to walk. It was a warm day; the intermittent clouds didn't look particularly menacing. Amelia liked them for the simple reason that they blocked her view of the sky's blue color—a color too reminiscent of Patrick's eyes.

If one didn't know better, one would never guess that final exams at the Hibbing School were only a week and a half away. The stately brick dormitories ringing the campus lacked air-conditioning, and through the open windows poured a cacophony of rock music, jangling telephones and screeching female voices. The grass quadrangle at the center of the campus was strewn with students sprawled on blankets, their skin shiny with baby oil as they labored to acquire preseason suntans. A few of the girls were studying while they basked in the sunlight that battled through the clouds, but most were either dozing, gossiping, or listening to portable boom boxes, which blasted more rock music into the air.

Amelia surveyed the scene with mixed emotions. Eleven years ago, she and Mary had been seniors at the school, and they'd occasionally indulged in similarly vacuous behavior—although Amelia had steadfastly chosen classical music over rock and roll. She knew the blasé poses of the students masked their inner turmoil. With finals coming up, they were under enor-

mous pressure. Some of them would be going home to
spend the summer with parents they rarely saw and
scarcely knew. For a few of the special scholarship
students, summer break would mean returning to their
inner-city homes and undergoing severe culture shock.
Despite the students' apparent lethargy, Amelia sensed
an undercurrent of tension.

Strolling along one of the paved paths that criss-
crossed the quadrangle, she found herself remembering the lawn behind the main building at Keppler's. It,
too, had been flocked with people reading and enjoying the summery weather, but there hadn't been any
anxiety there. The atmosphere had been utterly tranquil.

Amelia suffered a sudden wistful pang of nostal-
gia. How much nicer it would be to cater to happy va-
cationers than to high-strung adolescents who believed
that a date to the mixer at Greenfield Academy was a
life-and-death issue. How much nicer to put one's efforts into maintaining a resort than into pulling strings
so a mediocre but filthy-rich debutante could get into
Mount Holyoke.

"Apples and oranges," she reproached herself under her breath. Why was she even comparing a prep
school to a resort? Why was she pining for a hotel in
the mountains when she had a rewarding job here?

It wasn't Keppler's she was pining for, she admitted sullenly. Keppler's wasn't any more her type than
Patrick was. She knew what she was pining for, and as
soon as she came to her senses, Hibbing would probably look a whole lot better than Keppler's, too.

With a melancholy sigh, she opened the door to the
administration building and entered.

"HELLO, AMELIA."

Amelia hadn't spoken to her parents since her precipitous departure from Wisherville five days ago, and as soon as she heard her mother's voice on the telephone, she realized she should have contacted them. They must have expected her to call with a full report on Mary's latest caper, but Amelia didn't have much of a report to give them. The two times she'd spoken to Mary since she'd gotten back to Connecticut, Mary had been decidedly cryptic about her legal status.

Dropping onto a chair in the small dining nook by the open kitchen window, Amelia filled her lungs with the hot sticky evening air. Although it was only the second week in June, a humid heat wave had descended heavily on the region. It was an apt reflection of her mood—out of sorts, out of season, weighted down by unseen masses of air, by invisible discontents. It was as if the universe had chosen to become as unsettled as she was—and with as little justification.

"Hello, Mom," she said, cradling the telephone to her ear.

"How's work?"

Amelia knew her mother hadn't called to talk about her job, but she played along. "More hectic than usual. You know how it gets before exam time." She didn't bother to mention the previous day's incident, when two sophomores had arrived for their French class stinking drunk, or the tedious lunch she'd endured with Dean Blanchard today, during which the dean had expounded at length upon her decision to reread the complete works of Charles Dickens over the summer, or the chaos her office was in as they scrambled to update the computer files of all graduating

seniors so that as soon as their final grades were entered their transcripts could be sent to the colleges
they'd be attending in the fall.

"Your father met Bartholomew for a drink at the
club today," her mother remarked in a deceptively
casual voice.

Amelia perked up. "Oh?"

"Bartholomew said that everything was once again
copacetic in Wisherville," her mother informed her.
"It's such a comfort having him to take care of Mary's
silly little imbroglios. He said the town's agreed to
drop all charges against her."

"That's wonderful," Amelia said, hoping she
sounded appropriately enthusiastic.

"Amelia." Her mother's crisp tone alerted Amelia
to the fact that the real purpose of the call was about
to be unveiled. "Bartholomew said something about
how you left Wisherville before Mary's situation was
completely straightened out. Now, I know Bartholomew is a whiz and we can trust him to do what has to
be done, but why did you leave? How could you
abandon Mary in her time of need?"

"Her time of need?" Amelia snorted. "Mary didn't
need me."

"She always needs you when she's on a tear. It's
your job to bring her under control, to keep an eye on
her until everything's back to normal. How could you
forget about your responsibilities and just run away
like that?"

Amelia almost blurted out that, with Bartholomew
and Patrick Levine on the scene, she'd become extra-
neous. She stopped herself, though. For all she knew,
her parents had no idea about Patrick's role as Mary's
attorney. If Bartholomew or Mary had informed

them, her mother would have mentioned it right at the start.

But then, maybe Patrick was no longer handling Mary's case. Amelia hadn't heard from him—not that she'd expected to—and Mary had been vague about what was going on in Wisherville. Amelia hadn't had the nerve to raise the subject of Patrick herself.

Thinking about him now, let alone explaining him to her mother, would be counterproductive. Amelia chose to focus instead on her mother's accusation. "I didn't forget about my responsibilities," she asserted, her voice taut with barely suppressed anger.

"You saw the newspaper articles about Mary, didn't you? It was bad enough having her appear in hand-cuffs on TV, but then those newspaper articles began to come out. You wouldn't believe the coverage the *New York Post* gave it."

"You don't read the *Post*, Mom," Amelia pointed out.

"And this is why. They sensationalize everything. With all this hysteria going on, I fail to see what possessed you to walk out on your sister, to turn your back on her."

"I didn't turn my back on her! Mary asked me to have some faith in her judgment. I felt—"

"Amelia. I love Mary, you know I do, but—have faith in her? She has no judgment whatsoever."

"That's not true," Amelia said, simultaneously defending both her sister and herself. "She does have judgment, and I felt she could handle things—with Bartholomew's help, of course."

"Thank God for Bartholomew," he mother exclaimed dramatically. "I'm beginning to wonder if *you* have any judgment, Amelia."

Once again, Amelia stifled the retort that rose to her lips. Maybe if she had less judgment, her parents wouldn't expect her to be so responsible all the time. Maybe they'd place less trust in her and more in Mary.

That would be fine with Amelia. "As it turns out," she said quietly, "Mary seems to be out of danger. So my judgment or lack of it really doesn't matter."

"There's still the problem of the sculpture," her mother noted ominously.

"Oh?"

"According to Bartholomew, Mary has acquired some sort of agent to sell the piece for her. Bartholomew said the darned thing is still in police custody. I confess, neither your father nor I could make heads or tails out of his explanation. How can an agent sell something that's been impounded by the police?"

"I don't know," Amelia answered, experiencing a creeping sense of uneasiness. She could guess who the "agent" was. "I don't know anything about the fate of the sculpture."

"You'll have to find out for us," her mother requested with an imperiousness that infuriated Amelia. "If it means going back to Wisherville—"

"I can't do that," Amelia cut her off. The last time she'd insisted she couldn't go to Wisherville, she'd wound up knuckling under and obeying her mother. This time she would have enough gumption to stand up for herself.

"Amelia, Mary could be doing something illegal with the statue—the *obscene* statue, may I remind you. She's never sold her work through an agent before. She has a gallery; she *is* an agent. There's something fishy about this arrangement, and I want to know what it is."

"Then *you* go to Wisherville."

"She's your sister."

"She's your daughter."

Her mother fell silent for a moment. "Amelia, I don't know what's gotten into you. It isn't like you to give me a hard time. Now be a good girl and find out what Mary's up to."

"I'll do what I can," Amelia promised, not bothering to add that what she could do didn't happen to include driving to Wisherville.

After saying goodbye to her mother, she spent a couple of minutes cooling off. Her mother's high-handed attitude wasn't unusual, but Amelia's intense resentment of it was. For as long as she could remember, her mother had been making similar demands on her. This time, though, she wouldn't be the "good girl" and do as she was told. She simply wouldn't. It was a matter of principle.

A smile teased her lips. For all Patrick's grandstanding, all his maneuvering and showmanship, she couldn't dismiss the rationale underlying his actions: that certain principles needed to be defended. He was fighting for the constitutionally guaranteed freedom of artists, and Amelia was fighting for freedom, too—her own freedom. It might be a more personal, limited issue, but her convictions were as strong as Patrick's. In refusing to go to Wisherville, Amelia was in her own small way fighting the good fight, too.

Even though she wasn't going to rush to Mary's aid, Amelia figured it wouldn't hurt to try calling her sister, if for no other reason than to make sure Mary wasn't doing anything illegal by trying to sell her sculpture while it was still in police custody. Amelia dialed Mary's home phone number, but nobody answered. Nor did anyone answer the phone at the gallery when Amelia attempted to reach Mary there. She could be anywhere—visiting friends, conferring with Patrick, cloistered inside the shed she'd converted into a ceramics workshop in her backyard, beyond the reach of her telephone. Or she could be in police custody herself. With Mary, anything was possible.

Amelia occupied herself cleaning up the dishes from her dinner, then tried Mary's home telephone number again. No answer. Although it was getting close to seven o'clock, and Mary generally closed the gallery at six, Amelia tried her there. No answer.

She leaned her elbows on the windowsill, cradled her chin in her hands and ruminated. There was another way to find out what was going on in Wisherville. She was loath to contact Patrick, afraid he'd misinterpret her motives if she did. But she owed at least this much to Mary, and to her parents. She was supposed to be the responsible one, after all.

After obtaining Patrick's office and home telephone numbers from directory assistance, she dialed the office number, assuming that no one would answer at this late hour. Her assumption bore out, giving her an extra few minutes to reconsider before she tried him at home.

I'll do what I can, she had promised her mother. Surely one thing she could do was have a civil conversation with the man over the phone. Squaring her shoulders, she dialed his home number.

"Hello."

The sound of his voice awakened a series of unwelcome emotions within her—a memory of how alive she'd felt when he had kissed her, how much she'd longed for him during those few crazed moments on her sister's front porch, and how many times she'd felt that same restless longing since her departure from Wisherville. She gave herself an instant to contemplate hanging up without speaking, then decided that would be discourteous and said, "Hello, Patrick. This is Amelia Potts."

"Amelia!" He was obviously delighted to hear from her. "Hello! I've been expecting your call."

"You have?" She felt a twinge of indignation at his presumptuousness—and a twinge of bewilderment. "Why?" she asked.

A low husky chuckle rumbled along the wire and into her ear. "Because you're a smart lady, and I knew that if you thought long enough about what happened the last time we were together, you'd see the light."

"That's not why I'm calling," Amelia said quickly, eager to concentrate solely on the business at hand. "I'm calling to discuss Mary's case."

He paused for a moment. "Haven't you spoken with her?"

"Not in great detail. I—I understand the charges against her have been dropped."

"Almost," he confirmed. "It's just a matter of dotting the i's and crossing the t's. I reckon I'll have her name cleared from the books by the end of the week."

His statement implied that he, and not Bartholomew, had achieved that goal. "You're still representing her?" Amelia asked.

"Of course I am. Did she say I wasn't?"

"No. I just... As I said, she hasn't gone into detail. I assume this means you're not going to press charges against the town of Wisherville?"

"You assume wrong," Patrick drawled, a touch of cocky self-assurance tingeing his voice. "I didn't cut any deals with the town to get her off. I never cut deals when civil liberties are at stake."

"Spare me." Amelia didn't want to be subjected to any patriotic lectures, although she couldn't ignore the sudden boost her spirits experienced at the news that Patrick hadn't turned his back on his principles. She ought to be concerned that he was still exploiting her sister, but instead she found herself admiring his devotion to his ideals. "What's going on with the statue itself?" she asked.

"Well, we've just begun collecting bids—"

"Bids?"

"With the publicity Mary's received, interest in the sculpture has skyrocketed. Rather than act in haste, I've convinced Mary to let me run an advertisement announcing that the piece is up for auction. The ad should be appearing this weekend in a number of publications. I think we'll get a good response."

"But Patrick, who's going to bid on a sculpture they haven't even seen?"

He laughed. "Three people have so far. The piece is still in police custody. Given its inflated value, I'm just as glad it's there. Nobody's going to try to steal it from the police."

"Its inflated value," Amelia echoed beneath her breath. "Patrick, that's ridiculous."

"Ridiculous or not, it's going to earn your sister a tidy profit, so stop being so negative."

"I'm not being negative," Amelia said testily. "Just because I find it hard to imagine why anyone would want an X-rated statue standing on a coffee table in the living room—"

"Not only are you being negative," Patrick chided her, his tone becoming gentle, "but you sound like you're in a funk. What's wrong, Amelia?"

"I'm not the least bit in a funk," she said gruffly.

"Mary's worried about you," he went on. "She said it was very unlike you to disappear in the dead of the night."

"You—you didn't tell her why I left, did you?" If Mary knew how unglued Amelia had become over Patrick's kiss, she would die of embarrassment.

"Me? What could I tell her?" he asked with phony naïveté. "I don't even know why you left, do I?" She could hear the laughter in his voice.

"No," she said coolly. "I don't suppose you do."

"So, when are you planning to come back to Wisherville?"

"Not in the foreseeable future."

"That's too bad."

"I've got a ton of work to do here at Hibbing, and Mary is apparently in the clear, thanks to you. There's no reason for me to come back. I'm sorry to have bothered you at home, Patrick. I just wanted to make sure everything was all right with Mary."

"Everything is just swell," he assured her.

"Thanks. Well . . . goodbye, Patrick."

She hung up the phone and returned to the open window. The sky had grown darker, but the air was still stagnant and muggy. The robins roosting in the branches of the maple tree that stood between her building and the one next door seemed jittery, fluttering their wings and fidgeting as they tried to get comfortable. They didn't chirp.

They probably wished they were in the cool, shadowy forests of the Catskills, Amelia thought disconsolately, wiping a few beads of sweat from her brow.

HIS FIRST THOUGHT, as he steered the Jeep along the narrow road open to motor vehicles on the campus of the Hibbing School, was that the place was unreal, with its quaint courtyards and its Gothic buildings overgrown with ivy. His experience with prep schools was limited to having read *Catcher in the Rye* and *A Separate Peace* as a youngster, and having endured countless late-night arguments with a jerk named Chauncey Phillips or Phillip Chauncey—Patrick could no longer remember—who had lived down the hall from him in college and maintained that the most valuable lesson he'd learned at Exeter was that people who were poor invariably deserved their fate. Perhaps the Hibbing School provided its students with a more enlightened view of the world, but judging by its appearance, Patrick wouldn't count on it.

He found the visitors' parking lot without too much difficulty. Climbing out of the Jeep, he fingered the loose knot of his necktie and considered whether he ought to neaten his appearance before he located Amelia. It was awfully muggy out, too hot for his jacket, which he had removed somewhere around the state line. During the course of his drive, he'd also unfastened his collar, loosened the tie, and rolled his shirtsleeves up to his elbows. He probably should have changed his clothes before leaving Wisherville, but he'd wanted to hit the road as soon as possible after completing his work at the office, so he'd kept on his business suit. Now that he was in New Milford, he wondered whether he should go the whole route and impress Amelia with his sartorial splendor.

The hell with that. He hadn't come all this distance to prove to her that he was reputable. He'd come to prove to her that, deep in her heart, she didn't give a damn about reputability.

The truth was, he'd come because she had called him. She'd had the guts to call, but not the guts to tell him the real reason she'd called: to hear his voice, to connect with him, to let him know he was still very much alive in her thoughts. He'd come to get her to admit the truth.

It had been a hectic week, what with a few intense meetings with the condominium developer who wanted to buy land from Rae Keppler, a preposterous negligence suit filed against a summer camp where an allergic camper had contracted a severe case of poison ivy, and a careful orchestration of Mary's legal situation. Even before his announcement appeared in the area newspapers inviting bids on *Liberty*, Mary's gallery was doing a lively business. So was the police station's property room, where *Liberty* was still being held.

The main door of the Hibbing School's administration building was unlocked. Entering, Patrick waited to be assaulted by a blast of air-conditioning. None came, and he realized that the building was too old to have an efficient ventilation system. Raking his floppy hair back from his face and pondering the practicality of a crew cut in hot weather, he stared down the long high-ceilinged corridor, smiling to himself at the looks of undisguised curiosity he received from the young ladies roaming the hall.

He reached a stairway at the end of the hall without having spotted the Dean of Students' office. Retracing his steps, he stopped a couple of girls with punkish hairdos. "Excuse me, can you tell me where I might find Amelia Potts?" he asked.

The two girls eyed each other and giggled. "Amelia Potts?" one repeated. "Isn't she that stuck-up freshman who lives in Morris House?"

"*Rilly*, Ashley—that's Emily Peters."

"Peters, Potts . . . like, what's the difference?"

Patrick intervened. "Amelia Potts works for the Dean of Students."

"Oh, no!" The two girls squealed and twitched their noses in distaste. "Blanchard! Yuck! That's, like, yuck!"

Impatience mingled with amusement as Patrick tried again to wrest a coherent response from the two girls. "Can you tell me where the dean's office is?"

"Down at the other end of the hall," one of the girls said, pointing a silver-painted fingernail toward the opposite end of the building. "But, like, stay away from Blanchard. She's, like, give me a vaccine, you know?"

He didn't know, but he smiled just the same. "Thanks," he said, starting down the hall. Behind him, he heard one of the girls assess him as "one foxy dude," and then they both giggled.

At the end of the hallway he discovered a heavy oak door with a frosted glass window consuming the upper half, and a sign reading Dean of Students fastened to the pale yellow wall beside it. He twisted the knob and shoved open the door.

The room he entered was fairly large and well lit with fluorescent overhead lights. Tall windows lined the far wall; an electric fan stood on one of the sills, valiantly churning the steamy air. A scarred wooden counter extended nearly the entire length of the room; on his side of the counter stood a gaggle of students jabbering at a harried-looking secretary. When the secretary spotted Patrick, the students turned and fell silent. Then one blurted out, "Who are you?"

He looked past the girls to the secretary. "I'm looking for Amelia Potts," he said.

The girls buzzed among themselves: "Who's Amelia Potts? Is he her boyfriend? Check him out!"

"Girls! Girls!" The secretary silenced their frenzied whispering. Then she eyed Patrick dubiously. "She's in the back," she said, angling her head toward an open door behind her. "You may as well go on in. I'm up to my ears out here."

Patrick grinned, pleased that the secretary wasn't going to announce his arrival and give Amelia an opportunity to refuse to see him. With a nod at the apparently awestruck students, he sauntered around the counter to the open door, slowing as he neared it.

It led to a stuffy, windowless conference room, most of which was taken up by a long table. Amelia moved methodically along the table, collating an assortment of papers and brochures and stuffing them into oversize envelopes. She had on a white camisole blouse and a flowered skirt; she'd wisely worn her long black hair off her neck in a ponytail. A few loose tendrils curled at the nape of her neck.

He was struck, for not the first time, by the graceful way she moved and by her proud posture. Even when she bent over the table she had a certain regal bearing about her, something that spoke of an inner confidence that wasn't always evident on the surface.

She was reserved—and that was part of her appeal, as far as Patrick was concerned. She wasn't the sort of woman who bared her soul and enumerated the petty tragedies of her life the first time you met her. She wasn't emotionally sloppy.

The sound of his footsteps as he approached the door alerted her, and she looked up from her work. Seeing him, she gasped in shock and leapt back, flinging the brochures she'd been holding into the air.

Patrick smiled and leaned casually against the doorjamb. "Do I look strange to you? Or is it that the young inmates of the Hibbing School never see men?"

She stared blankly at him, then pursed her lips and bent over to gather up the brochures she'd dropped. "You look strange," she said.

"A couple of girls I met in the hall thought I looked foxy."

Amelia's scowl deepened. "I'm not surprised. Sixteen year-old girls have such ghastly taste."

"Whereas a mature woman like you prefers men who look dignified," he rejoined with an amiable smile. He knew she was startled by his unexpected appearance; he'd forgive her sarcasm.

She turned away from him and busied herself straightening her brochures into a neat stack. He took advantage of the opportunity to admire the feminine slope of her shoulders and the graceful contours of her upper back, visible beneath the narrow lace straps and scooped neck of her blouse. "You're looking well," he observed.

"Thank you," she said in a clipped voice as she slid the brochures into an envelope.

"Mary told me she thought you might be sick."

"I'm sure what she meant was that I wasn't feeling like myself when I was in Wisherville." Amelia favored him with a steady, dark-eyed stare. "I *am* feeling like myself now, though," she said pointedly.

"Meaning, if I come any closer you'll holler for help?"

"Meaning, come as close as you like," she said with a noble show of confidence. "I'm not afraid of you."

As soon as she spoke, she realized her mistake. Smiling broadly, Patrick entered the conference room and perched himself on one corner of the long table. He tossed his jacket down beside him and swung his legs playfully. "That looks like incredibly boring work," he remarked. "What is it?"

Amelia glided along the table, collecting another round of brochures and inserting them in an envelope. "Information packets for incoming students."

"I see." He watched her glide the length of the table yet again, her slender hands gathering the pamphlets, her eyes focused on the stacks. "When do they have to be sent out?"

"August first."

"Mmm. And it's already the middle of June. You'd better get moving, sweetheart."

She shot him an irritated look. "What are you doing here, Patrick?"

"Visiting you."

With another disgruntled look, she bowed over her task. "I'm not in the mood to entertain visitors—certainly not a visitor who ought to be in Wisherville, taking care of my sister's legal situation."

"You know as well as I do how good her legal situation is," Patrick said, trying to smother the urge to gloat. "The town officially dropped all pending charges against her this morning. And according to the local Chamber of Commerce, the tourist business was up ten percent in Wisherville this past week, thanks to the publicity she's stirred up. And the bids are still coming in on *Liberty*.''

"How can you handle the bidding when you're here in New Milford?" Amelia scolded.

"One of my many talents. Besides, your buddy Bart is supposedly arriving in Wisherville this evening to keep an eye on Mary in my absence."

"Lucky Mary," Amelia muttered.

Patrick studied her thoughtfully. Her restrained anger implied that she might still be carrying a torch for Bartholomew. Patrick might be facing a greater obstacle in romancing her than merely her stubborn resistance to him.

Not quite sure how to break through the barrier she'd constructed around herself, he plucked a rubber band from a cup on the table and twirled it absently between his fingers. Then he stretched it taut and shot it over the table.

He wasn't aiming at Amelia, and the rubber band missed her by a couple of feet. She shrieked anyway. "Honestly, Patrick, are you trying to take out my eye?"

"No," he said, hopping down from the table to retrieve the rubber band. "Your eyes are much too pretty."

"Hush," she snapped, edging away from him and devoting herself to the pamphlets.

Why couldn't the lady take a compliment? he wondered. Her eyes *were* pretty, slanting exotically above her pronounced cheekbones, the irises a rich brown and the lashes long and thick. Amelia might not have the sort of looks that would automatically turn men's heads, but she certainly turned *his* head.

Still unsure of how to get her to relax, he lifted the rubber band, looped it around the index and middle finger of his left hand and shoved it in front of her face. "Watch this," he commanded, then gave his fingers a twitch, flipping the rubber band to his ring and pinkie fingers as if by magic. It was an old trick— and a remarkably simple one, if you knew the secret of arranging the rubber band in the right configuration at the start.

Obviously Amelia didn't know the secret. She gaped at him in astonishment.

"Yet another of my many talents," he said, deftly setting up the rubber band to repeat the trick. He performed it and she gasped.

A small reluctant smile tugged at the corners of her mouth. "How did you do that?"

"Tell me you love me and I'll show you."

"Forget it," she said with a wry chuckle. She gathered another stack of brochures, edging away from him along the table. He trailed her, closing the distance between them and then grabbing an envelope from the pile. Her eyes met his as he handed her the envelope, and she pressed her lips together, all traces of her smile gone. "I remember when you told me you were all thumbs."

"I remember, too," he murmured, putting down the rubber band and easing the packed envelope from her clasp. "I'm not all thumbs, Amelia. I think you know that."

Her gaze shifted from his face to his hands, which were rising to embrace her. She seemed to fortify herself, her back growing rigid and her chin rising defiantly. "I really don't want you to do this," she insisted in a low, tense voice.

Yet she didn't push him away, even as he let his hands come to rest on her shoulders. "What are you so afraid of, Amelia?" he asked.

She lowered her eyes to his hands, then ran her gaze up his arms to his open collar, to his neck, his jaw, the shaggy blond hair framing his face. "I don't know. Your earring, maybe."

"I'll take it off."

"No." She inhaled shakily. "Don't, Patrick. I don't want you changing for me. I just want you to admit that you're not the right kind of man for me."

"I'll admit to anything if you kiss me," he promised. "Come on, Amelia. What harm can one little kiss do?"

"Your definition of 'one little kiss' differs from mine," she said, reminding them both of what had happened the last time they'd been together.

"I'll behave myself this time," he said.

She tilted her face back to confront him. Her smile seemed to lose its nervous edge, growing bold, almost mocking. "I don't believe you."

He returned her grin. "I knew you were a smart woman," he whispered before bowing to capture her lips with his.

"Amelia?" A high-pitched voice sliced through the air with razor-sharp precision, splitting them apart. Amelia spun around to face the woman who stood in the open inner doorway. The woman appeared to be in her late middle age, her short hair a gunmetal gray, her eyes the same harsh gray, her skin so tight across her skeleton the tendons in her neck stood out. She wore a nondescript navy-blue dress with long sleeves;

the humid June heat seemed to have no effect on her. Her disapproving glare journeyed from Amelia to Patrick and back again. "What in heaven's name is going on here?"

"This—this is Patrick Levine," Amelia mumbled, taking a safe step away from him and then presenting him to the intruder. "Patrick, this is my boss, Mavis Blanchard."

He politely extended his right hand. "How do you do, Ms. Blanchard?"

"It's *Miss* Blanchard," she growled, giving his hand a hard brusque shake. "You may call me Dean Blanchard. Why are you attacking my assistant?"

"He isn't—"

"I'm attacking her," Patrick said, smoothly overriding Amelia, "because she's gorgeous and sexy and irresistible. Every time I see her she turns me into a raving lunatic. I can't seem to help myself." For emphasis, he lifted her ponytail and pretended to take a bite of her neck. Then he straightened up and grinned. He knew what he'd done would embarrass Amelia, but her harridan of a boss seemed to be in dire need of some shaking up.

His ploy worked; Dean Blanchard did, in fact, seem shaken up. Amelia glanced away and coughed, doing her best to recover. "I'm sorry, Mavis. He's...a friend of mine," she said hesitantly, "and on a whim he's driven a long distance to see me, and...and I guess this heat has gotten to him."

Ah, yes. The heat. His hand tightened slightly on her shoulder, and she tossed him a swift look of warning.

The dean fixed him with a steely stare. "I would suggest, young man, that you go somewhere else and cool off. Amelia has work to do."

He nodded. "Oh, indeed. As I understand it, these mailings have to be completed inside of two months. If she doesn't do them this minute, she may never finish in time."

"Patrick," Amelia cautioned him in a whisper. He realized that he might have gone too far, but he felt no remorse. He'd always had an adversarial relationship with authority figures, ever since his parents had described to him the treatment they received at the hands of fabric-mill managers. He could force himself to behave respectfully toward the Wisherville Police Department when it was necessary for the proper settlement of a case. But when the authority figure was a puritanical martinet who seemed incapable of smiling, he couldn't resist cutting up a bit.

The dean narrowed her eyes and assessed Amelia. Then she turned to the table. "If you feel it would be wise to escort this gentleman off the premises, Amelia, then please do so. I don't like this sort of nonsense going on in the office. We have to set an example, you know."

"I know," Amelia agreed, wriggling out of Patrick's clasp and heading out of the conference room, with Patrick and Dean Blanchard at her heels. "I'll take care of him, Mavis. Just let me get my purse." She vanished through another door, stranding Patrick with the dean.

Dean Blanchard inspected Patrick with her hawklike gaze, then issued a disdainful sniff. "It's mutual, lady," he muttered under his breath.

Amelia reappeared, carrying a leather clutch purse, and ushered Patrick toward the counter. He wondered whether she was as aware as he was of the gaping students on the opposite side of the counter. As much for them as for himself, he said sarcastically, "It's been a real pleasure, Dean."

Amelia winced and then smiled apologetically at her boss. "I'll come in tomorrow to finish collating the mailings," she promised before Patrick swept her out of the office.

"What do you mean, you'll come in tomorrow?" he questioned her as soon as they were outside the office.

Her smile fading, she stalked down the long echoing corridor in brisk, resolute strides, weaving past students and administrators and forcing Patrick to scamper to keep up with her. "What's wrong with my coming in tomorrow?" she snapped over her shoulder.

"Tomorrow's Saturday."

"People work on Saturdays. I bet even you do sometimes."

"When it's important. I certainly wouldn't go into the office on Saturday to stuff envelopes that don't even have to be mailed for seven weeks."

"Patrick, you were rude to Mavis." She had reached the main entry and shoved open one of the thick doors. "How could you behave so badly?"

"She was a prig."

"She's my boss," Amelia retorted. "I work for her."

"You have my sympathy," he said, following her down the concrete steps and into the quadrangle, once again aware of the number of uniformly female eyes riveted to him. "Maybe you ought to look for a new job."

"Don't say that," she argued with surprising fervor. She took a deep breath and slowed her pace. "Mavis comes across as an iron maiden, but she's really quite charming once you get to know her."

"Yeah. People said that about Hitler, too."

"I'm serious. She's a very intelligent woman. Just last week, she told me, she decided to reread *Bleak House*."

"I wonder why that doesn't surprise me," Patrick muttered.

"She gets hung up on the way we behave at the office because we do have to set an example. If those students had seen you flirting with me that way, they'd think it was acceptable behavior."

"It is acceptable behavior if the flirtation is welcome—which it was, Amelia, so don't deny it," he hastened to add when he saw her open her mouth to object. "I've got my car," he continued, touching her elbow and guiding her toward the visitors' parking lot.

She let him lead her down the walk to the lot. Her eyes remained on the path in front of them, assiduously avoiding Patrick's probing gaze. He thought back to the way she'd, if not welcomed, at least stopped fighting his overture, and tried to predict how long it would take him to persuade her all over again to allow him a kiss. Then his thoughts skipped forward to the way she'd reacted to his suggestion that she find another job.

"Amelia." He stroked her arm gently, not in any way seductively. He only wanted to get her to listen to him objectively. "Dean Blanchard seems like such a hard, cold lady, and—please don't take this the wrong way—if you aren't careful you could turn into her thirty years from now."

Amelia flashed him an enigmatic look. "Would that be so terrible? To you she may seem like a hard, cold lady. But I happen to know that she's a bright, well-organized woman, with a solid career—"

"And the personality of a tarantula. Amelia, that woman looked like she hadn't exercised her smile muscles in years. That's not the proper example to set for anybody."

"You're right," Amelia said in such a quiet voice he almost didn't hear her.

Nearing his Jeep, he pulled her to a halt. When he turned her toward him she tilted her head up to view his face, but there was nothing inviting in her expression.

That was all right, because he didn't intend to kiss her now. He intended to straighten out something more important first. "Why don't you get out of this place? Why don't you find a new job?"

Her eyes, dark and shiny, searched his as she mulled over her answer. The motion of her lips was nearly enough to convince him that kissing her was definitely more important than talking right now. But she began to speak before he could act on that impulse.

"I've been giving some thought to it," she admitted. "I don't know why, and I'm sure I'll come to my senses soon, but—"

No, he silently implored her, *whatever you do, don't come to your senses.* "You think you might want to do something more exciting with your life than stuffing envelopes?" he asked carefully, trying to keep his bias hidden even though it was undoubtedly too late.

"I don't stuff envelopes very often, Patrick," she informed him.

"I guess you spend the majority of your time setting a proper example for the students, huh."

She started to argue, then broke into a crooked, curiously poignant smile. "You may be closer to the truth than you realize."

"About setting examples for the students? Or about the fact that you should consider a career switch?"

Again she lapsed into thought. Then she shook her head. "It's just this oppressive heat wave. We haven't got air-conditioning in the office, and my apartment's stuffy, too, and the humidity is so high, and..." She sighed. "I'm sure that's the only reason I've been feeling restless."

Patrick was sure it wasn't. Mary had told him she thought something serious was bothering Amelia, and now that he'd seen her for himself he believed the diagnosis was accurate. "Let's take a drive," he recommended. He sensed that Amelia needed to talk, and he truly wanted to listen. As much as he admired her reserve, he wanted to break through and touch her, to find out what made her tick. He knew that if he came right out and asked her to tell him everything that was on her mind and in her heart, she'd clam up for good. But if they drove, if the passing scenery lulled her and her tension unwound, maybe he could get her talking.

"Okay." She moved away from him and climbed into the Jeep, allowing him to close the door behind her.

He got in behind the wheel and started the engine. "Where to?"

"We could ride over to Lake Candlewood, if you'd like. Maybe it'll be cooler there."

"Sounds good." He heeded her directions, cruising through the center of the modest town, which had sprung up a century ago on the shores of the Housatonic River. It was a pretty town but too built up for Patrick's taste. He had grown used to the dense forests and rolling hills of the Catskill region, the deer that ventured out of the woods surrounding his house to browse in his backyard, the wide-open sky and the clean pine-scented breezes.

Except for the directions, Amelia didn't say anything. Exercising what little patience he had, Patrick didn't question her right away. Instead he tried to gauge her mood, to interpret her pensive expression. After a few minutes the silence began to gnaw at him. "Mary's worried about you," he said, figuring such a statement would jar a response out of her.

Amelia grimaced. "That's ridiculous. I'm the one who's supposed to worry about her."

"Maybe she forgot to read the cast list," he remarked. "She thinks you've gone off the deep end."

"What deep end?" Amelia sounded indignant. "Just because I left town before her latest crisis played itself out? Just because I didn't hang around in Wisherville and nag her into settling her case quietly?"

Patrick sent her another measuring gaze. "Personally I think what you've done bodes well."

"Why? Because if I'd stayed in Wisherville I would have convinced her to fire you?"

"You wouldn't have," Patrick said with certainty. "Deep in your heart, Amelia, you know my approach is right."

"Deep in my heart—" she cast him a skeptical look "—I think you're a show-off using Mary as an excuse to make headlines. The sculpture was obscene—you and I both know it. Mary could have kept it out of the gallery's window, and none of this would have happened. But she likes stirring up trouble, and so, apparently, do you."

A deep clap of thunder sounded to the west. Patrick glanced upward and noticed the dark clouds drifting overhead. "Thank goodness there are a few of us left willing to stir up trouble," he countered. "If no one was willing to stir up trouble, we'd still be British subjects."

"Please! Not another lecture on the American Revolution!" Amelia protested, although Patrick detected a small grin playing across her lips.

"Not a lecture," he assured her. "All I'm saying is—" Another rumble of thunder rippled across the sky. "What was the weather forecast for today?" he asked, glancing upward.

Before Amelia could answer, a dagger of lightning shot down from the sky, followed by a much closer crack of thunder. And then the clouds opened up, releasing a stunning torrent of rain onto the earth. It flooded the asphalt; it hammered against the cars navigating the road, and they all immediately slowed to a crawl and turned their windshield wipers on at high speed. The world darkened beneath the deluge; the rain slashed down in blinding sheets.

And two passengers in a roofless Jeep got very wet, very fast.

Chapter Six

It took at least ten minutes for Patrick to maneuver the Jeep off the road in the downpour, weaving through the sluggish traffic until he found a safe place to park on the shoulder. It took several more minutes for him and Amelia to secure the detachable canvas roof. By the time they were safely inside the car again, Amelia was drenched. Her hair was heavy with rainwater, her clothing glued to her body, and drops of moisture beaded her eyebrows, lashes, cheeks and chin. She tried to wipe her face with her hands, but they were too wet to do any good.

Above her, the rain pelted the canvas roof. Around her, it rattled the windows. Although the air remained warm, she shivered slightly.

"Here you are, wet again," Patrick murmured. "It suits you, Amelia."

She shot him an impatient look. But the retort that sprang to her lips died as soon as she saw how soaked he was. His hair hung thick and long, darkened to a golden brown by the water streaming from its limp ends. Since he'd rolled his shirtsleeves to the elbows, his bare forearms glistened with the drops of rain. His shirt adhered to his body, revealing his streamlined chest, hinting at the strong frame of his ribs and a shadow of hair across his pectorals. His trousers were saturated, plastered to his thighs as he turned and leaned his back against the driver's door in an unsuccessful attempt to stretch his legs out beneath the steering wheel. His tie appeared to be ruined.

Her first thought was that being wet suited Patrick—suited him much too well. Given the way he looked right now, with his body slick and damp, its contours teasingly revealed by his clinging clothing, she felt a shocking, urgent awareness of him—and of herself.

She didn't know how to deal with such feelings. All week long she'd endured a certain restlessness about her job, about New Milford and her apartment and the monotonous temper of her existence. Now all of a sudden the restlessness had transformed from intellectual to physical, forcing her to reassess not the external facts of her daily existence but, rather, the internal truth about who she was and what she needed.

She was supposed to be the sensible one, the Potts sister who lived a calm, stable life. There was no place in it for overheated yearnings and reckless acts. And yet, for not the first time that day, she felt a compelling desire to do something reckless. With Patrick.

"I wish you wouldn't keep saying things like that," she said, glancing down at herself and discovering that her clothing was just as revealing as his. The thin cotton of her camisole had become nearly transparent thanks to the rain, and the delicate points of her nipples stood out in relief against the cloth. Embarrassed, she plucked the soggy fabric away from her chest.

"I'm saying it because it's true. You look great when you're dry, but when you're wet—"

"Patrick—"

"—your skin gets a kind of glow, and your eyes become incredibly dark, and your clothing—"

"Patrick."

"It makes me want to grab you and—"

"Shut up!" she snapped, then turned away and stared through the side window at the silvery cascade of rain. "I'm sorry," she mumbled.

He remained where he was, resting against the door, his left arm slung over the steering wheel and his right leg encroaching on the floor space in front of her seat. To her great relief, he didn't follow through on his desire to grab her. He only studied her, absently shoving his hair back from his face and then wiping away the moisture it left behind on his cheek. "Why are you sorry?" he asked.

"Saying 'shut up' like that was rude." She plucked again at her blouse, peeling it away from her chest, and kept her eyes focused on her lap.

She was surprised to hear a low husky laugh coming from him. "*I* was rude, Amelia. And I'm not going to apologize for it."

"I wouldn't expect you to," she muttered, intending the insult.

He continued to chuckle. "Sometimes you've got to be a little rude if you want to shake a reaction out of a person."

"And what reaction do you want to shake out of me?" she asked, still refusing to look at him. "Anger? Discomfort?"

His laughter faded into a sigh. "Anything that might prove to you that you're not the goody-two-shoes you try so hard to be."

"I don't try so hard to be a goody-two-shoes," she retorted.

"You mean it comes naturally to you? I don't believe that."

"Patrick—" she struggled to maintain her manners "—please stop goading me."

"*Please,*" he mimicked with a snort. "Back to minding our manners, are we?" Straightening, he twisted the key in the ignition and started the Jeep. Amelia watched him withdraw his leg from her side of the car. In spite of herself, she felt strangely bereft when he directed his attention from her to the traffic.

As soon as he'd coasted back onto the flooded road, however, he spoke again. "You were more than ready to kiss me at the school. And now all of a sudden you're doing your virginal-twit routine again."

"It's not a routine."

He cast her a quizzical look. "You are a virginal twit?"

"I'm not a twit," she shot back, then went on before he could pose the obvious next question. "I'm not a virgin, either, although I hardly consider that any of your business."

He opened his mouth, then shut it. His lips curved into a lazy smile.

Amelia tried to sort her thoughts. The click-clack of the windshield wipers distracted her, as did the ceaseless drumming of the rain, the arching sprays of water leaping at the Jeep from the tires of other cars, the sporadic bolts of lightning and the booms of thunder. Even more distracting was Patrick's Cheshire Cat grin, his sparkling blue eyes, his rain-soaked body—and the tiny flash of gold on his earlobe.

"Can we be honest with each other?" she asked cautiously.

He glanced at her, and his smile waned. "I'd like that very much. But first give me some directions back to your house. Somehow, I don't think this is a great day to visit the lake."

Nodding, she told him to take a right at the next intersection. After a few more turns she navigated him back onto the main route in the opposite direction, heading toward New Milford.

The rain showed no sign of letting up. Patrick hunched over the steering wheel, his gaze riveted to the road. But his concentration clearly allowed room for her. "Go ahead and say something honest, Amelia. I'm all ears."

She drew in a deep breath and turned to him. "Funny you should mention ears," she began. "Your earring... well, it doesn't really bother me as much as it should."

A small grin played across his mouth. "Should? *Should* has nothing to do with it." The oversize tires of the truck ahead of him shot blinding torrents of water against the windshield, and Patrick pulled out to pass. Once he was back in the right lane and cruising at a safe speed, he elaborated, "If we're going to be honest, Amelia, let me give you my honest opinion of what your problem is."

"I haven't got a problem," she objected.

He ignored her claim. "Your problem is, you're too hung up on 'should,' And 'supposed to' and 'ought to' and being polite. You've got this mind-set that balks every time something runs counter to it. So you've never dated a man with an earring before. So what? So you think saying 'shut up' is rude. Big deal. What matters, Amelia, is what you feel inside."

"Well, thank you, Dr. Freud."

"I'm not exactly sure what you feel toward me," he went on, undeterred. "But whatever it is, the fact remains that you telephoned me the other night—"

"To discuss my sister," she insisted.

"Like hell."

"I called you to find out about Mary's situation."

"Skip the rationalizations," he said. "I've spent the last week thinking about you and wondering why you ran away from me just when we were finally hitting it off, and praying for you to call me. And then you did call me—but you hedged and fudged and refused to say what you were feeling. So I came after you. I'm here. And deep down in your heart, you're glad I am. You know you are."

His arrogance appalled her. Regardless of how close to the truth he'd come, she resented his accusations and his attempts to psychoanalyze her. "That's just your ego talking," she scolded.

"It's the truth. If you really want to be honest, sweetheart, then you can start by admitting that when we were standing in your office no more than a half hour ago, you wanted to kiss me as much as I wanted to kiss you."

"In other words, all that matters is lust?" She shook her head. "I don't view things so simplistically, Patrick."

"What's wrong with lust?" he asked, then held up his hand to silence the protest he anticipated. "Just kidding, Amelia. Lust is great, but I think we've got more going for us than that."

"And what might that be?"

"You're a lot of fun to talk to."

"We argue more than we talk, Patrick."

He shrugged, unconcerned. "You're a lot of fun to argue with. I like to argue. That's one of the reasons I became a lawyer."

"Maybe you like arguing," she granted. "I don't. I like peace."

"Peace is okay every once in a while, too," he said agreeably. "However—" he shot her another quick look, then turned his gaze forward again "—I think you've got enough intelligence to realize that sometimes maintaining the peace isn't as important as fighting for what's right."

"And *I* think you're imposing your own opinions on me."

"But you admit that what I'm fighting for is right," he pressed her.

"I didn't say that," she grumbled, though she privately had to concede that he'd read her pretty accurately.

"I think," he continued, his tone now quiet and devoid of humor, "that there's someone inside you who likes things wild and exciting and totally unmanageable. And that someone is just straining to burst free."

Amelia mulled over his statement, trying not to become defensive. Before last weekend she had never considered that the way she conducted her life wasn't completely satisfying. She'd never felt notably moody or confused or unable to answer such epic questions as *Why am I doing what I'm doing? Would I rather be someplace else? Am I happy?* She'd never even entertained such questions.

Ever since her trip to Wisherville, though, she had been entertaining them. And she was troubled by the answers that kept taking shape inside her head, answers that she'd so far succeeded in fending off, but that Patrick seemed willing to force her to address.

She didn't like him dissecting her and speaking as if he knew her better than she knew herself. His attitude seemed patronizing—and his perceptiveness left her feeling exposed.

"We all have little inconsistencies inside us," she said, choosing her words with care. "Turn left at the next light. We all have inconsistencies," she resumed, "but that doesn't mean we have to turn ourselves upside down and inside out."

"Is that what you think I want to do to you?"

"Yes."

He slowed to make the turn. "Maybe you're right, Amelia. Maybe I do."

"Why?"

He thought for a minute. "Partly, I guess it's just the way I am. I like overturning tables—I've told you that. But it isn't just me, Amelia—it's you. I want to get to know all of you, up and down and in and out. I want to discover who you really are."

"Why? What's so special about me? Why me and not Mary?"

He shot her a quick glance. "Why you and not Jacqueline Bisset, or Barbra Streisand, or Margaret Thatcher? Why the hell do you keep comparing yourself to Mary?"

"She's my twin sister," Amelia reminded him.

"A quirk of birth. She's someone, and you're someone else. I want to have her as a friend, and I want to have you—" his voice trailed off enigmatically "—any way you let me," he finally concluded, tossing her a smile. "A friend, yes. But, since we're being so honest here, I want much more than that from you."

"So, we're back to lust," she said as calmly as she could. She preferred to reduce his expressed desire to its basest level. It seemed somehow safer than considering the deeper implications of his statement.

"There's a lot to be said for lust, Amelia," he teased. "Don't knock it if you haven't tried it."

She wasn't knocking anything she hadn't tried. She had lost her virginity to a classmate she'd been dating during her senior year in college. It had been a rite of passage, appropriate for her twenty-first year; she'd viewed it as part of her education. The possibility of her marrying Bartholomew was already being bandied about among her relatives back then, and they had gone on a couple of dates. He'd let slip somewhere along the line that he'd acquired some sexual expertise thanks to his encounters with women during his college years, so Amelia had decided that she, too, ought to bring a bit of know-how to their relationship.

But the truth was, what she'd shared with her classmate could scarcely be considered lust. It had been interesting, it had answered some clinical questions she'd had about the mechanics, and it had satisfied the young man's physical demands, but it hadn't been anything like what Mary had described to her when she'd lost her virginity a couple of years earlier. According to Mary, the moment was supposed to resemble fireworks, earthquakes, volcanic eruptions and the like. Amelia's few tame encounters with her college boyfriend hadn't included such rhapsodic splendors. Maybe what she'd experienced wasn't lust, after all.

Subdued, she directed Patrick to her street. She wanted to be honest with him, but the honesty passing between them had left her feeling stripped down to her nerves. Perhaps once she was in the familiar environment of her apartment, in some dry clothing, she would feel better. "That's where I live," she said.

Patrick followed her outstretched finger to a three-story house with scalloped teal-green shingles and white gingerbread ornamentation. The rhododendron bushes bordering the front steps were rife with bright pink blossoms, their petals drooping slightly in the driving rain.

He parked at the curb, pulled his jacket, his briefcase and a small overnight bag from the back seat, and followed her up the front walk and inside. If they hadn't already been waterlogged, the brief dash from the street to the vestibule would have done the job. Small puddles pooled on the hardwood floor at their feet as they stopped to catch their breath, and when they ascended the stairs to the second floor they left two parallel streams of water in their wake.

Inside her apartment, Amelia locked up while Patrick surveyed the living room. It was furnished in an understated style: the camel-back sofa, two armchairs and window-seat cushions were all upholstered with the same material, dark blue with tiny white flowers flocked across it. The drapes were a complementary blue held back with white swags, and the parquet floor was covered with a plush Persian rug. The fireplace screen was a modest brass-trimmed stand, and the mantel held several antique sepia portraits in oval frames. The overall effect was one of quiet elegance.

Amelia watched Patrick as his gaze skimmed the room from the arched doorway. Turning to her, he smiled and stepped out of his soggy loafers. "Where can I change my clothes?" he asked.

She led him down the hall to the spare bedroom. "Right in there," she said, gesturing inside. With a smile of thanks, he entered and closed the door behind himself.

Continuing down the hall to her own room, Amelia passed the linen closet and hesitated. Patrick was going to need something to dry himself off with. She pulled a thick brown bath towel from a shelf and returned to the guest room. "Patrick?" she called, rapping the door lightly. "I've got a towel for you if you want one."

"I want one." He swung open the door to take it. He had already removed his tie, and his shirt hung unbuttoned outside his trousers. Amelia's gaze locked onto his naked chest—the chest she'd attempted to picture through his wet shirt. The golden hair spreading across the upper portion of it and then tapering toward his abdomen was just as she'd imagined, as were his streamlined muscles, his flat stomach and his enticingly deep navel, visible just above the buckle of his belt.

Ashamed that he should see her admiring him so blatantly, she dragged her eyes from him and handed him the towel. "Here," she said in a rusty voice.

Slinging the towel around his neck, he said, "Thanks." With a dimpled smile, he closed the door.

Amelia hurried to her bedroom at the end of the hall and shut herself inside. Why had she thought she'd be better off on her home turf? Being alone with Patrick in her apartment wasn't the least bit safe, not when those astute blue eyes of his were able to read her so well.

He must have noticed the way she was looking at him. He must have sensed her attraction—and her panic. He must know that, despite her lack of personal familiarity with lust, she was more than a little susceptible to the affliction—at least when she was around him.

She couldn't very well have barred him from her home, though, not when he'd driven so far to see her and not when he was soaking wet. She would follow through on her original plan and put on some dry clothes. Then she'd fix them something to eat, and she'd explain to him that, just as she didn't want him to change for her, she had no intention of changing for him. If he wanted to turn someone inside out, he'd have to find another woman.

Then she headed to her bathroom for a quick shower. Then she donned a pair of pleated slacks and a short-sleeved sweater—an outfit she considered utterly unsuggestive—and brushed out her hair until it was smooth and shiny.

She headed for the living room, expecting to find Patrick there. "In here," he called to her from across the hall. She found him slouching against the kitchen counter, snacking on a handful of puffed wheat. "I was starving and this was the first edible thing I found." He eyed the box on the counter beside him and made a face. "Do you really eat this stuff?"

"Yes, I do."

"It's what I imagine Styrofoam packing tastes like," he said, although he helped himself to another handful. "I bet you eat stewed prunes, too."

"I'm not *that* much like Dean Blanchard," she joked, moving past him to the refrigerator. "You don't have to eat dry cereal for supper, Patrick. I'll fix us something."

He perked up. "What?"

She surveyed the contents of the refrigerator. "How about tuna salad?"

Making another face, he ambled over and inspected the shelves with her. "How about omelets? You've got a carton of eggs, and there's some . . . American cheese," he muttered, grimacing. "Not real cheese, but it'll do." He pulled out the ingredients. "Bowl?" he asked.

She supplied him with a mixing bowl and a whisk, and he set about making the omelets. She ought to have found it odd that he, and not she, was making their supper, but for some reason it seemed quite natural. She liked the way Patrick looked in his dry blue jeans and a fresh cotton shirt, with his hair beginning to dry to its usual tawny blond shade and the golden hair on his forearms glinting in the light from the ceiling fixture. She liked the way he appropriated her utensils, the way he beat the eggs and tossed a splash of water onto the skillet to test the heat of its surface, and even the way he curled his lip as he peeled the cellophane wrap from a couple of squares of cheese.

"Let me guess," he said, slapping a lump of butter into the skillet and swirling it around with a spatula. "Your favorite sandwich is American cheese and mayo on white bread."

She smiled tenuously. "I wouldn't say that's my favorite," she told him as she pulled two plates from a shelf, "but it's a tasty combination. What's wrong with it?"

"It's so Waspy." He poured in the eggs and then turned to her.

"I see." She pulled some silverware and napkins from a drawer and carried them to the circular table in the dining nook by the window. "What sorts of sandwiches do half-Irish-half-Jewish people prefer?"

"Corned beef on rye," he said without missing a beat.

Amelia grinned. If they could keep the atmosphere this light and playful, she would be able to survive Patrick's visit without much difficulty.

The double-size omelet Patrick was preparing smelled wonderful, dripping with butter and packed with cholesterol. "We're both going to have heart attacks," she commented, watching as he sliced the omelet in two and slid the halves onto the two plates she'd left by the stove.

"Every time I think of you I have a heart attack," Patrick confessed, smiling wistfully.

Amelia hadn't expected him to say anything so corny—so romantic. She tried to remind herself that she and he were acting at cross-purposes—that he desired her and had no qualms about it, while she desired him and had more than enough qualms for both of them. But in spite of herself, she let his gentle compliment thaw her resistance.

"This is delicious," she said after tasting the omelet. "Thank you for cooking it. I wish I had some wine to go with it, but—"

"You didn't know I was coming," he bailed her out before taking a long drink of milk. He ate for a minute, then said, "So tell me about this job crisis of yours."

"I don't have crises," she corrected him wryly. "That's Mary's department."

"Forgive me. What would you call it, then? A dilemma? A quandary?"

"A . . . bit of reflection, that's all," she said, knowing deep inside that it was much more than that. "It's really silly, Patrick, but every now and then, I've found myself wishing I could work at a place like Keppler's."

She waited for him to laugh at her. His respectful silence prompted her to lift her gaze. He was studying her thoughtfully. "In what capacity?"

She was enormously pleased that he was taking her seriously. "I don't know," she said.

"Well, I can't very well see you working the reception desk like Sue. And if your idea of cuisine is American cheese, Rae would never let you near the kitchen. You're a good swimmer. Maybe you could be a lifeguard there."

"Don't be ridiculous."

"I'm not being ridiculous," he said calmly. "Of course, you'd have to be Red Cross certified. Besides, lifeguard work is seasonal. What would you do come September?"

"What does Rae do in September?" Amelia asked.

Patrick measured her with his gaze. Then he ate a bit more of his omelet. "It's a year-round resort, so she does plenty," he informed her. "Business falls off somewhat after Labor Day, so Rae uses the autumn months to do inventory, repairs and so on. Then the ski season begins. She's about fifteen minutes from Holiday Mountain and Big Vanilla, so the place tends to fill up every weekend. Things quiet down again in the spring, which is when she oversees painting, major cleanup projects, landscape work and prepping the boats for the lake." He drank some more milk. "She works hard."

"But she loves it," Amelia noted.

"Yeah. She's been thinking about retiring because of her age and because she'd like to be able to spend more time with her grandchildren. But if her kids lived nearby, there's no way she'd retire."

"What a life." Amelia sighed pensively. If she had hoped that hearing about the rigorous nonstop labor of running Keppler's would quell her fantasies of working there, she'd obviously been wrong.

"Do you want me to talk to her?"

Amelia's eyes widened in puzzlement. "About what?"

"About finding you a job there."

"As what? You just said yourself that I wouldn't be suitable behind the registration desk or in the kitchen."

"Of course not. You'd run the place."

"Run it?" She laughed.

Apparently he wasn't joking. "You'd run the place," he reiterated, enunciating each word. "You've got administrative skills. You're a jack-of-all-trades at the dean's office. With that kind of background, you must have the flexibility it would take to run a place like Keppler's."

"But—but I've got no experience."

"You'd learn. You'd become Rae's apprentice." Patrick's mouth spread in a broad smile. "You could be her surrogate daughter—the child she always dreamed of having follow her into the business—and then you could take over the place when she retires."

"She told me she's looking for someone to *buy* the place," Amelia said, desperate to quash the idea before she got too caught up in its appeal. "She needs someone with the financial wherewithal—"

"You're rich," Patrick said simply.

"Not that rich. I don't know where you got that notion—"

"From your spiffy European car," he told her, "and your charming apartment here, and your wardrobe and your finishing-school poise. Even if Mary hadn't told me about your parents' eight-room East Side apartment, the housekeeper and the summer place in the Hamptons—right by the yacht club, if I'm not mistaken—and your diploma from the Hibbing School, I still would have figured you for rich. You've got the polish, Amelia."

"Maybe I have the polish," she conceded, once again unnerved by Patrick's powers of perception, "but I haven't got that much money. I supplement my salary with the income from a small trust fund, which helps me to pay for the Saab and a few antiques. But I certainly don't sponge off my parents, and I'm not an heiress."

"But the money's there if you need it."

"If I was facing an emergency, yes, of course my parents would help me out. Buying a Catskill resort hardly qualifies as an emergency."

"Didn't your parents help Mary start her gallery?"

Amelia brushed off the comparison with a wave of her hand. "They're always helping her financially," she explained. "Bartholomew helps her with her accounting, and when he absolutely can't make the numbers line up, my parents make a donation. But that's Mary. I'm the self-sufficient one.''

"Self-sufficiency is an admirable trait," Patrick remarked, pushing back his chair and stretching his legs beneath the table. "As a matter of fact, it's probably one of the most important things you'd need to run Keppler's."

Amelia closed her eyes, fighting against the desire to get swept up in Patrick's enthusiasm. So what if she was self-sufficient and flexible and in possession of administrative skills? The whole thing was a pipe dream. She was a fool to get so deeply drawn into the whimsical picture Patrick was painting. "This is silly," she said quietly. "I'm not going to become Rae Keppler's surrogate daughter and take over her hotel."

"We just came up with a whole bunch of good reasons why you should. Can you give me one good reason why you shouldn't?"

She bravely met his challenge. "Here's a good reason: I am who I am, Patrick. I'm not a cause you're fighting for. I'm not a case you're arguing before the court. Turning me upside down and inside out won't change who I am. I don't belong running a Borscht Belt hotel. I belong in a place like Hibbing."

"Even if you're miserable here?"

"I'm not miserable."

"Then what? Bored out of your skull?"

She sighed. "Maybe I'm bored. But this is who I am. Mary's the flamboyant exciting one; she can go around disrupting the world around her and reinventing herself whenever things get dull. But that isn't me, Patrick. I can't change my personality."

"You don't have to change your personality. All you have to do is liberate it."

"I can't. I'm the staid peaceful one," she claimed.

She was unnerved by the sheer force of his gaze, the clarity in his beautiful blue eyes. There was anger in his face, but compassion, as well. "I thought you were the sane one," he said.

"I'm that, too."

"Who decided this? Who established these roles?"

"Nobody established anything. It's just the way things are."

"Bull." He stood, grasped Amelia's hand and tugged her to her feet. She was afraid he was going to grab her, following through on the threat he'd made in the Jeep. But he only held her, his hands cupping her elbows, his gaze journeying over her upturned face. "If you were all that sane, Amelia, you'd know better than to stick with a job that's boring you to tears."

"I'm not bored to tears," she protested halfheartedly.

"Then it's tying you in knots."

"Don't be silly."

"You think everything you do has to fit this arbitrary role of yours. You've got to hold down a tedious job at the Hibbing School because it's your role. You've got to run away from me because it's your role."

"Nonsense," she scoffed, although she didn't sound terribly persuasive.

"No, Amelia, it's not nonsense," he said, his voice low and persuasive, a hypnotic drawl. "Quit the damned role, sweetheart. Walk out on it. Be yourself." His hands slid slowly up her arms to her shoulders. "Kiss me."

"One little kiss?" She felt her pulse begin to accelerate, felt her soul succumb to an intoxicating blend of fear and inevitability.

"For starters," he said—and she knew there would be more than one kiss. Patrick's eyes told her. Her heart told her.

She waited. She watched him, her lips parted, her breath trapped somewhere inside her throat. She waited for him to kiss her, but he didn't.

"Kiss me," he whispered, and she realized what he was asking of her: not to let him free her from her role, but to free herself. Closing her eyes, she rose on tiptoe and touched her mouth to his.

He must have recognized how hard it had been for her to make the first move, because as soon as her lips merged with his he took over, winding his arms around her and pulling her snugly to him. His lips moved sensuously on hers, boldly, his tongue forging deep into the soft warmth of her mouth, his fingers weaving through her hair to hold her head steady. She accepted his kiss, melted into it, gave herself over to its intensity.

She had understood before they started that Patrick didn't know the meaning of a *little* kiss. She had been expecting something like this. But she hadn't expected to relish it so much. She hadn't expected to respond to it in her belly, in her bloodstream and most of all in her mind. Thoughts skittered through her head, thoughts of earthquakes and fireworks and all the other wonders Mary had once described to her. Thoughts of liberation, of breaking out, of knots being untied and a spirit bursting free.

"Patrick," she moaned, her breath mingling with his.

He slid one hand down her to her waist and pressed her to him. Through their clothing, she felt his hardness against her. "Do you want this as much as I do?" he murmured.

Her eyes came into focus on him. His question told her much more than simply that he was aroused. It told her that he was prepared to back off if she asked him to. It told her that, as strongly as he longed for her, he wouldn't push.

She struggled to find her voice. "I . . . Patrick . . . is this why you came here?"

"I had hopes," he confessed, his lips curving in a heart-melting smile. "And if you start handing me a lot of bull about how I'm not your type I'm going to be mighty angry. But—" his hips moved subtly against hers, causing every muscle in her body to clench reflexively "—I came here to get to know you better. This way—or any other way. The decision is yours, Amelia."

He moved against her again, fitting himself against the crevice between her thighs, allowing her to feel his hunger and compelling her to acknowledge her own. Closing her eyes, she imagined their clothes falling away, their bodies joining as their mouths had joined, deeply and completely. Then she opened her eyes and chased away the fantasy.

She had spent too much time wondering lately, and too little time living. Patrick was here, real and solid. She didn't have to fantasize about him.

Without a word, she took his hand in hers and led him down the hall to her bedroom.

Chapter Seven

As soon as they crossed the threshold he gathered her into his arms again. He brushed his lips over her brow, down to the tip of her nose, to the dainty point of her chin and up again to her mouth. "Are you frightened?" he asked, searching her upturned face.

"A little."

He smiled gently. "Don't be," he whispered before bowing to kiss her. He captured her lips with his, sliding his tongue along the sensitive inner flesh of her lips. She shuddered slightly within his arms, then hesitantly returned his embrace, ringing her arms around his waist. "Hold me tighter," he requested, lifting his mouth to her hair and burying his lips in the silken strands. His warm breath caused her scalp to tingle.

She tightened her arms around him, flattening her hands against the small of his back. She felt his reaction instantly in the sudden lurch of his hips against hers, the sudden catch in his breath. "Like this?" she asked, already knowing the answer.

"Mmm. Like that."

Determined not to retreat to her usual stifling reserve, she dug her fingers into the supple muscles above and below his belt. When he leaned back to savor the massage, she pressed her mouth to the warm hollow of his neck. He groaned, a soft, indisputably erotic sound that reassured and inspired her. Reveling in her power over him, she slid her hands down to his hips. She would let herself be free, free to touch him everywhere, free to arouse him, free to respond.

He grasped the edge of her sweater and tugged it up, breaking from her embrace so he could pull her arms through the sleeves. He tossed the sweater behind him, but before she could see where it landed his fingers were on her bra, undoing the hook, drawing the lacy material away.

"I'm skinny," she warned as he slid his hands forward to cup her breasts. "I don't even need a bra...."

"But you're a goody-two-shoes, so you wear one anyway," he teased, flicking his thumbs gently over her flushed nipples. They beaded into two tight points, and when he ran his thumbs over them again she gasped at her body's instantaneous reaction, a hot heavenly throbbing that pulsed from her chest down to the tips of her toes. "You aren't skinny, Amelia. You're perfect. Don't let Rae Keppler fatten you up."

"I wasn't planning to," she said, amazed by the breathless quality of her voice.

His hands fell away, but before she could beg him to caress her some more he was busy elsewhere, unfastening the button and then the zipper of her slacks, sliding them down over her hips until they dropped to the floor. He spent several exquisitely frustrating moments running his fingertips along the elastic trim of her panties, gliding across the flat stretch of her belly, around to the back and then down over the softness of her bottom. His hands imparted their warmth through the wispy cloth, tickling her skin in a decidedly stimulating way. Her hips moved, writhing against his palms.

"I like that," he whispered, molding his hands firmly to her and drawing her against him. His plain words of encouragement prompted her to rise on tiptoe and seek him, to move against him. There was nothing practiced in what she was doing, nothing deliberate. She was operating on instinct, on reflex, on a secret knowledge that had lain dormant inside her all her life, just waiting to be discovered—waiting for her to set it free.

Waiting for Patrick, as well. He crooked his fingers around the edge of the panties and pulled them down, guiding them over her hips and then letting them fall. "Take your clothes off," she implored him in a thick, husky voice.

He grinned. "Where are your manners, Amelia? I didn't hear you say please."

"Please."

He gave her mouth a swift solid kiss, then set to work on the buttons of his shirt. He grinned as she contributed to the effort, unfastening the lower buttons. As soon as his shirt joined her clothing on the floor he attacked the buckle of his belt. She wanted to offer her assistance in removing his trousers, too, but she was abruptly seized by shyness. With a bashful sigh, she averted her eyes.

He shed his jeans without her help, and then his briefs. She stared at his feet, at his strong sinewy calves with their fine covering of dark blond hair, at his firm, muscled thighs. There she stopped.

He tucked his hand beneath her chin and lifted her face to his, allowing her the opportunity to glance at him along the way if she chose to. She did. He was full and hard. Merely glimpsing him caused a warm, fluid rush of sensation to sweep through her body.

"Still frightened?" he asked, urging her to meet his gaze.

"No." Hearing herself say the word convinced her of its truth. She was excited, anxious, apprehensive about whether a woman with her relative lack of experience could satisfy Patrick. But she wasn't frightened.

He kissed her again, this time slowly and thoroughly, plundering her mouth with long hungry strokes of his tongue. His hands traveled the length of her back, exploring every creamy inch of skin, lingering at the hollow of her waist, at the slope of her shoulders and the pliant curves of her derriere. She touched him as he touched her, running her hands up his sides, around his waist to his smooth, lean back, to the taut muscles of his buttocks. When her fingers grazed the outer surfaces of his thighs he gasped and then scooped her into his arms.

Still kissing her, he carried her across the room to the bed. Gently he laid her down, pulled his lips from hers and sat on the edge of the mattress beside her. He brushed a few strands of her hair back from her flushed cheeks and gazed down at her, his smile poignant, brimming with affection. "Are you using any kind of birth control?" he asked.

The question astounded her—in large part because she should have raised the subject herself. She'd been too distracted to think of it, too caught up in what Patrick was doing to her, too transported. Wondering whether this was going to bring everything to a crashing halt, she answered with a meek shake of her head.

He kissed the tip of her nose. "I figured as much. I'll be right back."

She watched him stride out of her room, totally uninhibited in his nakedness. His back looked as strong and graceful as it felt, and his hair shimmered with blond highlights in the rain-dimmed evening light that filtered through the window. Comprehending his thoughtfulness, his striking male beauty, his confidence in himself and his sense of responsibility toward her, she felt another tide of warmth flow through her, stronger than the last, brought on not by his nearness but by her own emotions.

Any man as sweet and funny and considerate and persistent as Patrick was simply had to be her type.

He reentered the room, crossed to the bed and dropped a handful of foil-wrapped packets onto the night table. Then he switched on the table lamp, warding off the encroaching darkness of the rainy night. In the amber glow of the lamp, Amelia counted the packets, her eyes widening in shock. "Six?"

He shrugged and stretched out on the bed next to her. "There must be a drugstore somewhere in New Milford. We can always buy more if we run out."

She let out an uncertain laugh. "If we run out?"

"Call me a cockeyed optimist," he said, dazzling her with a dimpled smile before he kissed her. She thought hazily about the pile on the night table, about Patrick's brashness in having brought contraceptives with him at all—let alone in such quantity—and about how he'd said, earlier, "I had hopes."

She had hopes, too. She had hopes of straying every once in a while from what was expected of her, of being noticed, of being more than merely the "sane" one. Of being loved for who she was, rather than for the fact she was placid and well behaved. She had hopes she'd never even acknowledged—until Patrick had forced her to acknowledge them.

Overwhelmed by a heady combination of love and gratitude, she returned his kiss, tangling her tongue with his, twining her legs around his, using her arms to pull him higher onto her. The wiry hair on his chest abraded her breasts, sending another barrage of fiery pulses deep into her. She wanted more, more of him, and although she didn't know consciously how to get what her body ached for, she knew intuitively. She knew to arch against him, to edge her hips beneath his, to clutch his back and press him to her.

He resisted, fighting her grip and bowing to kiss her throat. He ran the tip of his tongue along her collarbone and she sighed, wondering whether it would be considered improper to ask him to move faster, to take her now and end this agonizing suspense.

"What?" he asked, lifting his head to gaze at her.

His lips glistened with the moisture of his kisses. They looked enticing, and she longed to haul him back down to her and lock his mouth to hers.

"There," he said, tracing her lower lip with his index finger. "What's that mysterious smile about?"

"Smile? Was I smiling?"

"Don't deny it."

"Maybe...maybe I'm just happy," she suggested.

He smiled, too, a smile that reached his eyes, that spread its magic down into his body and into hers. He bent to kiss her, but it wasn't the devouring kiss she'd been anticipating. He lifted his head again. "You were smiling about something else, weren't you?"

"Well...if you really must know..." Her cheeks blushing a dark pink, she confessed, "I was wondering about the etiquette of a situation like this."

A low rollicking laugh bubbled into the air from deep in his chest. "The etiquette, sweetheart," he drawled, "is to go about this exactly the way we're doing it. You make me feel good, and I make you feel good. You make me feel better—" he slid one of his legs between her thighs, flexing against her and awakening a fresh burst of sensation within her "—and I make you feel better. I don't think Miss Manners would find anything to criticize in what we're doing."

"Miss Manners would advise you to stop laughing at me," Amelia pointed out, sliding her hands into the luxuriant depths of his hair. She combed her fingers through the soft blond locks to his ear, then traced its curve. Detecting the tiny gold jewel adorning it, she paused and then fondled the lobe, tracing the rim of it, stroking the crevice behind it and then roaming back to his earring. It felt wonderful to her, and it looked wonderful, too. "Have you turned off the electricity?" she asked, remembering the joke he'd made the first time she'd touched it.

His body had grown exceedingly tense above hers as she indulged in her provocative caress of his ear. "The electricity," he whispered hoarsely, "is very much on." Then he overwhelmed her with a fierce kiss.

She discerned the change in him. There was nothing playful in his attitude now, nothing teasing. His hands journeyed with authority over her, kneading her breasts, stroking her belly and legs. He eased off her so he could touch her, and when his fingers slid through the damp thatch of curls between her thighs she bit back a cry.

"God, Amelia, you're beautiful," he murmured against her lips. As his fingers skillfully fed the fire inside her she closed her eyes, moving with him, urging him deeper, adopting the rhythm of his masterful strokes.

"Please," she mouthed, scarcely able to breathe, let alone speak. "Please, Patrick..."

"Always so polite," he murmured, leaving her for an instant and then returning to her, rising fully onto her, nudging her legs apart with his knees. She felt him straining against her, so close to satisfying them both...and then he wedged his hands beneath her hips and raised her to meet his conquering thrust.

For an instant the world seemed to stop. Patrick held himself motionless deep within her, his eyes shut and his body rigid as he struggled for control. Eventually he let out a groan and relaxed his hands on her. As the universe once again stirred to life around her, she heard the muffled patter of the rain against her windows, the thudding of her heartbeat, the slow broken rasp of his breath as he withdrew and thrust again. Before she could accustom herself to his tempo, he ground his hips in a circle, igniting an unexpected flare of sparkling sensation inside her. He did it again, and she jammed her fist to her mouth to stifle her ecstatic cry.

He pulled her hand from her lips and kissed her knuckles. "Let me hear you," he demanded, surging inside her.

"Yes." It was half a sigh, half a sob. She closed her eyes again and cradled his head against her, moaning her pleasure, too enraptured to worry about being loud or conspicuous or unladylike. She loved him with her voice as he loved her with his body, compelling her beyond anything Mary had every described, beyond anything Amelia had ever dared to imagine—beyond feelings she hadn't dared to imagine. She felt freer than she'd ever felt before, liberated from herself, from the boundaries of her past. She was someone entirely new, awed but unafraid of the heat and pressure building inside her, the sensations expanding beyond her ability to contain them. She loved Patrick, loved him completely, and as she surrendered her soul to him her body followed, erupting in a stunning cascade of pulses, her existence reduced to trust and energy and passion pounding at the core of her like the heartbeat of love itself.

After a long while the throbbing faded. Slowly, gradually, she became conscious of her surroundings, the weight of Patrick upon her, his lips browsing wearily along her hairline. She became conscious of the tears beading along her lashes, and then of the hushed sound of her ragged breathing and his as he cuddled her protectively to himself.

When at last she grew still, he loosened his hold enough to peer down at her. His face registered concern. "Was that the first time?" he asked, gliding his hand consolingly over her cheek and into her hair.

"No." Her voice emerged brokenly, and she looked away. "I told you I wasn't a virgin."

"That's not what I meant."

Bravely turning back to him, she saw love in his eyes, love and profound caring—and an unspoken reminder of her request, earlier that day, that they be honest with each other. "Yes," she admitted. "It was the first time."

He smiled tentatively. "I don't know whether I should be thrilled or sorry." He brushed her temple with his lips again, then settled beside her on the bed, wrapping his arms around her and guiding her head next to his on the pillow. "I'm thrilled that I'm the one who did it, but I'm sorry you went so many years without."

"Don't be sorry," she said, addressing his chest. She wanted the honesty to continue, but it was easier to speak candidly when she didn't have to confront those omniscient eyes of his. "I'm the modest one, Patrick. I'm not supposed to get carried away. That's Mary's—"

He touched his fingers to her mouth to silence her. "Don't say it, Amelia. Don't even think it."

She laughed, feeling twenty-eight years of conditioning slip away. "It's too late, Patrick. I *can* say it and think it, because we've just proven it all wrong. *You've* proven it wrong," she amended.

"No, Amelia. *You* have."

She traced an abstract pattern through the swirls of hair on his chest. He sighed, flattening his hand over hers and molding her fingers to the curve of his ribs. She understood the gesture as a tacit request, and it caused her a twinge of remorse. "You did it all, Patrick. I hardly did any of it. I'm not very experienced, as you probably guessed, and I'm not creative. I hardly even touched you...."

His chest vibrated beneath her fingertips as he laughed. "You touched me in all the right ways," he assured her.

"I could have done better," she said contritely.

He tilted her face up to his so she could see his contented expression for herself. "If you insist, I'll be happy to give you all the practice you need. But right now you're probably a little sore." He pressed his

hand gently between her legs and her body clenched,
then relented. Despite the luscious echo of his lovemaking brought on by his light caress, she did feel a bit
sore. "How about a bath?" he suggested.

She smiled crookedly. "You'll do anything to get me
wet, won't you?"

"Just about," he confirmed, swinging off the bed
and heading for the bathroom.

She remained in bed for a few minutes, listening to
him as he moved around in the bathroom. She ought
to help him—but he'd told her to stop worrying about
"ought to." So, feeling utterly decadent, she lay lan-
guidly atop the rumpled blanket, cushioning her head
with the plush down pillows and trying to come to
terms with what had just happened to her: not simply
Patrick's spectacular lovemaking but her rapturous
response, her discovery that she didn't have to be so
sane and sensible and well behaved, that sometimes it
was thrilling to go to extremes.

He appeared in the doorway, casually displaying his
lean, beautifully proportioned body. She noticed the
tan line above his hips, the well-shaped muscles of his
upper arms and thighs, the firm length of his torso. He
looked just as glorious now as when he'd been
aroused. Recalling the marvels his body had performed caused yet another faint spasm inside her.

She was almost embarrassed to be so attuned to
him, so overwhelmingly turned on by him. As recently as a week ago, she would have been mortified.
But not anymore. Modesty was fine under certain circumstances—but these were clearly not those circumstances.

"Her highness's bath awaits," he said, waving her
over.

She stood, feeling strangely light-headed and jelly-kneed, and walked across the room to him, aware that he was gazing at her naked body with the same intense appreciation with which she'd scrutinized his. When she reached his side he closed his hand around hers, kissed her brow and led her into the small steamy bathroom. He chivalrously helped her into the tub, then climbed in behind her, arranging his legs on either side of her and offering his chest as a backrest.

She leaned back into him, and he curled his arms around her waist. "You have nice feet," she observed. They happened to be one of the few parts of him visible to her.

"I have ugly feet," he refuted her good-naturedly. "They're strictly funtional." He nuzzled her hair with his lips, then relaxed against the sloping porcelain wall of the tub. "Feeling better?"

"Patrick, I have never felt better in my life."

He flexed his fingers gently against the feminine curve of her stomach. She watched the ripples the movement of his hands made in the warm soothing water. What might have been arousing on the bed was supremely tranquilizing in the tub. "Your feet are small," he noted, peeking over her shoulder. "What size shoe do you wear?"

"Six and a half."

"Mary really crowded you, didn't she?"

"In the womb, you mean?" Amelia chuckled. "She wears a size eight shoe, if that's any indication."

He kissed her hair again. "Why did your family force you into such absurd roles?" he asked.

She nestled against him and sighed. Jokes about her shoe size were no longer appropriate; Patrick had become serious. "They didn't force us into anything," she said in defense of her parents. "You talk about it as if it were some sort of malicious plot on the part of my family. It wasn't."

"Then what happened? You don't really believe this was all decided in the womb, do you?"

"Maybe it was." She considered the notion for a minute, whisking through a lifetime of memories— memories of how her role and Mary's had been shaped. "According to my mother, Mary was bigger and hungrier and more active as a baby," she informed Patrick. "She was colicky and high-strung. I was much less demanding."

"So she got all the attention."

"She needed it. It wasn't my parents' choice any more than hers. She needed the attention then—and now. I guess she's had it so long she's used to it."

"Only now, she does have a choice," Patrick remarked.

Amelia analyzed his tone and found no condemnation in it. She twisted sideways within the cozy enclosure of his legs, resting her cheek against his damp chest. "You can't really blame Mary for wanting attention all the time. People can't overcome their backgrounds that easily."

He ran his hand up her back to the nape of her neck and angled her head so that he could see her face. "Isn't that what you've just done?" he asked.

His smile was as warm and soothing as the bathwater. She let it wash over her, then lowered her head back to his chest. "If I have, I assure you it hasn't been easy."

"You're a lot stronger than you know," he said. "That's one of the things I sensed in you, right from the start. You're strong enough to overcome anything if you try.''

She was moved by the enormous faith he had in her—not necessarily convinced, but incredibly moved. ''Do you have any sisters or brothers?'' she asked, beginning to grow uncomfortable as the sole focus of their conversation. She might be capable of overcoming her modesty to some extent, but she couldn't imagine seeking the spotlight on a regular basis, as Mary did. Too much attention, and she began to fidget and look for a place to hide—or a way to change the subject.

''I've got an older sister,'' said Patrick.

''Since you're flamboyant, I take it she's quiet and well behaved.''

''No. We don't have specific roles like you and Mary.''

''I bet you do,'' Amelia argued gently. The way her family had evolved seemed so obvious, so inexorable, she couldn't believe that other families didn't evolve similarly.

Patrick twirled his fingers through her hair while he collected his thoughts. ''Terry is seven years older than me,'' he told her. ''When I was born, I guess she thought at first that I was an interesting toy. Then, when she saw the way everybody was always fussing over me, she grew to resent me. Eventually she learned to ignore me.'' He chuckled in reminiscence. ''I reckon we were pretty rotten to each other. She pretended I didn't exist, and I spied on her when she was necking with boys on the living-room couch. I think the happiest moment in both our lives was the day she left for college.''

"What about your parents?" Amelia asked. "Didn't they try to bring you together?"

"They both worked," he reminded her. "By the time I was five, my mother was back at the mills, working full-time with my father. Poor Terry got stuck baby-sitting me. Some of her most heated fights with my mother were over how much money she deserved to be paid for keeping an eye on me. Not that she did keep an eye on me, of course. She'd sit around reading her fan magazines, and I'd get into mischief."

"That I can believe," Amelia said with a smile. She found it quite easy to picture a young towheaded Patrick gleefully disturbing the status quo all over North Carolina while his sister hid in her bedroom. "Are you any closer with your sister now that you're both adults?"

Patrick shrugged, the motion causing the water to lap against the sides of the tub in gentle waves. "I wouldn't call us close," he allowed. "We get along these days. We don't fight much. We've got a lot in common actually. She's a lawyer, too, a public defender down in Atlanta. She married a nice guy a couple of years ago."

"Do they have any children?"

His chin nudged her hair as he shook his head. "No desire for any. She must have had her fill of children when she was stuck taking care of me. I guess," he added, his tone laced with humor, "she discovered she wasn't too good at it. Look at how I turned out."

"You turned out magnificently," Amelia assured him. She contemplated the childhood he'd described, so very different from her own. Not only because his mother worked outside the home—years before that was fashionable—but because, from the sound of it, he and his sister truly didn't have to squeeze themselves into assigned roles. "Maybe if your parents had been around more, you would have developed the way Mary and I did."

"I doubt it," Patrick countered. "I would have rebelled. If Terry had so much as tried to claim the sexual-pleasure role for herself, I would have had her summarily shot."

Although she knew he was only kidding, Amelia bridled. It wasn't as if Mary had deliberately set out to deprive her of the ability to enjoy sex before now. "I love Mary," she said. "Please don't say anything bad about her."

"I didn't mean to. I like her fine, myself." He bent to kiss the crown of Amelia's head. "I just can't understand how come she got dibs on all the fun. It doesn't seem fair."

Amelia lapsed into thought, breathing in the clean fragrance of Patrick's skin and relishing the wiry texture of his chest hair against her back. "It must have been obvious to you that Mary was the... more fun sister," she said carefully. "Why didn't you pick her, Patrick? Why did you come after me instead of her?"

"I've tried to tell you, Amelia. I didn't *pick* you," he corrected. "I've known Mary for some time, and sure, she's a lot of fun. She's also offered me a fascinating professional opportunity. I like Mary." He closed his arm snugly around her shoulders. "But the minute I saw you, I thought: Wow! I want that woman!"

She laughed again, a bewildered, dubious laugh. She simply couldn't believe that anyone would ever look at her and think *wow*. "I bet what you really thought was that I'd offer you a table to overturn."

He considered her mild accusation, winding his fingers through her hair, shifting his leg along her hip. "Sure, that was part of it. You were a challenge—and you still are."

"How am I still a challenge?"

"You're as opinionated and stubborn as I am," Patrick pointed out. "That's saying a lot. And you're almost as intelligent as I am."

"Almost?" She gave him a playful poke in the ribs with her elbow.

He grunted at the jab, then laughed and tightened his arms around her. "See? If I said that to Mary, she'd probably giggle and say, 'Oh, I'm just a fruitcake. Amelia's the intelligent one.' You, however, have the spirit to argue. And I love a good argument, Amelia. Especially if I can have it with you."

She smiled and, leaning sideways, brushed her lips over one of his wet knees. His affectionate words fed her love for him and her desire, filling her with a heavy, visceral longing. He shifted behind her again, and his condition informed her that the longing was mutual.

"How are you feeling?" he asked, his lips close to her ear, his breath feathering across her neck and feeding her arousal.

"A lot warmer than the bathwater."

She couldn't see his smile, but she could imagine it. He released the stopper with one of his spectacularly functional feet, then climbed out of the tub and helped Amelia out. "Let's go overturn another table," he murmured, wasting little time toweling her off before he hurried her back to bed.

SOMETIME AFTER MIDNIGHT the rain finally stopped. Amelia was asleep, but Patrick had been drifting in and out of a shallow slumber, and the sudden silence outside the window startled him awake.

He lay motionless beside her, waiting until his vision adjusted to the dark. Once it did, he indulged in a leisurely perusal of her: her small, lovely, magnificently ravished body half-hidden beneath the lightweight blanket, her black hair splayed across the pillow, her lips parted, unconsciously shaping a kiss. Desire fluxed through his body, and he considered waking her up, but he thought better of it. Throwing back the blanket, he got out of bed and walked to the window. The screen was mottled with rainwater, and beyond it the world was gloomy and sodden. "Thanks for the rain," he whispered heavenward. It was definitely worth the sacrifice of a silk tie and the dry-cleaning costs of his suit to have been forced by the weather back to Amelia's house. He hadn't really wanted to discuss her professional dilemma that afternoon, anyway.

They'd discussed it that evening. After making love a second time, they'd reluctantly abandoned the bedroom for the kitchen, where their dinner dishes lay caked with dried egg. They'd wound up leaving the dishes in the sink to soak overnight, then returned to the bedroom to talk.

She was serious about wanting to leave the Hibbing School, for which he couldn't blame her. She was equally serious about wanting to work at a place like Keppler's, and while that might have surprised anyone else, it didn't surprise Patrick. He had always believed that instinct was more powerful, and often more trustworthy, than logic. If Amelia's instincts told her she wanted to work at a resort hotel in the mountains, he saw nothing wrong with that.

In fact, he saw plenty right with it. Rae Keppler needed an heir of sorts, someone she could rely on to learn the business and keep it running as her father-in-law and husband had meant it to run. She'd met Amelia only once, but her first impression had been positive. Amelia had the smarts, the levelheadedness and the dedication it would take to enable Keppler's to survive and flourish. Patrick didn't doubt for a minute that she'd do well there.

And, of course, if she worked at Keppler's she'd be near Wisherville. She could live closer to the sister she adored—and closer to Patrick, close enough that their meetings wouldn't always have to be planned, that they could be spontaneous and easy—and not just on weekends. He could meet her for lunch at the resort, or for a drink after work on a Tuesday night, if they chose. They could argue whenever they felt like it, debate principles and critique erotic art, and love each other, not just physically, but emotionally, constantly. They could be a couple, truly together.

Resting against the windowsill, he gazed across the shadowed room, his eyes loving what his hands and lips and entire body had already loved so exhaustively all evening. As petite as Amelia was, she struck him as voluptuous in sleep, as she had in love. He felt like a dauntless explorer, the discoverer of thrilling new territory, wild and beautiful—and his. He found it; it was his to claim.

That was an egotistical view of things, and Amelia had already scolded him about the size of his ego. As egotistical as he was, he also happened to be a realist. He knew Amelia wasn't his, and she never would be.

She was free now, free to love him, but more important, free to be herself and to discover her own destiny. Patrick only hoped she would remember that he had helped her to untie the bonds. And, in celebrating her wonderful new freedom, he hoped she wouldn't leave him behind.

Chapter Eight

Patrick entered his office humming on Monday morning. The exhilarating aftermath of his weekend with Amelia had mellowed into a sweet warmth that he hoped would be enough to satisfy him until he could be with her again.

They'd spent most of Saturday at her office at the Hibbing School, where he had helped her to finish collating the mailings. Due to the fact that he was a male who didn't happen to be a member of the faculty or somebody's father, he'd received an inordinate amount of attention from the girls on campus. He'd been surprised at how busy the dean's office was on a weekend—although Amelia had explained to him that things tended to be abnormally frenetic during the last two weeks of the term. Students had darted in and out of the office all day, choosing Amelia as the target of their whining once they learned that Dean Blanchard wasn't in. While Amelia had attended to their various needs with impressive calm and efficiency, the adolescent girls had ogled Patrick, nudged each other and tittered. One outspoken young student had asked Amelia if Patrick was her boyfriend, and Amelia had blushed several shades of pink.

"Yeah," he'd answered for her, "I'm her boyfriend."

He liked the way that sounded. "I'm her boyfriend," he mouthed to himself as he swung into the reception area and greeted his secretary with a cheerful wave. "Marilyn, could you get Rae Keppler on the phone for me?" he asked. It wasn't too soon to start sounding Rae out about the possibility of a position for Amelia at the hotel. A mere fourteen hours after having said goodbye to her, he was already impatient to find a way to get her to move to Wisherville.

Marilyn answered his request by shifting her eyes toward the right, drawing Patrick's attention to a woman waiting to see him. She had on a demure brown suit, a peach-colored blouse and leather pumps, and she was sitting so quietly on the couch, partly hidden by the overgrown rubber plant on the end table, that he couldn't be blamed for not having immediately noticed her.

"Mary?" he asked, astonished by her conservative attire and her unobtrusive bearing.

Mary Potts smiled meekly and rose to her feet. "Can you spare me a couple of minutes, Patrick?"

"Of course." He turned back to Marilyn. "I'll talk to Rae later. Hold my calls," he instructed his secretary before opening his office door and ushering Mary inside.

His private office, like the reception area, was furnished haphazardly. His desk was huge and tolerably neat, but the swivel chair he used squeaked whenever he shifted in it. The chairs for clients showed signs of wear, and the shelves lining the walls were constructed of industrial steel. He hadn't wanted to waste a lot of money decorating the place; the clients he served weren't the sort to care one way or the other about the decor of their attorney's office.

As soon as Mary was settled, he strode to his swivel chair and sat. They regarded each other across the wide desk, Mary smiling and Patrick curious about the reason for her visit—to say nothing of her uncharacteristic outfit. A vague uneasiness gnawed at him. For all he knew, Amelia might have told Mary all about their blossoming love affair. Mary might resent the idea of her attorney sleeping with her sister. But, even if that was the case, Patrick had nothing to hide, nothing to be ashamed of. Still, he'd rather not discuss the relationship until he felt more secure about it.

"What's up?" he asked, deceptively casual.

Mary's smile lost some of its voltage. Patrick realized that she was just as uneasy as he was. "Did you have a good weekend?" she asked.

"Yes," he said noncommittally. "How about you?"

"Yes."

"How's Blond Bart?" Although he maintained an indifferent tone, he was growing tenser by the second. What if Mary and Bartholomew Driscoll had spent the entire weekend plotting Bartholomew's wedding to Amelia? What if they suspected that Patrick had become involved with Amelia, and Bartholomew was at this very minute buying a shotgun with which to come after Patrick? What if—

"He's fine. We had a—a very nice time," Mary stammered, lowering her eyes for a moment and working through her thoughts. When she lifted her gaze again, her smile was bright in a way that struck Patrick as artificial. "Patrick, I think we ought to forget about suing Wisherville."

Was that all? Was that why she was fidgeting and faltering, refusing to look directly at him? Patrick permitted himself a moment of glorious relief that Mary hadn't come here to chew him out for spending the weekend with her sister.

Then her announcement registered fully on him, and his relief was replaced by a healthy surge of outrage. "What do you mean, you want to forget about suing Wisherville? I filed the papers Friday morning, Mary."

"Can you un-file them?" she asked, her expression partly coy, partly pleading.

"Why the hell should I?" he shot back. "Why would you want me to? Dunphy and the police department deprived you of your rights. They tried to deny you your constitutionally protected freedoms. And then they added insult to injury by arresting you when you attempted to defend those rights and freedoms. We can't back down now."

"Well, they did drop the charges against me," Mary pointed out.

"I thought we already established that this isn't a quid-pro-quo situation. The charges were dropped because the town realized how wrong it was to arrest you. The fact that they've all but admitted they were wrong gives us that much more ammunition for our case against them."

"I know, but—" Mary pressed her hands together and beamed another pleading smile at him "—if they've admitted they're wrong, why should we harass them?"

"Harass them?" Patrick erupted. "Mary, for God's sake, there are principles at stake here. You've become a symbol to artists everywhere! A municipality condemns your art for no good reason, and then compounds its crime by refusing to protect you and your property from a violent gang of rock-wielding thugs! If you withdrew the suit now, it would be like giving the green light to hundreds of other narrow-minded towns across the country. It would be like saying, 'Go ahead, censor your artists and deliver them to lynch mobs. It's okay, nobody's going to prosecute you for it.'"

"Patrick, I know there are principles at stake, but..." Mary sighed and squeezed her hands more tightly together. "As you just said, there'll be other cases. You can take one of them to the Supreme Court if you like, can't you?"

Leaning back and cringing at the plaintive squeak of his chair hinges, he assessed Mary thoughtfully. It wasn't like her to undergo such a drastic change of heart. She had always loved a good battle, and from the start she'd been enthusiastic about his decision to take on Wisherville in her name. Why was she suddenly defecting from the cause?

Why, for that matter, was she wearing a senator's-wife suit instead of something typically outlandish? "Is this Bartholomew's idea?" Patrick asked suspiciously. "Did he change your mind for you?"

"Of course not," she said too quickly.

Damn. That tweedy blond Brahmin had turned Mary against her own ethics. Bartholomew had had the entire weekend alone with her; somehow he'd succeeded in persuading her to abandon the cause. "What did he do?" Patrick asked, struggling to keep his irritation in check. If he wanted to win Mary back to his side, he couldn't run the risk of insulting her. "How did Bartholomew convince you that your constitutional rights weren't worth fighting for? How did he talk you into discarding your principles?''

"Really, Patrick, you can't blame him. It has nothing to do with principles,'' she swore, her eyes flickering to the window, to the faded carpet, to the pen stand on his desk, to the steel shelves behind him—everywhere but to Patrick.

"It has everything to do with principles, damn it,'' he asserted angrily. "Right from the start, Mary, that's what this case has been about.''

"I thought it was about getting the town to pay for my broken front window, and maybe pulling in a few high bids on my sculpture.''

"The auction of the sculpture is just a sidelight, Mary,'' he explained, his patience stretched to the breaking point. "As far as getting Wisherville to pay for the window, that's also a matter of principle. It's the town's fault the damned window got broken in the first place.''

"You don't have to curse so much,'' Mary chided him.

Patrick's hands fisted in his lap. What the hell had gotten into her? He took a deep breath to regain control. "As I recall, last Friday you were gung ho to fight this case. Then Bartholomew swung up here for the weekend, and now, lo and behold, you're ready to wave the white flag all of a sudden. Something must have happened over the weekend, Mary, and as your attorney I have a right to know what it is.''

Mary's gaze circled the room again. "What happened was, Bartholomew was good enough to remind me that fighting my case could bring a lot of unwanted publicity down on my family. That isn't fair. My family hates publicity.''

"Your family." After the job Mom and Dad Potts had done on Amelia's self-esteem, Patrick wasn't particularly interested in protecting them from publicity—or anything else. "The hell with your family," he snapped. "They're *your* civil rights."

"My parents would rather I keep things quiet," she mumbled.

"And when has that ever stopped you from doing what you wanted to do?" He scrutinized her, looking for chinks in her argument. "What happened? Did they threaten to stop supplementing your earnings from the gallery?"

"Patrick." She gave him a scathing look, then said, "It has nothing to do with money."

"What is it with your parents, anyway? Is it a power game with them? They'd sell their souls to keep their precious daughters in line?"

"Patrick! These are my parents you're talking about! Where do you get off saying such awful things about them?"

Patrick jammed his lips together to keep from telling her exactly where he got off saying such awful things: from learning firsthand what Mary's wonderful, above-reproach parents had done to Amelia, making her believe that she had to be quiet and courteous and self-contained to win their approval. Whether out of malice or simple thoughtlessness, the senior Pottses seemed to have made a career out of restraining their daughters' instincts.

His silence gave Mary courage. "Bartholomew is not my parents' puppet," she said, her voice rising in pitch and her cheeks flushing with indignation. "He is not their mouthpiece. All he did was remind me that they have feelings, too, and that, as their daughter, it wouldn't be a crime for me to respect their feelings.''

"Right," Patrick scoffed. "How come you didn't feel so obligated to respect their feelings last week? You've already been on television and in the newspapers, waving your fist in the air and shouting about the Bill of Rights. You've already embarrassed them. Now it's time to rush the goal line, to make whatever embarrassment that might have cost them pay off. We've gone too far to quit, Mary."

"It's always possible to quit," she retorted, then subsided in her chair. "Not that I feel we'd be quitting if we withdrew the suit," she added, giving him an ameliorating smile. "We got the charges against me dropped. We made our point, Patrick. We won."

"What about defending the Constitution?" he muttered. "What about Martin Luther King and the American Revolution?"

She giggled nervously. "I know it's a noble cause, Patrick, but don't push it, okay? Find another test case. I want to keep a low profile from here on."

"Why?" He was less accusing than merely bewildered. It would be the ultimate irony if Amelia finally broke loose, only to have her rowdy twin sister abruptly turn mousy and meek.

"I just want to," she insisted vaguely. "I'm entitled to change my mind. I'm the crazy one, right?"

He groaned. If she wanted to cling to her role, the least she could do was put her craziness to a worthwhile purpose. "Okay, Mary," he said, forcing himself to remain calm and reasonable. "All I'm saying is, don't rush into a decision you're going to regret. Give yourself a little time to reconsider. This is quite an about-face you're proposing, and you owe it to yourself to think it through very carefully."

"I've already thought it through."

"Think it through some more," he urged her, then tossed her a placating smile. Inside he was simmering—not only because he thought her parents were trying to lay some sort of trip on her, but for the more selfish reason that he didn't want to drop her case. Years of work and training and a lifelong commitment to civil liberties had led him to this legal battle, a suit through which he could further the cause of justice. Sure, there might be other cases in other venues, but Patrick couldn't count on the slim chance that he would have the opportunity to argue them. *Mary Potts v. the Town of Wisherville, et al* belonged to him. He wasn't going to let it slip away, no matter how much Ma and Pa Potts and Bartholomew Driscoll had brainwashed her.

Mary let out a long sigh. He took heart in the fact that she seemed torn. "Patrick, what exactly is the status of my suit right now?"

"The papers are getting processed through the bureaucracy. There'll probably be a preliminary hearing in a few weeks."

"So if we do nothing, we've got a few weeks before the you-know-what hits the fan?"

"That's my best estimate."

"Okay." She stood, smoothing her prim skirt and straightening her blazer. "I'm going to be out of town for a few days. I promise that while I'm away I'll give some thought to what you've said."

Her failure to commit herself fully to the suit frustrated him, but he couldn't push her any harder on it right now, not without risking everything. "Where are you going?'' he asked, rising as well. ''Will I be able to reach you?''

She shook her head. ''I need some time to figure things out. If you get any more bids on the sculpture, you can leave word with Mina Josephs. She's going to be running the gallery while I'm gone.''

''I'll do that.'' He walked Mary to the door. ''Whatever you decide,'' he murmured, giving her what he hoped was his most winning smile, ''just remember, the future of the country is resting on your shoulders.''

''Thanks a heap.'' Her eyes flashed with grudging amusement. ''Take care, Patrick. I'll be in touch in a few days.''

He watched her stroll through the reception area and out the front door. As soon as it swung shut behind her, Patrick shifted his gaze to his secretary. ''What was that all about?'' Marilyn asked.

''Cold feet, I think,'' said Patrick, running his fingers through his hair and mentally reviewing his conversation with Mary. ''She's not sure she wants to follow through on her suit against the town.''

''But you intend to use your ample powers of persuasion to convince her otherwise,'' Marilyn guessed. ''Do you want me to try Rae Keppler for you now?''

Patrick shook his head. ''Later,'' he grunted, stepping back inside his office and closing the door. He needed to sort his thoughts first, to rework his strategy on Mary's case. That she might be retreating from the struggle was a serious problem, but he refused to let it defeat him. Fighting for one's rights was never easy—but if nobody did it, nobody would have any rights.

He hoped he hadn't scared her off for good with his show of fury. He felt a bit guilty about having blown up at her, but dammit, the issues at stake were too important to let her parents and Driscoll get in the way. If Mary kept her promise and gave the case all the thought it deserved, she would have to agree with Patrick. He prayed that she would.

Because he wasn't going to give up. He knew when something was worth fighting for—like Amelia's love or Mary's legal rights. He'd won one battle; his victory gave him the courage to keep fighting.

"I DON'T USUALLY make it my habit to read the Metropolitan News," Dean Blanchard said as she stalked into Amelia's office carrying an inside section of the *New York Times* beneath her arm. As usual she was dressed in one of her severe dresses, the long sleeves and high collar of which seemed a deliberate denial of the fact that summer was less than two weeks away. "The section," she continued, "carries too many stories about turnstile jumpers in the Bronx and bag ladies with hearts of gold."

She dropped the newspaper onto Amelia's desk, scattering the pile of below-average grade reports Amelia had just finished arranging in alphabetical order. Amelia bit her lip to keep from screaming at the destruction of her morning's major accomplishment.

At least a dozen times in the past three days she'd been tempted to hand in her resignation at the Hibbing School. She was eager to relocate to Keppler's and start her new life as a brave adventurous woman open to new experiences. But when she'd discussed her prospects with Patrick on the phone the past few evenings, he'd suggested that she hang on at Hibbing a little while longer. "I've mentioned your interest to Rae and she's receptive," he had assured Amelia. "Maybe you could come to Wisherville this weekend, and I'll get you and Rae together for a talk."

"I can't this weekend," Amelia had explained. "Next week is finals, and the week after that is commencement. I'm so buried in work here, Patrick."

"Then maybe you ought to sit tight till the end of the school term," he'd advised. "There's no real rush with Rae—she's survived without an apprentice for years. Wait until things are calmer at your end, and then— Hey, does this mean I can't see you this weekend?" he'd asked abruptly, as the full implication of her statement sank in.

"You could come here."

"I can't. You think you're the only one snowed under at work?" He had sighed. "Things are crazy here, too, Amelia. Maybe I could make a day trip on Sunday. Let's see how it plays out." He'd sighed again. "I miss you."

"I miss you, too," Amelia had murmured, surprised by her newly burgeoning romantic streak. She had never before told a man she missed him, not even Bartholomew. But then, she *hadn't* missed Bartholomew, not with her body and her heart and her mind, not in such a way that it hurt and paradoxically felt good at the same time. Not to such an extent that it simultaneously sapped and motivated her, that she felt dreadfully lonely yet secure in the knowledge that she wasn't truly alone.

Now, peering up at her unsmiling boss, she felt her newfound strength gathering inside her. "Is there something in this newspaper I ought to know about?" she asked Dean Blanchard in a carefully modulated voice. She didn't want the dean to realize that her formerly staid, compliant underling had transformed into a mooning, lovesick flake, one who could easily blow her top over her boss's cavalier attitude toward the alphabetizing chore she'd just completed.

"I think so." Dean Blanchard pointed at an article with the headline: Small Town, Big Issue: Freedom of Expression Debated in Catskill Village.

Amelia's teeth closed around her lower lip again. She skimmed the article, which offered a reasonably accurate depiction of Mary's recent escapade in Wisherville. Mary was quoted as describing her sculpture as the ultimate expression of human love, just as she'd been describing it from the start. The grand oratory about the Bill of Rights was reserved for Patrick, who referred to the Constitution four times in explaining why he was pursuing Mary's case against the town of Wisherville even though he'd already persuaded the town to drop all charges against her. Far from being vexed by his impassioned defense of Mary's legal rights, as she might have been a week ago, Amelia found his statements inspiring.

"I am shocked," Dean Blanchard declared piously, "to think that an alumna of the Hibbing School could be embroiled in such notoriety."

Amelia unflinchingly returned Dean Blanchard's stony stare. "I should think you'd be honored to know that a Hibbing alumna is willing to fight for everything this country stands for," she shot back.

Dean Blanchard eyed Amelia with a quizzical frown. "The lawyer mentioned in the article, Patrick Levine. Isn't he that strange-looking fellow who tried to assault you last Friday?"

"He didn't try to assault me," Amelia retorted, still striving to keep her voice level. "He's a friend of mine."

"A boyfriend, as I understand it." Dean Blanchard crossed her arms over her chest and glowered at Amelia.

She wondered who the dean's source might be on that information. Not that it mattered—Amelia had nothing to hide regarding her relationship with Patrick. "As a matter of fact, Mavis, yes, he is my boyfriend."

"That fellow has scandalously long hair. And he was wearing an earring," the dean chastised her.

"So he was." Knowing that she wasn't going to remain at this job much longer gave Amelia the freedom to speak without fear. No—her fearlessness wasn't a result of her plans to quit her job; it was a result of having gotten to know Patrick, having learned from him that it was acceptable not to be a goody-two-shoes, that it was all right to let one's feelings out. "Having the freedom to wear his hair the way he wants it—and wear an earring, too—is also what this country is all about."

"The histrionics are unnecessary," Dean Blanchard continued, apparently unnerved by Amelia's nonchalance. "Let us focus on the most salient issues here. I understand that this *boyfriend* of yours—" she clearly had difficulty using the word "—was here at the office on Saturday, fiddling with our mailings."

"He wasn't fiddling with them," Amelia assured her boss. "He was helping me to collate them."

"He was flirting with the students."

"No, Mavis. He was flirting with me."

Stunned by Amelia's flippant attitude, Dean Blanchard floundered for a moment. "What in heaven's name has gotten into you, Amelia?"

"Love," Amelia answered blithely. "Love and liberty. If you'll excuse me, Mavis, it would appear that I've got to sort these report cards again." She handed the newspaper back to the dean.

"What are you going to do about your sister?" Dean Blanchard inquired.

"Nothing."

"Amelia, your apathy is most inappropriate. Here in the dean's office we need to set an example for the students. They must learn that certain behavior is objectionable—and that includes inviting one's boyfriend to barge in at will, and encouraging one's sister to stir up trouble in the newspapers—"

"What, exactly, are you saying?" Amelia rose to her feet. Given that she was at least four inches shorter than Dean Blanchard, the effectiveness of her position was limited, but Amelia threw back her shoulders and faced her superior squarely. "Are you dissatisfied with the way I'm doing my job?"

"Well..." Obviously the dean hadn't expected the question. She took a minute to collect her thoughts and then said sternly, "In a sense, yes. The past several days you haven't been yourself, Amelia, and—"

"The past several days I *have* been myself. If you don't like it, Mavis—"

"I don't like it."

"—then I quit." Her announcement was premature; she had arranged nothing concrete with Rae Keppler yet. But Amelia didn't care. The words had arisen from her heart. She didn't want to be at the Hibbing School anymore, suppressing her emotions and behaving decorously. She wanted to do the unexpected.

Evidently she'd succeeded on that score. "Let's not be hasty," Dean Blanchard cautioned her, reflexively blocking the door with her body.

"I want to be hasty," Amelia declared, then tossed back her head and laughed at the sheer joy her recklessness brought her. "I don't want to be predictable. I don't want to be well behaved. I don't want to set an example for anyone. I just want to leave." With that, she grabbed her purse from a side drawer of her desk and slipped past the formidable obstacle her boss presented. Romping through the outer office, Amelia waved a farewell to the secretaries, then swept past the anxious students crowded around the opposite side of the counter and headed out the door.

She had never felt so free in her life. Making love with Patrick had been the most liberating thing she'd ever done, but this ran a very close second. She wanted to dance, to sing, to pull off her shoes and stockings and sprint barefoot across the lawn of the quadrangle. As soon as she passed through the main entrance to the administration building, she dropped onto one of the steps, plucked off her shoes, then discreetly slid down her panty hose and stuffed the wad of nylon into her purse. With a girlish laugh, she leapt down the stairs and into the grass.

She should have been mortified by the puzzled stares she attracted from the students on the lawn, hurrying frantically in and out of the classroom buildings and juggling stacks of textbooks and notebooks, but she wasn't. She didn't want their attention, but she didn't mind it, either. All that mattered was that for the first time in her modest existence she was free, truly free.

Passing one of the dorms, she heard music blasting through an open window—Michael Jackson wailing that he was bad, so bad. Amelia sang along.

She was still humming the catchy tune as she sauntered down the sidewalk to her house, the unprotected soles of her feet becoming encrusted with tiny concrete pebbles. Exuberantly oblivious of her surroundings, she didn't immediately notice the beige Mercedes with the New York State plates parked in front of her house. But as she neared the front walk, she spotted the car—just seconds before her mother tripped daintily down the front steps and called out, "Amelia! Thank heavens you're here. You've got to do something about your sister!"

"I don't have to do anything," Amelia retorted under her breath. Yet she was sobered by the sudden presence of her mother in New Milford, looking characteristically refined in a blue silk dress and a string of pearls, her dark hair pinned into an elegant knot at the nape of her neck and her feet shod in spectator pumps. Amelia slowed her pace to a halt. She traced her mother's astonished gaze to the shoes she was carrying, and then to her naked legs.

"What are you doing here?" Amelia asked, suddenly feeling sheepish and more than a little foolish about her outburst on campus.

"Mary has vanished," her mother announced. "Why are you barefoot?"

Amelia thought it odd that, with Mary missing, her mother should care one way or the other about the condition of Amelia's feet. She didn't comment on it, though. The news of Mary's disappearance was too horrifying. "What do you mean, she's vanished?"

"Come inside and pack some things," her mother ordered her. "I just got here a few minutes ago. Since you weren't home I was about to go and look for you on the campus. But now you're here, so we can get going."

Amelia's heart began to pound faster as fear about Mary's fate overtook her. "Get going where?"

"You're coming home with me. We need you in New York."

"Wait a minute." She sank onto the front step and shook her head, trying to unscramble her thoughts. "How do you know Mary's missing?"

"No one has answered the phone at her house since Monday. She's left the gallery in the hands of a woman I've never heard of before, some neighbor of hers named Mina Josephs who swears she has no idea where Mary went. Your father spoke to a man named Patrick Levine whose name was mentioned in an utterly dreadful article concerning Mary in the *Times*, but he claimed to know nothing of her whereabouts. He also claimed he was representing Mary in a civil suit against Wisherville. It's all in that article. I'm beside myself, Amelia. Mary has always been a fruitcake, but vanishing into thin air like this...well, she's gone too far." Amelia's mother tugged a scented linen handkerchief from her purse and dabbed at the perspiration forming on her forehead.

"Have you talked to Bartholomew?" Amelia asked, her alarm fading. If Mary had arranged for someone to run the gallery in her absence, then her disappearance was obviously intentional, not the result of a kidnapping or an accident. Whatever she was up to, Mary probably wasn't in any danger.

"Bartholomew is in Washington, D.C. on business. We couldn't reach him."

"How about the police?"

"Don't be silly, Amelia. The last thing we need is more publicity. The situation is too humiliating as it is."

Amelia mulled over the possibilities. If Mary had been gone since Monday, she could be anywhere. She had friends and professional contacts all over the country, to say nothing of that colleague of hers who'd moved to Patagonia a year ago. Perhaps Amelia could figure out where her sister was if she could figure out *why* her sister had left Wisherville. But the only answer she could come up with to that question was that Mary had left because it was unexpected, and she loved doing the unexpected.

"Our prime suspect is that lawyer, Patrick Levine," her mother went on.

"Prime suspect? Do you think he abducted her?" Amelia laughed at the absurdity of the idea.

"Not abducted her but contributed somehow to her disappearance. He's obviously a master at manipulating the media and gaining publicity for his clients. That appalling article proves it. Maybe he thinks this will get more publicity for her."

"That doesn't make any sense," Amelia debated. "Patrick's only interest is in seeing that justice is served."

"I take it you're acquainted with this Mr. Levine?"

Amelia lifted her eyes to her mother and smiled hesitantly. Now certainly wasn't the proper time to tell her family that she was in love with Patrick. "I met him when I went to Wisherville a couple of weeks ago," she admitted. "He's very smart, and extremely committed to his ideals. I'm certain he didn't have anything to do with Mary's disappearance."

"I'm not certain of anything. Bartholomew assured us that the entire matter had been settled, and now there's this article claiming that the fight has only begun—and that this other lawyer is representing Mary. And all of a sudden Mary's vanished."

Amelia looked away, gazing at the Mercedes parked behind her Saab. It didn't seem possible that she'd quit her job just minutes ago, that she'd been waltzing down the street chanting a rock-and-roll song and feeling ebullient and carefree. Too much was happening too fast. She was suddenly exhausted.

"Why did you drive all the way up here?" she asked her mother. "Why didn't you just telephone me?"

"The last time I telephoned you, you refused to go to Wisherville. I don't know what got into you, Amelia, but I couldn't run the risk of your refusing us again. Mary is your sister and she needs your help. Now, let's go inside and pack your things. We've got to get back to New York."

"There's nothing I can do in New York that I can't do here," Amelia pointed out. "Why don't you go to New York, Mom, and I'll go to Wisherville?" *And see Patrick,* she added silently. *And enlist his help.* She knew he would offer his assistance. He had to be as troubled by his star client's disappearance as the Potts family was.

Her mother looked at her askance. "Can I trust you to go to Wisherville?"

"Of course you can," Amelia answered, not as offended by her mother's doubt as she might have been.

It was perversely satisfying to know that she could keep her mother off balance, that she could shake off her role as the dependable one.

"Last time you refused," her mother recalled.

"Last time Mary wasn't missing."

Her mother sized her up with a long dubious stare. "Let's go upstairs and pack your bags," she finally said, apparently not willing to trust Amelia enough to let her pack on her own.

Sighing, Amelia preceded her mother up the stairs to her second-floor apartment. There would be time later to celebrate her unemployment and figure out her future. For now, she would do what was necessary to rescue her sister. She issued a silent prayer that this would be the last time she'd ever have to bail Mary out.

To her great annoyance, her mother shadowed her into her bedroom. "Mom, I'm an adult," she protested. "I know how to pack a suitcase."

"You'll have to pack for several days," her mother instructed her, as if she hadn't spoken. "I don't know how long this is going to take. And, of course, you'd better bring some nice dresses, in case we do have to go to the police."

If Patrick could represent a client at an arraignment wearing a slogan-embossed T-shirt and frayed jeans, surely Amelia could make a missing-person report without dressing to the nines. She refrained from sharing this observation with her mother, however. She needed to preserve her strength for the bigger battles she anticipated.

"I suppose you ought to call the dean and tell her you'll be missing work for the remainder of the week," her mother went on. "Is that going to be a problem?"

Amelia gave her mother an incredulous look. "Do you care?" she asked, her voice tinged with sarcasm. Every time her mother ever called upon her to rescue Mary, Amelia had always put her job and her life on hold, and her mother had never expressed any concern about it before. Why was she acting so solicitous about Amelia's career now, when for once it didn't matter?

"Of course I care. As a matter of fact, I'm wondering what you're doing home from work now. Are you on your lunch break?"

Amelia checked her watch: almost one o'clock. She didn't want to lie, but she couldn't tell her mother she'd just quit her job. That bombshell would have to be saved for a more tranquil time. "I'll go and call Dean Blanchard," she mumbled, choosing diplomacy over candor for the time being. With a parting glance at her mother, who was rummaging through the closet in search of dresses suitable for paying visits to police departments, Amelia headed down the hall to the kitchen.

Halfway there, she heard her telephone ring. She picked up speed, entertaining the hope that Patrick might be on the other end, and answered the phone with a breathless "Hello!"

"Melie!" Mary boomed. "What's going on? I just tried you at your office, and a secretary said you left in a huff. Are you okay?"

Amelia took a deep breath before responding. She was thrilled to hear Mary's voice, but until she had a clearer idea of what was going on she didn't want to attract her mother's attention. "Mary," she said in a muted voice, "where are you?"

"In Wisherville," Mary answered glibly. "Where do you think?"

"Mary, be honest with me." Amelia cupped her hand around the mouthpiece to insure that her mother wouldn't hear. "You've been missing for three days. You've got some stranger running your gallery, and—"

"Okay, okay," Mary cut her off with a sheepish laugh. "I'm not in Wisherville. Mina Josephs isn't a stranger. She's a neighbor of mine and she can use the part-time work."

"Where are you?" Amelia persisted.

"I . . . I'm at a rest stop on the New Jersey Turnpike, all right? I was thinking maybe I could come straight to New Milford."

"Here? What for?"

"To see you," Mary said simply.

If Mary wanted to see her, she could do so in Wisherville. Amelia had no need to be in New Milford, now that she was unemployed. And in Wisherville she could see Patrick. "Why don't you go home instead? I'll meet you there in a couple of hours."

"Okay. Let's do it that way." Mary spoke slowly, carefully. "We . . . we have some things to talk about."

"What things?"

"Things," Mary said. "We'll talk when I see you."

"If you want." She was puzzled by her sister's cryptic reply, but not too troubled by it. If Mary had something serious to discuss with her, a long-distance telephone call wasn't the best medium, particularly when their mother was within eavesdropping distance.

The truth was, Amelia had serious matters to discuss with Mary, too. She wanted to tell Mary about her having quit her job, about her interest in working with Rae Keppler, about her relationship with Patrick. Especially that.

"So, you should be happy about that, at least," Mary was saying.

Amelia struggled to catch her end of the conversation. "What should I be happy about?"

"The fact that I'm dropping the suit against Wisherville. I know it seems like a kind of gutless decision, but really, I've come to realize that you and Bartholomew were right all along. Principles are great in theory, but sometimes you've got to be practical. So we'll just call this the one that got away, right? Some things are more important than the Bill of Rights."

Amelia didn't think her brain could accommodate any more confusion. She herself had read the article in the *Times* in which Patrick had expounded on the legal battle he was planning to wage against the town on Mary's behalf. It had been published that very morning. What Mary was saying now made no sense.

"What?" she challenged. "What's more important than the Bill of Rights?"

Mary didn't answer immediately. When she did, she sounded as puzzled as Amelia felt. "Lots of things, Melie. Discretion, for instance. Respect for Mom and Dad."

"You can respect them and still disagree with them," Amelia argued. Principles were as important as respect for one's parents. Patrick had helped her to recognize that—and she'd assumed that Mary was of the same opinion.

"Melie, let's not talk about this now, okay? I've made my mind up. I'm dropping the suit."

"Does Patrick know about this?" Amelia asked.

"Yes. I told him."

Amelia frowned. Patrick's statements in the newspaper article indicated quite clearly that he had every intention of pursuing the case as far as it would go. How could he and Mary have crossed wires so badly?

Maybe they hadn't crossed wires. Maybe Mary had told him she'd changed her mind about the suit, but he'd chosen to disregard her wishes. Maybe he'd willfully ignored her.

No, he wouldn't do that. He couldn't. Lawyers weren't supposed to file suits behind their clients' backs, not even if their clients were retreating from a good constitutional battle. No matter how much they wanted to continue the fight, no matter how long they'd dreamed of arguing before the Supreme Court, lawyers weren't supposed to try their cases in the newspaper when their clients had cut them off.

But that was apparently what Patrick had done. Mary had told him to drop the suit and then she'd left town, and while she was gone Patrick had supplied the *New York Times* with a story about Mary and her fight for justice. Perhaps he'd hoped to embarrass her into continuing the case. Perhaps he didn't give a hoot how she felt about it.

Perhaps all he cared about was himself, his reputation, his lofty ideals. Mary had been little more than a tool to him, an excuse to make a name for himself as a great champion of justice.

He was exploiting Mary. He was fighting for himself, not for her. It wasn't a matter of right or wrong.

It was a matter of a slick lawyer taking advantage of a flighty artist for his own glorification.

Anger began to build inside Amelia, anger and all her protective instincts toward her sister. How could Patrick have been so two-faced? How could he be so obstinate, so egotistical, so selfish, so insensitive to Mary? How could he have broken her trust?

How could Amelia believe in him after this?

"I'm on my way to Wisherville," she said into the phone. "I'll see you in a couple of hours. We've got more to talk about than you know." Hanging up the phone, Amelia left the kitchen with a sense of purpose fueled by profound indignation.

She wouldn't let Patrick take advantage of Mary this way. She wouldn't let him turn Mary into some sort of martyr to his cause. If ever Mary deserved to be rescued, it was now. And if ever Amelia wanted to rescue her, this was the time.

Chapter Nine

Patrick's secretary was on the telephone when Amelia marched into the reception room in his suite of offices. At first Marilyn just smiled at Amelia in recognition, but when she realized Amelia was headed straight for the door to Patrick's office, she clamped her hand over the mouthpiece and called out, "You can't go in there. He's with a client."

Ignoring her, Amelia shoved open the door and stormed into Patrick's office. She found him seated at his desk conferring with an older man in a neat gray suit. Patrick was in shirtsleeves, his necktie dangling loose and his collar open. He'd been speaking and scribbling notes on a lined pad when Amelia entered; at the interruption, he broke off in midsentence and glanced impatiently toward the door. His annoyed expression dissolved into such a wonderful dimpled smile that the indignation Amelia had been nursing all the way from Connecticut began to falter.

"Amelia!" His blue eyes luminous with delight, he sprang to his feet and shot an apologetic grin at his client. "Excuse me for a second," he said, hurrying across the room to her and giving her a brief but heartfelt hug. "What a fantastic surprise!" He gazed into her upturned face for a moment, then shrugged off his sense of propriety and planted an exuberant kiss on her lips.

Amelia was keenly aware that a stranger was in the room watching their reunion. During the drive to Wisherville, she had decided that when she got to Patrick's office she would make a big commotion and suffer no qualms about it. She'd figured she would barge in on him as irreverently as he'd barged in on her last weekend, and order him to drop whatever he was doing and explain to her why he was taking advantage of her sister.

If there were witnesses, if she had to disrupt Patrick's schedule and interrupt a conference, so be it. One thing Patrick had taught her was that sometimes it was acceptable to be rude.

At least that had been her feeling during the drive. She'd been so enraged about the way he was using Mary's situation to promote himself that she'd actually been looking forward to shedding her inhibitions and raising a ruckus. But now, with his arms around her and the familiar taste of his kiss on her lips, she was flooded by other emotions just as intense as anger, emotions she most certainly preferred to keep hidden from Patrick's no-doubt curious client.

Either she could run away in embarrassment or she could counterattack. She hadn't driven all this distance to run away. "Patrick—" she wriggled out of his embrace and tried to compose herself "—how could you let the *New York Times* run that story about Mary? How could you say all those things in the paper when you knew she wanted to drop the case? All your high-minded talk about justice and principles— what a load of garbage!"

Taken aback, Patrick scowled. After a long, intense scrutiny, he touched her arm to silence her and then turned to the man at the desk, who had twisted in his chair and was flagrantly gawking at them. "Excuse me, Mr. Sloan. I'll be back in a minute." Tightening his grip on Amelia's arm, Patrick propelled her out of his office.

"I'm sorry," his secretary called from her desk. "I tried to stop her, but—"

"It's all right, Marilyn." Patrick guided Amelia to the conference room and shut the door behind them. Enclosed in the dimly lit room with him, Amelia fortified herself against the dressing-down she expected for having disrupted his meeting.

She should have known better. While obviously bemused, Patrick gazed at her with what could only be interpreted as admiration. "You've developed quite a flair for drama," he said, the corners of his mouth quirking upward in a grin. "I'm impressed."

His compliment disconcerted her. Closing her eyes, she reran in her mind the various speeches she'd rehearsed during her drive to Wisherville. As soon as she got her thoughts back on track, she pinned Patrick with a scathing stare. "Let me impress something else upon you, Mr. Levine. You had no right to feed the *Times* all that garbage about my sister."

His smile lost some of its sparkle, although he didn't quail beneath her gaze. "Uh, would I be way out of line if I said hello first? It's good to see you, Amelia. You look wonderful. Have you made any plans for dinner?"

The only plans she'd made were to give Patrick a piece of her mind and then bid him goodbye. She was incensed that he would allude to the fact that they had a relationship totally divorced from Patrick's representation of Mary. She didn't want to be reminded of how deeply she loved him, and how demolished she was going to be once she shut him out of her life.

"I didn't come here to talk about dinner," she said. "I came here to tell you off."

"So I gather." Running his hand haphazardly through his hair, he sorted his thoughts before speaking. "I thought the *Times* did a pretty good write-up, myself," he said with deceptive casualness.

"I don't care how nicely it was written up. It was a lie!"

Something hardened in his eyes. "What are you talking about, Amelia? Every word in that article was true."

"Maybe the words are true, but the message behind them isn't. You have some gall announcing to the world that you're going to continue to press Mary's case when you know very well she doesn't want you to."

He took a deep breath, then let it out slowly, turning his gaze from her to the windows. Late-afternoon sunlight spilled in through the blinds, striping his face with shadows. "Amelia," he said slowly, "have you ever heard of attorney-client confidentiality? Just because you're Mary's sister—and the love of my life— doesn't give you the right to interfere in my handling of her case. That's between her and me alone."

Amelia bristled. The nerve of him, hiding behind confidentiality! His job might be to handle Mary's case, but Amelia's job was to protect her scatterbrained sister from sharks like him. "Here's what's between her and *me*," she roared, hating herself for losing her temper but unable to stop herself. "She told me she wants to drop the suit against the town. She told me she told you that. She wants to put the whole thing behind her.''

"I can't discuss this, Amelia—"

"You can! You have to!" She grabbed his arm, thinking to shake him out of his complacent professionalism. The contact between their bodies startled them both, however. His gaze flew to her fingers where they curved around his biceps, and her grip grew gentle, almost beseeching. Dismayed that merely touching him could have such a strong effect on her, she let her hand fall and lowered her eyes. "Don't evade me, Patrick. If Mary's telling you something different than she's telling me, I want to know. And if she isn't . . ." *If she isn't, then you're doing something terribly wrong,* she concluded silently. She had to know that, too, even though she didn't want to.

He reached for her hand, hanging limp at her side, but she shot him a forbidding look and he shoved his hands into his trouser pockets instead. "We obviously have a problem here," he said quietly. "And it's too important to rush through while I've got a client waiting for me in my office. Let me finish up with him, and then we can talk about this calmly and rationally. If you can just sit tight for a few minutes—"

"I can't," she retorted. To her amazement, she discovered that the mere act of asserting herself infused her with a sense of her own power. She moved away from Patrick, refusing to let his logical suggestion dull the edge of her anger. "I spoke with Mary just a couple of hours ago—"

"Amelia, please." Patrick moved, too, in the direction of the door. "We can talk about this all you want, but not now. I'm billing Mr. Sloan by the hour."

She sensed that Patrick was grappling with his own temper, and that his eagerness to get away from her had something to do with wanting to cool off before anger got the better of him. Not that she cared. She had right on her side; she was happy to continue with her attack. "Oh? Mr. Sloan isn't another of your righteous freebies?"

"No," he replied in a strained voice. "When a client can afford it, I bill him for my services. Call me crass, Amelia, but I've got this strange notion about wanting to pay my secretary a living wage, so on occasion I do something really unethical, like charge clients a fee."

"I'll gladly call you crass," Amelia complied bitterly. "And I'll call you unethical, too. You're taking advantage of my sister, Patrick. You're refusing to represent her the way she wants to be represented. And what's worse, you're bragging about it in the media."

"You want to talk about ethics?" he railed. "You want to talk about principles? You were the one who wanted to sell Mary out in the first place, Amelia. You were the one who wanted her to plead guilty to disturbing the peace, for God's sake."

"Well, she did disturb the peace."

"So you figured she should be punished for it. You figured she should hang her head in shame and confess to being a bad girl. That's your idea of ethics." He shook his head, his eyes cold with loathing. "You don't know what you're talking about."

"I'm talking about Mary, and your inflated ego. You want to be in the newspapers, you want to be the famous hero of the next American Revolution? Go right ahead, Patrick! Be my guest. But leave my sister out of it.''

He was clearly torn; he knew he had to return to the client waiting in his office, yet he didn't want to leave the conference room without rebutting Amelia's accusation. He curled his hand around the doorknob, twisted it, but hesitated before opening the door. ''This has nothing to do with my ego, Amelia,'' he said, his tone bristling with a fury that matched hers. ''Stick around. We'll straighten this thing out as soon as I'm free.''

''I will not stick around!'' Amelia shouted. She had never given herself over to anger so completely, and she found the experience as cathartic as giving herself over to the passion she'd found in Patrick's arms. Just as when they'd made love, her emotions were exposed, full-blown, running rampant with nary a concession to etiquette or sensitivity. The feeling was curiously liberating—and frightening. She wrestled with the compulsion to apologize for her outburst, to revert to the decorous, well-behaved young woman she was supposed to be. But it was too late; hiding behind a veneer of good manners would be absurd at this point.

Releasing the doorknob, Patrick walked toward her, his arm outstretched. She recoiled from him, and he let his hand drop. ''Please stay, Amelia,'' he implored her, although the look of wary resignation in his eyes implied that he doubted she would. ''Whatever it is that's bothering you, I know we can work it out.''

Her only response was a stony glare.

Sighing, he pivoted and stalked out of the conference room. Amelia heard the muffled sound of his voice as he said something to his secretary, and then the distant click of his office door closing.

She stared at the unlit overhead lights, the long oak conference table, the angled vertical shades across the windows. She wrapped her arms around herself, closed her eyes and tried to reassure herself that she didn't love Patrick. What they'd experienced together over the weekend meant nothing to her. His tenderness, his sensitivity, his enthusiasm and humor and his alleged principles—none of it mattered. She couldn't possibly love a publicity-hungry hypocrite.

Straightening her back and lifting her chin, she strode out of the conference room. "Patrick asked me to make sure you didn't leave, Ms. Potts," the secretary said as Amelia hurried across the reception area.

"Patrick can go to hell." With a violent yank, Amelia opened the outer door and stormed out of the building.

AMELIA ARRIVED at Mary's bungalow feeling frayed and disoriented—and exhausted. Her nervous system seemed to have responded to the day's overload of tension by shorting out, leaving her bleary and achy. The muggy late-June weather of the previous week had been replaced by a breezy mildness more reminiscent of early May, but Amelia was too drained to appreciate the crisp mountain air and the darkening blue of the evening sky.

Mary's van stood in the driveway; behind it was a silver Porsche, indicating that Bartholomew was here. No doubt he'd returned from Washington in time to receive word from the Pottses that Mary was once again running wild, and he'd hastened to Wisherville to lend his assistance.

How decent of him, Amelia thought with genuine fondness. The poor man must be tired from his business trip. Scarcely a minute after he'd stepped off the shuttle plane, her parents must have tracked him down and begged him to help them with Mary. And he'd done it. Even though she would never marry him, Amelia loved him for his devotion to her sister. Unlike Patrick, Bartholomew would never exploit Mary for his own professional advantage.

Locking her car and heading up the front walk, Amelia was visited by an unwelcome memory of the night Patrick had kissed her on Mary's porch, the night he'd forced her to acknowledge her attraction to him. As she approached the screen door she willfully shook off the memory. The inner door was open, and after announcing her arrival by rapping on the frame, she entered the house. The living room was empty, but she heard voices drifting out from the kitchen. "Mary?" she called. "Hello?"

"Melie? Is that you?" Mary raced into the living room from the kitchen, Bartholomew right behind her. Before Amelia could speak, Mary was hugging her exuberantly. "I'm so glad you're here! We have a lot to talk about."

"I know," Amelia said, casting Bartholomew a smile of greeting over Mary's shoulder. She wondered whether they'd seen the article in the *Times*, and whether that was what Mary wanted to talk about. Or maybe Mary had learned about Amelia's relationship with Patrick and wanted to sound the alarm about him.

In which case, Amelia thought as she extricated herself from her sister's smothering embrace, Mary's advice wouldn't be necessary.

"I was surprised when you said you were coming to Wisherville," Mary said, clasping her hands in front of her and smiling sheepishly. "I know what it's like at Hibbing this time of year. I didn't think you'd be able to get away."

"But here I am." Amelia didn't want to get side-tracked with a conversation about her job—or lack thereof. Right now what mattered most was learning why Mary had disappeared, where she'd been, and why Patrick had misrepresented her in her absence.

And why she looked so nice. She had on a modest shirtwaist dress in subdued peach, and her usually untamed hair was pinned back from her face with attractive tortoiseshell combs. "I love your dress," Amelia said.

"Do you?" Mary laughed bashfully. "I guess that's no surprise."

"It *is* a surprise. I never like your clothes."

"No...I mean..." Mary eyed Bartholomew nervously, then turned back to Amelia. "Amelia, we've got to talk."

"No kidding. Where have you been? Mom was so worried she drove all the way to New Milford to enlist my aid in person."

"Well, she didn't have to worry." Mary shot another swift look at Bartholomew, who nodded slightly. "I wasn't in any danger."

"What Mary's trying to say," Bartholomew interjected, "was that she was with me."

"But I thought you were in Washington." Puzzled, Amelia shifted her gaze from her sister to Bartholomew and back again.

Mary's smile grew increasingly brave. "I was in Washington, too, Melie. Bartholomew had to attend a business meeting, and I . . . I was with him."

"You were with him," Amelia repeated, not yet sure of what Mary was getting at.

"Why don't you have a seat, Amelia?" Bartholomew chivalrously ushered her to the couch and pressed down on her shoulder until she had no choice but to sit. "Can I get you a drink?"

Recalling the bizarre selection of beverages in her sister's liquor cabinet, Amelia declined. "I don't want a drink. I want to know why Mary went to Washington with you instead of staying in Wisherville and keeping an eye on Patrick."

"Patrick? He has nothing to do with this," Mary insisted, succumbing to a giggle. She plopped down next to Amelia on the couch and let her smile fade. "When I phoned you today, Bartholomew and I were prepared to drive straight to New Milford to talk to you if it came to that. But then you said you were coming to Wisherville so we decided to meet you here. You see—" Mary swallowed, then took a deep breath "—we're in love."

"You're in love," Amelia echoed, her head beginning to throb.

"Yes." Mary gathered Amelia's hands in hers. Bartholomew confirmed the statement with a nod.

"With each other?" Amelia asked incredulously.

Mary smiled. "You must think we're both nuts," she said. "You're probably shocked. . . ."

Amelia closed her eyes and stared for a moment at the silvery fireworks dancing across the inside of her lids. "Shocked" scarcely scratched the surface. She was dumbfounded. She was staggered. She couldn't take it in.

"I thought..." She opened her eyes and stared glassily at Bartholomew. "I thought we were..." What little strength she had left seemed to fail her, and she let her voice fade away.

Bartholomew sat on her other side on the couch. "Amelia, we've known each other for so long, we've been such good friends... If there was any way I could avoid hurting you—"

"Hurting me?" A dazed laugh escaped her. At the moment her hurts were so deep she couldn't even begin to sort out their causes—except to know that Mary's and Bartholomew's announcement was nothing compared to the understanding that Patrick was a two-faced liar.

"If you're upset, Amelia, please let us know," Mary begged her. "If you had always hoped to marry Bartholomew—"

"No, Mary," Amelia cut her off. She recalled once more the first time Patrick had kissed her, after which she'd come indoors and acknowledged that she could never marry Bartholomew. "I wish you'd said something, though. I wish you'd given me some... some warning or something. It's just so sudden."

"We've always liked each other," Mary explained. "But the love... You're right. That happened kind of suddenly."

"Not that we're unsure of our feelings," Bartholomew interjected. "Sometimes these things evolve rather quickly."

"When the brouhaha erupted over *Liberty*, we spent so much time together discussing tactics." Mary gave a little lovesick sigh. "The more time we spent together, the more time we found ourselves focusing on other things, like each other and our feelings."

Bartholomew nodded in agreement. "Your sister, well, there's something so...so zany about her, something so fragile. You *look* delicate, Amelia, but you're really the strong one. Mary's the one who needs me. And, well, I need to be needed."

"We stand as living proof that opposites attract," Mary declared cheerfully.

"She keeps me on my toes," Bartholomew pointed out.

"And he keeps my feet on the ground," Mary chorused. "When he found out he had to go to Washington on business, I decided to go with him. We wanted to get away from the mess here and our families in New York, and just isolate ourselves from everything to see if what we felt was real. It was."

"We wanted you to be the first to know, Amelia," Bartholomew said earnestly.

"That's very sweet of you." Amelia sank against the upholstery, fighting the fatigue that threatened to overcome her. At least Mary's news was joyous, and Amelia hung on to it as an antidote to the far less pleasant events of the past few hours. After quitting her job and learning that Patrick was a first-class manipulator, all she wanted to do was concentrate for a while on her sister's happiness. She would enjoy that happiness vicariously; she would try not to be jealous of the fact that, when it came to love, Mary was triumphant and Amelia had gotten crowded out, left in the shadows. "I'm delighted, really," she managed.

"Thank you," Mary and Bartholomew said almost simultaneously. "It means a lot to us to have your blessing," Mary added.

"Then you have it," Amelia assured her. "I don't know how Mom and Dad are going to take this development...."

"They're going to be shocked," Mary remarked firmly. "So are the Driscolls. I'm sure of it."

"I'll do what I can to help you to win them over," Amelia promised. "Have you made any plans?"

"About marrying?" Mary glanced up at Bartholomew, took note of his reproachful expression, then turned back to Amelia and chuckled. "He wants to. He's so insufferably respectable, Melie. I myself think it would be more fun to live in sin."

"Obviously, we have a number of details to work out," Bartholomew muttered.

"What about the gallery?" Amelia pressed on. "Are you going to move to New York City?"

"Mary's friend Mina can run the place during the week, and Mary can work there weekends—if she wants. This will be our vacation house—and, of course, she'll need the studio."

"I'm not giving up sculpting," Mary explained. "Even Bartholomew wouldn't hear of it, now that it's proven to be so lucrative."

"Has it?" Amelia asked dubiously.

"According to Mina, Patrick has received more bids on *Liberty*. You won't believe who's been bidding on it."

"Who? The Museum of Modern Art?" Amelia guessed. "Playboy Enterprises?"

Laughing, Mary silenced Amelia with a wave of her hand. "Try this—the Wisherville Chamber of Commerce, the Wisherville Town Council, a museum in Monticello and two resort hotels. They've all bid over a thousand dollars, Melie. Can you believe it?"

Frankly, Amelia couldn't. "Why?"

"Why? Because it's a tourist attraction. The tourist business here in town is nearly double what it was a year ago at this time. People go to the police station to look at the sculpture, and then they wind up spending some money at Main Street Curios, or Frannie's Gifts and Notions, or the T-Shirt Shoppe, and they have lunch at Melbourne's Patio, or ice cream at the Davenport Creamery. Every town around here has pretty scenery and good restaurants and a store that sells overpriced souvenirs. But only Wisherville has a Mary Potts original."

"So, what are you going to do? Create obscene sculptures for all the other towns in Sullivan County?"

"No, but there's clearly a demand for my stuff. Patrick's handled the marketing so magnificently. I figure I'll have to pay him a commission once *Liberty* is sold, and maybe he can give me guidance in marketing my future work. Bartholomew is a marvelous man—" she batted her eyes at him "—but when it comes to erotic art he gets discombobulated."

"I wouldn't say that," he grumbled, heading for the kitchen. "I'm going to fix myself a drink. Are you sure you don't want one, Amelia?"

"Positive." Her reeling mind didn't need being clouded by liquor.

Mary gazed after him for a moment, then twisted around to face Amelia and smiled hopefully. "What do you think? Does any of this make sense?"

"It doesn't have to make sense," Amelia said. "You aren't the sensible one." She rested her head against the sofa back, assimilating as much as she could. In time, she would accustom herself to Mary's and Bartholomew's love. And Mary's news about the potential profitability of her sculpture filled her with pride. As far as Mary's plan to let Patrick assist Mary in marketing her works, however, Amelia balked. "You really can't trust Patrick," she said.

Mary rolled her eyes in irritation. "Oh, please, Melie. I know you haven't trusted him from the start—you think he's a goof just because he wears an earring. But he happens to be very shrewd—"

"Too shrewd," Amelia maintained harshly.

Mary's eyebrows rose. "How can he be too shrewd? Do you think there's something wrong with the way he's solicited all these bids on my sculpture?"

"No, Mary. I think there's something wrong with the way he's pushed your civil suit against the town of Wisherville. You told me on the phone you decided to drop the case."

"Yeah." Mary shrugged pensively. "It means a lot to Bartholomew that I keep my nose clean and shun publicity. He works for such a respectable law firm and all. Cripes, Melie, I hope I can be respectable enough for him!"

"You can do it," Amelia encouraged her. "But not if Patrick keeps thrusting you into the public eye."

"He won't do that. I've asked him to drop the case."

"He ignored you," Amelia told her. "He's going forward with it."

Mary appeared surprised, but not terribly concerned. "No, he's not. I explained to him that I thought we ought to back off."

"There was an article about your case in today's *New York Times*," Amelia told her sister. Mary's startled expression implied that this was the first she'd heard about it. "It was all about how the fight Patrick's waging in defense of your sculpture represents all sorts of patriotic high-and-mighty principles, and how he intends to fight all the way to the nation's highest court if need be, because the issues at stake are that important. Your name was mentioned several times."

"Oh?" Mary frowned for a minute, then grinned slyly. "Did it say good things about my sculpture? Maybe we'll get some more bids. I'll bet that's why Patrick got the story into the newspapers—to increase interest in *Liberty*."

"How much more interest do you need in the thing?" Amelia felt her anger rising again, and she tried to push it back down. "Do you know how many people read the *Times*? Millions. Millions of people read about you and your lawyer and your obscene sculpture."

"Well, that's the way Patrick is," Mary said in his defense. "He likes making a fuss even more than I do."

"Exactly. And he's using you to make his fuss. Mom and Dad read the article. Dean Blanchard read the article. Half the population of the Greater Metropolitan Area read the article. You've said you want to drop the charges, and Patrick has blatantly ignored you."

As the ramifications of Amelia's words began to sink in, Mary frowned. "Maybe he misunderstood me," she said. "I thought I was clear, even though I promised him I'd give my decision more thought. He must have misunderstood."

"Deliberately," Amelia said with a snort. "He misunderstood because he wanted to."

Mary's cheeks began to lose their color. "It's just one article," she said, trying to convince herself more than Amelia. "I mean, it's not such a big deal, is it?"

"It's a very big deal," Amelia argued. "Do you think Wisherville's going to want to buy your sculpture for a thousand dollars if Patrick presses your suit against the town? His mule-headedness is going to cost you money, and even more, it's going to cost you your privacy. Patrick wants to grandstand, and you're the most convenient vehicle he's found. He's using you, Mary."

Mary glanced toward the kitchen, where Bartholomew was, and bit her lip. "I don't care about losing my privacy," she confided. "Let's face it, Melie, half the people in Wisherville saw me nude the time I went skinny-dipping. But Bartholomew won't stand for it. I promised him I'd try to keep a lower profile from now on. I love him, Amelia. I don't want to jeopardize what we've got."

"When did you tell Patrick to drop your case?" Amelia asked.

"Monday morning. Just before I left for Washington."

"What did he say when you told him you didn't want to continue?"

Mary rolled her eyes. "Oh, he started speechifying. You know how he is."

Yes, Amelia knew how Patrick was. He figured out what he wanted from a woman and then forged ahead, doing whatever was necessary to accomplish his goal and disregarding everything that stood in his way. From Mary, he'd wanted a political crusade, and he'd gotten it. From Amelia he'd wanted her heart and soul—and damn the man, he'd gotten them.

Maybe all he'd really wanted from her was what he'd wanted from Mary: the opportunity to overturn a table and fight a good fight.

The telephone began to ring. "Should I answer it?" Bartholomew hollered from the kitchen.

Amelia eyed Mary anxiously. "I've got a hunch it's Patrick," she whispered, swallowing to relax the knot of tension in her throat.

"Sure, go ahead and answer it," Mary called to Bartholomew before winking at Amelia. "If you're right about him, if he's been pumping up my lawsuit to the press, I'm going to set him straight. It was fun pretending I could be as important as the civil-rights movement, but Bartholomew's feelings are even more important. I'll go tell Patrick—"

"Amelia?" Bartholomew appeared in the doorway, confirming her worst fears. "It's Patrick Levine. He said he'd like to speak to you."

"Give him hell for me, will you?" Mary requested, rising and nudging Amelia toward the kitchen.

Amelia entertained the notion of having Bartholomew tell Patrick she wasn't there. Then she discarded the idea. She'd come to Wisherville anticipating a showdown with him. If she'd been courageous enough to confront him in his own office, she could certainly confront him over the telephone.

Drawing a deep breath, she crossed the kitchen and took the phone from Bartholomew. "Hello," she said with what she considered admirable poise.

"What the hell is Blond Bart doing there?" Patrick fumed, skipping any pretense of civility. "Coaching you in the art of surrender? Or giving you a ten-carat solitaire?"

"Blond Bart—I mean, Bartholomew—is here visiting Mary," Amelia said, forcing her words through clenched teeth to avoid erupting in rage.

"And why did you bolt from my office? I told you I'd be done in a few minutes."

"I wanted to see Mary," Amelia rationalized. "I wanted to make sure she was serious about dropping her suit against Wisherville. She was. Which means you're flying without a passenger, Patrick."

"That's between her and me," he claimed. "I want to talk about what's going between *you* and me."

"What's going on is, you hoodwinked my sister."

Patrick was silent for several long seconds. "If Mary wanted to drop the suit," he finally said, shaping each word carefully, "she was wrong. My job as a lawyer is to make sure my clients do what's right, both legally and morally. If I didn't follow her dictates rigidly, Amelia, it was because she was wrong."

Amelia winced at his confession. He'd all but come right out and admitted to everything she'd accused him of. Whether or not Mary's decision was wrong, Patrick had been wrong, as well. It had nothing to do with principles; it had to do with Patrick's smug self-righteousness.

And that meant he was unethical. It meant he was unprincipled.

It meant he was undeserving of her love.

"Amelia," he said when she didn't speak, "I'd like to see you. Can I come over to Mary's house?"

"No." She had to push the word past the lump of tears clogging her throat.

"Amelia—"

"If you honestly think you did the right thing, Patrick, then we have nothing more to say to each other." Before she could change her mind, before she broke down and wept, she hung up the phone.

Peering through the doorway, she saw Mary and Bartholomew standing together, gazing out the window. Bartholomew's arm arched around Mary's shoulders and she nestled her head into the hollow of his neck. They looked like lovers, Amelia thought wistfully. They looked satisfied.

They belonged together, and Amelia didn't belong here with them. From now on, Bartholomew would be the one to rescue Mary whenever she got herself into hot water, and Mary would make him feel needed. Amelia would no longer have to be the sane, sensible, responsible one, hurrying to bail Mary out on a moment's notice. That would be Bartholomew's role. Amelia would have to find a new role for herself.

She had never felt so alone, so unmoored, so utterly lost, in her life.

Chapter Ten

Keppler's was gearing up for dinner. Hungry guests milled around near the doors leading from the lobby into the dining room. A few men had donned sport coats, a few women fashionable summer dresses, but most of the guests were clad in casual attire. A couple of rambunctious young boys darted among the adults, playing tag.

Amelia hovered in the doorway for a moment, her attention drifting from the cheerful babble of voices to the desk where Sue, the pretty young clerk, was gluing postage stamps onto a stack of picture postcards, and from her to the silently spinning ceiling fan. She wondered whether she should have come here, and what she should do now that she had come. What if Rae Keppler was about to have dinner herself? What if she had no time to greet Amelia and no real interest in her? What if Amelia had made the biggest mistake in her life by quitting her job at Hibbing and chasing an empty fantasy all the way to this hotel in the Catskills?

No, she consoled herself, coming to Keppler's wasn't a mistake. Even if Rae refused to offer a job, Amelia was glad to be here. The air breezing into the lobby through the broad screen windows smelled sweet, and the building itself seemed to welcome her, its symmetrical extensions spreading outward like open arms. She knew in her gut that she'd done the right thing in coming.

Weaving among the throngs of guests, Amelia approached the desk. Sue peeled a stamp off her tongue and pressed it onto a postcard, then smiled. "Can I help you?" she asked, her vacant grin indicating that she didn't recognize Amelia. Not surprising, since the last time Amelia had been in this lobby, Sue hadn't even noticed her.

"I'd like to see Rae Keppler, if she's available," Amelia requested.

"I think she's in her office," said Sue. "What's your name?"

"Amelia Potts."

Sue turned to the telephone console and dialed a number. After a moment's consultation, she hung up and smiled. "Do you know where her office is?"

Amelia hadn't realized she was holding her breath. Now that she knew Rae was willing to see her, she let out a long sigh of relief and nodded at Sue. "Thanks," she said before heading down the hall to the office she'd once visited with Patrick.

Recalling that day brought Amelia up short. She remembered his playful flirting, his flattery, his seductive gaze. She remembered how inexplicably peaceful she'd felt that afternoon here at Keppler's, and yet how aware she'd been that Patrick could disturb that peace, that he could alter her world in unforeseeable ways.

She couldn't have predicted then that a few weeks later she'd be back at the hotel applying for a job. She couldn't have guessed that while she and Patrick had been here her sister and Bartholomew had been falling in love with each other back in Wisherville. She couldn't have imagined that her life was already transforming, that when she came back to the Catskills she would be a different person than she'd been when she'd left, that sometime between then and now her entire perspective would change.

But she *had* known, deep inside, that Patrick was somehow fated to become a significant part of her life. She had known, from the way he'd gazed at her and the way she'd responded to the potent message in his eyes, that things were no longer the same, that she was capable of experiencing yearnings she hadn't been conscious of before. She'd known, subliminally, that whatever murky dissatisfactions she'd refused to acknowledge until that moment were about to rise to the surface, that Patrick would stir them up until she could no longer deny their existence.

She had known, deep in her soul, that regardless of his questionable professional ethics, his brashness and his blind spots, Patrick had been destined to steal her heart.

She had also known that he wasn't her type. Now that she'd learned of his duplicity in his handling of Mary's case, she had added proof of that. She couldn't possibly love a man who committed unjust acts in the name of justice. She simply couldn't love him—although her emotions hadn't yet caught up with her logic. Once they did, once she could say with certainty that she no longer loved Patrick, she'd probably stop hurting so much.

At least she hoped she would. Because she was hurting now, hurting so deeply she was tempted to postpone her meeting with Rae and hide herself away somewhere where she could lick her wounds in solitude.

But she wouldn't. Amelia was desperate to get at least this much of her life settled—and Rae was in her office, waiting to help Amelia settle it. She took a few deep breaths and knocked on the door.

"Come in, come in!" Rae exclaimed, swinging the door open and gathering Amelia's hands in hers. "This is such a pleasure. Come in, darling—" she ushered Amelia over to one of the chintz sofas and sat with her "—and tell me how you've been. If I'd have known you were coming I would have had Roger fix up something special for you. You must be starving."

Amelia smiled, relaxing in the realization that she had, indeed, done the right thing in coming. Rae was wearing a casually chic slacks outfit, her fingernails polished pink and her platinum hair arranged neatly about her lively face. "Actually, I'm not very hungry at all," Amelia said.

"You should be," Rae scolded. "Look at you—there's nothing to pinch." She plucked at Amelia's cheek, then smiled. "So, we'll eat later. Now tell me, what brings you here?"

Amelia faltered for a minute. Patrick had said he'd broached the subject of her employment at the hotel with Rae. Had he lied? Had he been dishonest about this, too? "Well—" she swallowed, then plowed ahead "—I know this isn't the time to discuss it, but I've been thinking, if there were any way for me to find work here at Keppler's—"

"Yes, of course, but Patrick told me you planned to work at that fancy-schmancy prep school until the end of the term," Rae interrupted. "I was figuring we'd talk when you were free."

"I'm free now," Amelia informed her, feeling another wave of relief wash through her. Obviously Patrick had talked to Rae about Amelia in some detail.

"All right, so you're free." Rae sat back and grinned, her canny brown eyes shimmering in the light that filled the room through the west-facing windows. "It's already five o'clock, I've spent a long day dickering with some schmo from Montcello who's supposed to repair the roof of the barn down by the lake. So maybe we should talk tomorrow, on a full stomach."

"Whatever is best for you." Amelia realized her statement may have sounded too docile, and she added, "I'm here to speak for myself, Rae. I don't need Patrick speaking for me. I'm a hard worker and I'm willing to start at the bottom and work my way up. We can talk tomorrow if you'd like, but I want you to know I've handled all sorts of responsibilities in the dean's office, everything from compiling mailings to screening students for counseling, from overseeing menus to double-checking budgets. I've organized school dances and parents' weekends, I've done fundraising, I've run interference between the dean and the secretarial staff, I've written pamphlets and dealt with printers—"

"Whoa!" Chuckling, Rae held up her hand. "And all Patrick told me was that you were wonderful. Little did I know."

Amelia almost protested that Rae should be suspicious of anything Patrick had ever told her. But if his exaggerating worked in Amelia's favor, she saw no point in putting him down.

"So you've done all these things," said Rae, "and now you want to work at a resort."

"I'd like to give it a try," Amelia confirmed, unable to curtail her instinctive modesty. "I don't know how successful I'll be, but—"

"Nobody ever knows that going in," Rae finished for her. "It isn't easy, keeping this place running. And like you said, you're going to have to start at the bottom. We can talk pay tomorrow, but I'm warning you right now, it won't be much."

Amelia shrugged. "The Hibbing School didn't pay much, either."

"At least you're entitled to free meals while you're here. Which, if you don't mind my saying so, you could use. But I'll work you hard, and you'll probably burn off all the cheesecake I can stuff into you."

"I'm willing to work hard," she said.

Rae gave her a leisurely perusal. "You know, I'm beginning to think you're as much of a nudnik as that crazy sister of yours. I tell you, that sculpture—they've started car pools here, driving down to Wisherville to see the statue that started the fuss. Apparently the thing's in some office in the town hall."

"I'm not a nudnik," Amelia said. "I'm not even sure what a nudnik is."

"A nut," Rae explained. "A meshuggenah. When I talked to Patrick about you, he told me your sister was kind of crazy, but you had the potential to be even crazier. This from him was a compliment."

"I can imagine," Amelia said dryly.

"Of course, he's the craziest of all, with that wild hair and the earring. Crazy—but smart, Amelia. Smart and good-hearted. You hang onto him and don't let go."

A fresh, keen pain sliced through her, and she averted her face to hide her discomfort from Rae. Patrick might be smart and he might be crazy. But if he were all that good-hearted he would have listened to Mary and respected her decision. He wouldn't have run off to the newspapers and drummed up extra publicity for himself. He wouldn't have put his own needs before his client's.

She gamely fought off her bitterness. "I'm very grateful that you're willing to take a chance on me," she said, choosing not to comment on Rae's tribute to Patrick. "Of course, I can't say exactly when I'll be able to start working for you. I've still got my apartment in New Milford, and—"

"We'll work all that out tomorrow," Rae promised. "Not that I approve one way or the other, but are you going to be living with Patrick?"

Amelia's jaw dropped. What on earth had Patrick told Rae about her, other than that she was wonderful? Had he confided to Rae that they'd been lovers? Had he discussed the possibility of a future for them? If he had raised that particular subject with Amelia, she would have been happy to set him straight at once. "My sister has a house in Wisherville," she said, striving to maintain a calm facade. "I'll probably be staying there until I find a place of my own."

"Fine." Rae studied Amelia for a minute. "You and your sister are close?"

"Very close," Amelia replied.

"You're not really crazy like her, are you?" Rae leaned forward, her expression serious. "What I mean is, you're not going to come and work here just because it seems like a kooky idea, are you?"

Amelia gave Rae's question the solemn consideration it deserved. "You're asking me why I want to give up a secure job and try my hand at something I've never done before."

Rae nodded. "You've got to admit it's strange."

Amelia met Rae's searching gaze. "I can't exactly say why I want to be here, Rae," she conceded. "It doesn't make any sense. I've lived my whole life sensibly, though, and I'm no longer sure that's the way to go. Sometimes something just feels so right you've got to do it." She groped through her thoughts, trying to find a way to phrase them. "I was stagnating at the Hibbing School. I can't guarantee that I'll spend the rest of my life working at Keppler's, but it feels right to me. I feel as if I belong here." She smiled shyly. "I can't explain it any other way."

Rae absorbed her words, then nodded. "So, we'll try it and see how it goes. Now, how about some dinner? Roger's got a pot roast...."

"I think I'd rather just take a walk, thank you," Amelia said. Rae was going to take a chance on her, and she was going to take a chance on herself. The momentousness of the step she had just taken stripped her of what little appetite she might have had. "What time would you like me to come back tomorrow?"

"How about you come at noon and we'll have lunch," Rae decided. "One way or another, I'm going to fatten you up."

"Lunch it is," Amelia agreed, rising from the sofa with Rae and shaking her hand. "We can discuss a starting date then."

"Right. If you haven't come to your senses first." Rae grinned, then put her arms around Amelia in a warm hug. "If I had any sense, I'd sell this place to the condominium developer and be done with it," she remarked, escorting Amelia out of the office and down the hall to the lobby. "But my heart tells me otherwise, and that's what I wind up listening to. So maybe I'm a little crazy, too."

"YOU JUST MISSED HER," Mary said. "She left about five minutes ago. But come in, Patrick, and fill me in on what's going on." She held the screen door open for him.

"Where did she go?" Patrick asked, ignoring Mary's invitation. He'd fill her in some other time. Not now, though. Not when Amelia was off somewhere, hating him.

A tall hefty figure loomed behind Mary, nearing the door until he became identifiable as Bartholomew. A remote corner of Patrick's brain digested the fact that Mary was dressed as conservatively as the old family friend, just as she'd been dressed primly when she'd come to Patrick's office last Monday. Apparently Bartholomew's influence extended beyond legal counsel to sartorial advice. "Hello, Patrick," Bartholomew said without much warmth. "I was just on my way out to see if I could scrounge a copy of this morning's *New York Times*. According to Amelia, it contains an article about Mary."

Patrick checked his wristwatch. Every minute that passed conceivably put another mile between him and Amelia. He couldn't waste time explaining the article to Mary. "Let's meet at my office tomorrow at, say, ten o'clock," he offered, struggling not to sound brusque. "We can discuss your case then, Mary. Right now, I've really got to find Amelia."

"You've really got to explain the article first," Bartholomew insisted, placing his hand protectively on Mary's shoulder. "After you've explained yourself, we'll tell you where Amelia is."

Extortionist. Patrick hadn't known Bartholomew had it in him. He was too distracted to sit down with Mary and analyze her legal situation; he was too worried, too fearful of losing Amelia's love. But Bartholomew wasn't giving him a choice. "All right," he said, shoving his floppy blond hair back from his brow and stepping into the house.

The three of them sat in the living room, Mary and Bartholomew side by side on the couch and Patrick in an easy chair, facing them across the coffee table. He leaned forward, too edgy to make himself comfortable. He'd come here straight from his office, and although his tie was already loosened, he tugged the knot a bit lower, as if to prevent choking.

"Look," he said, hoping he sounded reasonable, "I got a call from a friend of mine at the *Times* Monday afternoon, asking about the status of Mary's case. As of then—" he directed his gaze to Mary "—you left me with the impression that you weren't totally committed to closing the book on this suit. I couldn't reach you, I couldn't confer with you, so I went with my instincts and fed my friend a piece about our fight for your constitutional rights."

Mary shook her head vehemently. "But I told you I wanted to drop the case."

"And I told you to give it some more thought," Patrick defended himself.

"Fine. I agreed to give it more thought. That didn't mean I was planning to change my mind."

"Dropping the case was changing your mind, Mary," Patrick retorted. "I thought you cared so deeply about the principles at stake that, whatever momentary lapse you were suffering, you'd come to your senses. I had that much faith in you, Mary—"

"And I had faith that you'd do as I asked! You were my lawyer, Patrick."

"Your lawyer, not your hired gun," he countered. "I don't necessarily do everything a client asks of me. I do what's legally sound and just."

"What's legally sound," Bartholomew interjected, his tone low and reproachful, "is to give your client fair representation. A client is entitled to change her mind and drop a suit. We both know that."

"Dammit!" Patrick abandoned all pretense of civility. "This issue was too important to be sacrificed by some fickleness on Mary's part."

"Too important to you, perhaps," Bartholomew retorted.

"And I'm not fickle," Mary added. "I love Bartholomew, and I have no intention of stopping."

Mary loved Bartholomew? The news brought Patrick up short. His astonished gaze shuttled between the two on the couch, and he easily perceived that her love was reciprocated. No wonder she'd decided to drop the case. The man she adored had asked her to, and she'd obeyed.

Patrick suffered a surge of anger that Mary had allowed love to interfere with the principles for which he was fighting on her behalf. His anger was followed by a sudden stab of joy. If Mary and Bartholomew were lovers, then Bartholomew wasn't going to marry Amelia. He didn't love her. Patrick had a chance.

Some chance. Amelia would probably never forgive him for having fed the *Times* the story about her sister. Her relationship with Bartholomew, whatever it might entail, was irrelevant. She hated Patrick.

"Where's Amelia?" he asked again. "I really need to talk to her."

"You really need to guarantee that you'll drop Mary's case," Bartholomew foiled him.

"Her case is too important," Patrick maintained. "It's the perfect test case. I've been waiting for something like this all my professional life. I'm not going to give it up so easily."

"*Your* professional life?" Mary exclaimed. "What about *my* life, Patrick? Whose case is it, anyway?"

He hesitated before answering. Mary's anger took him aback. He was used to her being fervently on his side, not against him. This case was neither hers nor his, but theirs. Patrick was fighting it for both of them, for artists everywhere, for the freedom of every citizen of the United States. How could he get it through her head that she was wrong, that a love affair was trivial compared with her case, that the Constitution was more important than making goo-goo eyes at Bartholomew?

Damn. It might take hours to convince her. And in those hours, Amelia might slip away from him for good. He couldn't let that happen.

"Fine," he said, his voice low and bitter. "I'll drop the case. I'll do whatever you want me to do, Mary. I'll send a retraction to the *Times*. But for God's sake, tell me where Amelia is."

Bartholomew and Mary exchanged a glance. Then Mary turned back to Patrick. "She's at Keppler's. What's going on between you two, Patrick?"

"Keppler's. Of course." He leapt to his feet and hurried to the door. "Thanks," he shouted over his shoulder as he bolted outside and down the front walk to his Jeep.

Not until he'd started the engine and cruised down the street away from Mary's bungalow did he acknowledge how easily he'd caved in to Mary's demands, and Bartholomew's. How easily he'd discarded the case, how easily they'd defeated him, how easily he'd turned his back on all those civil rights and freedoms to which he'd dedicated his career. And all because he wanted to find Amelia.

No. He'd given in, but it hadn't been easy. It had been one of the hardest things he'd ever done.

Until he caught up with Amelia. Much as it agonized him, he couldn't shake the suspicion that winning her forgiveness would be even harder.

AFTER INSISTING one final time that she didn't want any dinner, Amelia bade Rae goodbye in the lobby and left through the back door. She ambled across the grass to the lake, sifting through her feelings. As much as she wanted to rid herself of her dependence on what was sensible, she wanted even more to sort out what she'd done, to prove to herself that she'd done the right thing in coming here.

But it was impossible to make sense of anything when her thoughts were overshadowed by the understanding that in loving Patrick she'd done the wrong thing. She wanted to stop loving him, but she could think of no sensible way to go about it.

She reached the edge of the lake and lowered herself onto a granite boulder rising from a small stretch of sand between two groves of evergreens. Above her the sky had faded to a pearly pink streaked with lavender and royal blue. The pine-scented air vibrated with the rumbling song of bullfrogs.

No matter what happened between her and Patrick, Amelia knew she'd be happy working at Keppler's. That happiness had nothing to do with logic, common sense, or any of the other standards that had guided Amelia's life up to now. It had to do with forgetting what was expected of her, shedding her inhibitions and listening to her heart.

It was all Patrick's doing, she thought. She hated him for his hypocrisy and his stubbornness. But she loved him because he'd taught her to break free.

Why did she insist on believing she loved Patrick? What she felt for Patrick was only appreciation, gratitude, indebtedness. She could learn to listen to her heart when it came to Keppler's, but not when it came to Patrick.

Certain things simply had to make sense—and loving Patrick didn't.

HE WATCHED HER for several minutes from a distance. As the evening light waned, her features became less distinct until she was nothing but a silhouette, straight-backed and proud, her hair billowing back from her shoulders in the gusts of wind lifting off the lake.

During the trip from Wisherville his anger had drained away, leaving in its wake a deep, aching guilt. He could blame it on his ethnic background—or he could be honest and blame it on himself, on his dishonesty, on his foolish indulgence in what could be considered his own version of goody-two-shoes behavior. He could tell himself from here till tomorrow that he was right and Mary was wrong, but the bottom line was, he *had* been wrong, if not in principle then in practice. He should have taken Mary's Monday-morning announcement seriously. He should have held the story, eschewed the publicity, waited until he was sure he had Mary firmly in his corner once more.

All his noble intentions couldn't change that fact.

Digging his hands into the pockets of his trousers, Patrick watched Amelia now, futilely wishing for just a bit more light so he could decipher her mood from her face. She had on a long-sleeved blouse and tailored slacks, but she appeared chilled, her knees bent against her chest and her arms ringing her legs, holding in her body warmth. Perhaps if she accepted the offer of his suit jacket, she'd be more willing to accept the words he had to offer, as well.

With a grim sigh, he pulled off the jacket and loped down the hill toward her. She didn't hear him until he was only a couple of feet from her, and when she spun around and saw him she flinched.

"Careful," he murmured, covering the last few feet and extending the jacket to her. "If you fall off the rock, you might land in the water and get soaked, and then I might have to tell you how sexy you look."

"Well," she muttered, "we certainly wouldn't want that, would we?"

"The truth is, you look like you're freezing." He draped the jacket over her shoulders when she made no move to take it. "Come on, Amelia, put it on."

Reluctantly she slid her arms through the sleeves and shoved them up to free her hands. "Thanks," she grunted, her lips pursed in a tight scowl.

"Mountain weather can be tricky," he cautioned her. "Sizzling at noon, freezing at midnight."

"I'll bear that in mind," she said.

He didn't dare to take her offhand remark as a clue to her plans. Even if she intended to stay in the area, even if she took a job at Keppler's, she still might have every intention of cutting him out of her life.

And he would deserve it. How ironic. He'd pursued Mary's case out of self-righteousness, and Amelia seemed prepared to dump him out of self-righteousness. What a pair they made.

"Okay," he said, lowering himself to sit on a neighboring rock. "Spit it out. You hate my guts? You think I'm evil? What?"

"I think you're a lousy lawyer," she said, each word a bludgeon, bruising him.

"I'm a great lawyer," he argued fiercely. "I'm the best damned lawyer I know."

"You're the biggest damned egotist I know," she shot back, quietly adding, "Please forgive my language."

"Please! Language! Stop being so god-awful proper, Amelia. You could say damn a million times, and it wouldn't be as offensive as your casting aspersions on my professional integrity."

"Integrity?" She snorted. "You're a lying, cheating, two-faced—"

"Defender of principles," he interrupted, his voice rising in intensity. "Dumping tea into Boston Harbor was against the law, Amelia, but it was the right thing to do. Sitting in the front of the bus was against the law, but Rosa Parks was right to do it. And fighting for Mary's freedom of speech was the right thing to do, too."

"Except for one thing," Amelia reminded him. "She asked you to stop, and you misrepresented her. You were dishonest."

The anger and loathing that emanated from her was almost palpable. It chilled him more effectively than the brisk night breeze. "I wasn't dishonest," he muttered, turning to gaze at the lake so he wouldn't have to see her lovely face twisted with contempt. "I may have misinterpreted what she told me—"

"Deliberately."

"With decent motives."

"In your narrow-minded view."

"All right, all right!" He couldn't stand it anymore. He turned back to her and flung his hands in the air in surrender. "I was wrong! All right!"

"Oh?" For the first time since he'd joined her she looked directly at him. Her eyes appeared darker than usual in the encroaching night, her chin thrust forward defiantly and her mouth shaping a severe line. "You finally admit it?"

He cursed under his breath. Evidently she was determined to make this as difficult for him as possible. "I admit it, Amelia," he grumbled impatiently. "I pushed harder on Mary's case than I should have. All right?"

"You don't sound very sorry."

"I'm not," he confirmed irascibly. "I'm a little sorry, but not very."

"You should be," she reprimanded him. "Mary was your client. She had a good reason to want to let the publicity fade away."

"What good reason? Because all of a sudden she's head over heels with a stuffed shirt? Because the Potts family prefers the status quo?"

"It doesn't matter whether you approve of her reasons."

"It matters to me," Patrick flared, then took a deep breath and turned his gaze to the water until he simmered down. "I've still got to live with myself, Amelia. I've got to go to bed believing I've done everything I can to support what I believe in." He swallowed, and when he spoke again his voice was more subdued. "I know you think the only reason I overturn tables is for my ego. But that's not the reason at all. I have a healthy ego—which means I don't have to go out of my way to prop it up." He turned back to Amelia, studying her, searching for any hint that she still harbored a shred of respect for him. "I do these things because I believe in the principles underlying them. Mary was censored by Wisherville, and I hate censorship. I want to prevent it. Shaking hands with Mayor Dunphy solves Mary's problem, but it doesn't solve the problem of censorship. That's why I wanted to keep the case alive."

"But—"

"I know, she was my client, and I was under certain obligations to her," he said, preempting Amelia. "I know that. I should have done it her way. I just...I hoped she would stick with it. I didn't know she was jumping ship because she'd fallen for Bartholomew. That's a pretty stupid reason to withdraw her suit, if you ask me."

"She's in love," Amelia retorted, her anger burning brightly in her eyes. "Are you saying you think love is stupid?"

"No." He swallowed again, aware that they were no longer talking about Mary and her case. "If I thought love was stupid, I wouldn't be here apologizing to you now. Apologizing doesn't come easily to me, Amelia, but I'm here, doing it.''

Amelia stared at him. Did he detect a slight thaw in her attitude? Or was he just hoping for it? Then she spoke, her voice hushed and velvety soft. "Is this your way of saying you love me?"

"It's one of my ways," he answered. "Here's another." Rising to his feet, he gently took her hands and lifted her off the rock, enveloped her in his arms and kissed her. He wanted to taste her, to drink her in, to seduce her with his lips and tongue, but he held back. He knew very well the difference between love and lust. If she didn't return his love, there was no point in settling for lust.

She accepted his kiss passively, but when he loosened his hold on her she didn't pull away. Instead she rested her head against his shoulder and sighed. "Patrick…it's just that…Mary's my sister, and you exploited her."

"I didn't." He defended himself quietly this time, his anger spent. "She was with me most of the way, Amelia. She knew my philosophy, she knew my strategy, and she agreed with it. I exploited the legal opportunity she presented, but she knew from the start that was what I was going to do. I'm disappointed, Amelia. I don't want to give up this fight. It infuriates me that I've got to. Believe me, I'm hurt, too."

She sighed again, apparently unable to look at him. "I admire your principles, Patrick," she confessed. "Even at the beginning, when I tried to talk Mary into letting Bartholomew negotiate a settlement, I admired what you stood for. But I loved Mary, and I wanted to protect her."

"Sometimes…" He paused, then yielded to a truth he'd never before considered, a truth he'd learned thanks to Amelia. "Sometimes love is more important than principles."

"That bothers you, doesn't it?"

"Not as much as losing you would bother me." He tightened his hold on her and kissed her brow. "Which is the point, I guess."

"I'm scared," she whispered, ringing her arms around his waist. The shoulder pads of his jacket drooped down her arms, and the bottom hem fell to mid-thigh. She seemed so slight to him, so small and delicate.

"Why?"

"I quit my job at the Hibbing School today, Patrick," she revealed. "Rae Keppler is going to give me a job, but I feel so…so open-ended. I'm not even sure what I believe in."

"You know what you believe in," he reassured her, his lips close to her ear. "You believe in principles and love, not necessarily in that order. If anyone should be scared, it's me. All that's unsettled for you is your job situation. I've just had my entire way of thinking turned upside down."

She tilted back her head and gave him a crooked anxious smile. "So have I, Patrick," she claimed. "The whole world is in front of me, and I'm not sure where I'm supposed to go, or what I'm supposed to do."

"The first thing you should do is forget about 'supposed to,'" he urged her. "Freedom can be pretty intimidating. But I think you're tough enough to handle it."

She leaned back against his hands until her eyes met his. "Love can also be pretty intimidating."

"I think you're tough enough to handle that, too."

"Do you really love me?"

He kissed her again, gently but deeply. "I'm crazy about you," he murmured when they parted. "Now tell me you love me, too, so I can stop feeling insecure."

"You? Insecure? Ha!" But she kissed him, a kiss as deep and hungry and rich with emotion as the one he'd given her. "I have the feeling I'm going to wind up as crazy as you," she mumbled, drawing away at last.

"No," he said solemnly, looping his arm around her waist and turning with her to gaze at the lake. The breezes had died, leaving the surface of the water still enough to reflect the first stars glinting overhead. "You're going to wind up tough and free. That's a damned good combination, Amelia."

"Mmm." She smiled, a private little smile. "And you're going to wind up tilting at windmills?"

"Sometimes," he conceded. "Will I be able to count on you to patch up my wounds when I lose?"

"Yes," she promised. "I'm amazed to hear you admit you might lose some of your noble battles."

"I happen to be a pretty amazing guy," he reminded her, grinning.

She laughed. "Now there's the egotist I know and love."

He pretended to resent her teasing accusation. "I'm not—"

"That's a matter of opinion."

"Your opinion's wrong."

She laughed again. "You've got a lot to learn, Patrick Levine." He didn't miss the note of warning in her voice.

Her cheerful argumentativeness startled him. Then he grinned. Amelia had obviously learned how to take him by surprise.

Which, to Patrick's way of thinking, was another good reason to love her.

Epilogue

Wisherville's Independence Day parade wended its way through town. Leading the parade was Mayor Dunphy, who sat in an open convertible car and waved to his constituents, flashing the sort of cloying smile generally associated with politicians. Behind the mayor's car marched a combined troop of Brownies and Cub Scouts, and then Boy Scouts and Girl Scouts, two fire engines, a fife-and-drum corps in Revolutionary War garb, a few members of the local chapter of the Veterans of Foreign Wars wearing medal-encrusted uniforms, a baton twirler in a red-white-and-blue spangled leotard and, bringing up the rear, a horse-drawn wagon toting a mound of crepe paper that was supposed to resemble an ice-cream sundae, with advertisements for Davenport Creamery plastered on its sides.

It wasn't a glamorous parade, but Amelia was pleased to be standing between Patrick and Bartholomew, viewing the parade from its terminal point in front of the town hall. Most mornings found her behind the front desk at Keppler's, assisting Sue with the hotel guests when she wasn't calculating customer bills. Rae had decided to initiate her on several fronts at once: she was simultaneously being introduced to the hotel's bookkeeping system, familiarizing herself with the staff schedules and learning how to attend to the needs of the guests at the desk.

Less than an hour ago she'd been on the telephone with the housekeeping department, trying to locate a pair of foam pillows for a guest who complained that the feather pillows on his bed made him sneeze. Then Rae had materialized at the desk, smiled at Amelia's harried expression and said, "Go to Wisherville. I know they're going to be honoring your sister today. It would be a shame if you missed it."

Actually Wisherville had started honoring Mary two weeks ago, when Mary had accepted a hefty check in payment for her sculpture. According to Patrick, Mary had received two bids higher than the final offer from the mayor's office, but out of loyalty to her town she'd chosen to sell *Liberty* to Wisherville. "They've cleared out a room next door to the mayor's office in the town hall," Patrick told Amelia. "Actually it's a glorified closet. They're going to keep *Liberty* on display there, and they're going to restrict access so only adults can see it."

"That sounds like censorship to me," Amelia declared. In truth, it sounded quite reasonable given the particulars of the sculpture, but she'd learned that arguing with Patrick—especially over principles—was a whole lot of fun.

"It was one of the terms of the purchase, and Mary agreed to it," Patrick explained. "People are still coming to see the piece—and spending their money all over town. Let's face it," he added, his blue eyes twinkling with amusement, "sometimes principles have to take a back seat to practicality, right?"

"And besides, adults have more money to spend than youngsters."

"Well, youngsters will be able to see the new sculpture she's been commissioned to do for the town," Patrick reminded Amelia. That was what today's honor was about. Mary was going to unveil the clay model for an outdoor sculpture Wisherville had asked her to create for the tiny paved plaza in front of the town hall, across the street from the park.

Mary had driven to the town hall earlier that morning with the model of her statue in the back of her van. The model was now standing underneath an opaque white cloth on a table at the top of the stairs leading to the building's main entrance. Seated in one of folding chairs arranged in a row along the top step, Mary had been given a position of honor between Mayor Dunphy's wife and the chief of police. She was wearing a tangerine-colored jersey and a chartreuse miniskirt, and she grinned broadly at the crowds swarming at the foot of the stairs.

"I hate that skirt," Bartholomew griped under his breath. "I told her to dress in something more discreet, but she wouldn't listen to me."

"More power to her," Patrick said, needling Bartholomew. "Just because two people are in love doesn't mean they have to pay any attention to each other."

"Amen," Amelia whispered just loud enough for Patrick to hear. He pretended to appear wounded, and she laughed.

The fife-and-drum corps turned the corner of Main Street, their pounding percussion slightly out of sync. "Did you have a chance to talk to Rae about our idea?'' Patrick asked, slipping his arm around Amelia's waist and pulling her closer to him.

"You mean, having our wedding at Keppler's? She said it shouldn't be any problem, as long as we're willing to wait until after Labor Day when the place empties out a bit."

Patrick scowled. "I don't want to wait."

"Be patient," Amelia scolded, although she secretly shared his impatience. Ever since she'd sublet her apartment in New Milford and moved to Wisherville she'd been eager to legalize their relationship. She was still fairly traditional about certain things. So, to her great delight, was Patrick.

Even though he'd been anxious to have her with him, he had seconded her decision to return to the Hibbing School to help Dean Blanchard find a replacement for her. Fortunately one of the secretaries had been angling for a promotion for months, and within a couple of days Amelia had her reasonably well trained. She'd cleaned out her apartment, packed up and moved the bulk of her things to Mary's bungalow. However, she spent most of her time not at Mary's but at Patrick's sprawling ranch house on the outskirts of town. The sooner they got married, the sooner she would feel comfortable thinking of his house as her home.

"Oh, boy, check this out," Patrick said, nudging Bartholomew in the ribs and winking lewdly as the baton twirler pranced into view. "Get a load of those legs."

"Mary's legs are much nicer," said Bartholomew.

"Yeah, I noticed," Patrick teased. "So did the entire population of Wisherville."

Bartholomew glared at Mary in her skimpy skirt. "Maybe her outfit is a tad racy," he commented, "but at least she's assured me that her new sculpture for the town is tame."

"She's assured you?" Amelia exclaimed. "Haven't you seen it?"

Bartholomew shook his head. "You know she won't let me in her studio when she's working. Have you seen it?"

"Huh-uh."

Bartholomew appeared dyspeptic for a moment. Then he sighed. "Well, she did swear to me that it was tame. Patrick, have you—"

"Nope." Patrick's eyes began to sparkle in gleeful anticipation. "On the other hand, I did hear something about how there were going to be fireworks today."

"There aren't supposed to be any until this evening," Bartholomew muttered, his gaze narrowing on the mysterious shape beneath the cloth on the table.

With the appearance of the Davenport Creamery's crepe-paper sundae, which had sunken somewhat, as if the ice cream had melted in the July heat, the parade was officially over. Dozens of onlookers streamed from Main Street into the plaza in front of the town hall, eagerly awaiting the unveiling of Mary's sculpture. Before they could have their curiosity satisfied, though, they had to endure a speech by the smiling mayor.

"Ladies and gentlemen," he intoned, pulling a few index cards from an inner pocket of his suit jacket and speaking into a microphone standing on the table, "today we remember those brave patriots who stood up for liberty, who raised their voices and risked their lives, who sacrificed their property and their safety to make our nation free. We celebrate the bravery of those vigilant men—"

"And women," Mary interjected from her seat behind the mayor.

He glanced around, then smiled sheepishly and turned back to the microphone. "Those vigilant men and women who risked everything so that we may live in freedom today. Today is an especially proud moment for our town, because today we salute Wisherville's resident sculptor, Mary Potts, the owner of the Potts Gallery on Main Street, right across the way from Frannie's Gifts and Notions. Mary's work stands as a testament to the freedom of expression for which those brave men fought—and those brave women, too," he added hastily. "In honor of our hard-won freedom, Mary has been commissioned to create a statue for our town plaza here. Mary?" He turned to her, leading his audience in a round of applause.

Rising from her chair, Mary acknowledged the clapping with a buoyant grin. She strode to the microphone, bowed a few times, and waited for the applause to die down. "Mayor Dunphy, on behalf of all those brave women you were so thoughtful to remember, I thank you," she said, her smile taking on an ironic twist. Then she gestured toward the draped model on the table. "Mayor Dunphy asked me to share this model with you. When you look at it, please try to envision it cast in bronze and standing approximately five feet high, on a concrete base approximately three feet high, which Wisherville has generously volunteered to provide. The statue I've designed for our town is meant to commemorate liberty—and, as usual, I've taken some liberties myself."

With a flourish, she whipped the cloth from the table, revealing the model. The crowd pressed forward, temporarily blocking Amelia's view of the figure. From somewhere a few feet in front of her, a voice cried out, "They're stark buck naked, Dunphy!"

A higher-pitched voice rising from Amelia's left shouted, "Oh, my Lord! They haven't even got fig leaves!"

Dismayed but admittedly intrigued, Amelia angled her head and rose on tiptoe, anxious to see the model. Like *Liberty* it featured two naked forms, one recognizably male and one female. This time, however, they stood back to back, their arms extended outward as if to embrace not each other but the world.

As modest as Amelia was, she found nothing overtly sexual about it at all. "I like it," she whispered to Patrick.

"It's not obscene enough for my taste," he whispered back, grinning.

Next to Amelia, Bartholomew uttered an oath. Then a scuffle broke out, with some people trying to get at the sculpture and others trying to block them, and with nearly everybody shouting—at Mary, at the mayor, at one another. The chief of police stood and tried to silence the mob; someone began to sing the national anthem; a trio of women on the bottom step chanted, "Smut! Smut! Smut!" but they were shouted down by another trio of women who yelled, "Freedom of speech! Freedom of speech! Freedom of speech!"

Amelia felt a hand on her elbow, dragging her through the crowd. She tripped on a step, regained her balance, and stumbled again before the level pavement of the sidewalk was beneath her feet. Twisting around, she found herself face-to-face with Patrick.

He relaxed his grip on her. "Pretty nasty," he grumbled, gazing at the people raging on the stairs. "I hope they aren't going to start throwing rocks."

Amelia focused on her sister, who stood on the top step, above the fray, protected by the chief of police. Several other officers formed a cordon around the table to guard the clay model. "Look at Mary," Amelia said with an astonished grin. "She's having the time of her life."

Patrick looked. Mary was smiling, one hand held in a fist high above her head and the other acknowledging Amelia with a subtle wave. "So she is."

"If they smash her model, she might have to sue someone."

"She'll need a lawyer for that." Patrick and Amelia eyed each other with amusement. "She's engaged to Bartholomew."

"You mean, you wouldn't take her on as a client?" Amelia asked, feigning grave disappointment.

Patrick wrapped his arms around Amelia and gave her a loving kiss. "I've already taken on one of the Potts sisters, and that's enough for me."

COMING IN AUGUST

SOMETHING EXTRA

Jolie was ready for adventure after finishing college, and
going to Louisiana to find her family's ancestral home
looked more exciting than returning to the family farm.
Finding the house was wonderful; finding its new owner,
Steve Cameron, was an added bonus. Jolie fell in love with
Steve so quickly that his reputation as a womanizer barely
registered—but his beautiful girlfriend Claudine was quite
another matter....

Watch for this bestselling Janet Dailey favorite, coming in
August from Harlequin.

Also watch for *Sweet Promise* this October.

HARLEQUIN
American Romance®

COMING NEXT MONTH

#305 MOTHER KNOWS BEST by Barbara Bretton

Author of the "Mother Knows Best" helpful-hints column, Diana had a master plan: finish her book, lose ten pounds and on Labor Day, begin the Great Husband Hunt. But then a month at seaside Gull Cottage fell in her lap, and two months early, at exactly the wrong time, Diana met Mr. Right. Don't miss the second book in the GULL COTTAGE series.

#306 FRIENDS by Stella Cameron

As children, Tom, Shelly and Ben had been inseparable. Then they became adults and their friendship faced a challenge. Ben was destined for fame, while Tom and Shelly were destined for love. But would their love break the bonds of an unbreakable friendship?

#307 ONE MAN'S FOLLY by Cathy Gillen Thacker

Diana Tomlinson was justice of the peace in Libertyville, Texas, but her life was far from peaceful. Newcomer Mike Harrigan was insistent about his foster ranch—even though the town was up in arms, all hell had broken loose and there had been a rash of burglaries. Diana knew that where there was a will there was a way—but as she got to know Mike and his trio of boys she found her will rapidly fading....

#308 WHITE MOON by Vella Munn

Lynn Walker was a championship barrel rider without a horse—her dream was just out of reach. Then Bryan Stone found her a mare to match her spirit and her strength: proof that he believed in her and her dream. There are many ways to say "I love you," and White Moon was Bryan's.

Harlequin American Romance®

Gull Cottage

SUMMER.

The sun, the surf, the sand...

One relaxing month by the sea was all Zoe, Diana and Gracie ever expected from their four-week stays at Gull Cottage, the luxurious East Hampton mansion. They never thought they'd soon be sharing those long summer days—or hot summer nights—with a special man. They never thought that what they found at the beach would change their lives forever. But as Boris, Gull Cottage's resident mynah bird said: "Beware of summer romances...."

Join Zoe, Diana and Gracie for the summer of their lives. Don't miss the GULL COTTAGE trilogy in American Romance: #301 _Charmed Circle_ by Robin Francis (July 1989), #305 _Mother Knows Best_ by Barbara Bretton (August 1989) and #309 _Saving Grace_ by Anne McAllister (September 1989).

GULL COTTAGE—because a month can be the start of forever...

Have You Ever Wondered If You Could Write A Harlequin Novel?

Here's great news—Harlequin is offering a series of cassette tapes to help you do just that. Written by Harlequin editors, these tapes give practical advice on how to make your characters—and your story—come alive. There's a tape for each contemporary romance series Harlequin publishes.

Mail order only

All sales final
